PENGUIN BOOKS

WHERE IT LEADS US

Joy started writing stories on Wattpad at thirteen, convinced words were the best kind of therapy. After thirteen years in Qatar, she returned to the Philippines, pursued Creative Writing, and pivoted into freelance life—writing copy, web articles, and still squeezing in stories when she can. Now in her early twenties and based in Metro Manila, she writes about mental health, family secrets, and self-discovery with humour and heart. Follow her on Instagram @joy.pepito_

Where It Leads Us

Joy Pepito

PENGUIN BOOKS
An imprint of Penguin Random House

PENGUIN BOOKS

Penguin Books is an imprint of the Penguin Random House group of companies
whose addresses can be found at global.penguinrandomhouse.com

Published by Penguin Random House SEA Pte Ltd
40 Penjuru Lane, #03-12, Block 2
Singapore 609216

First published in Penguin Books by Penguin Random House SEA 2026

10 9 8 7 6 5 4 3 2 1

Where It Leads Us includes elements that might not be suitable for some readers. Depictions of mental illness, specifically psychosis and suicidal ideation are present in the story. Readers who may be sensitive to these elements please take note. Please note that no part of this book may be used or reproduced in any manner for the purpose of training artificial intelligence technologies or systems.

ISBN 9789815323634

Typeset in EB Garamond by MAP Systems, Bengaluru, India

www.penguin.sg

To Renzelle,
the muse to most—if not all—of my writings,
especially this one
I love you, B
Forever and always

1

6 August 2023

They say the brain decides before we even know there's a choice to make—ten seconds ahead, sometimes more. Like fate isn't something we run towards, but something that's already waiting, settled into place.

Ten seconds.

Just enough time to take a breath, to blink, to hesitate. Just enough time to change your mind.

Or not.

Elise made her choice in silence; in those ten seconds I never saw coming. One minute, she was there—solid, breathing, laughing. The next, she was gone. A decision slipping through the cracks, rewriting everything before I could even understand it had happened.

I used to think time dragged. Like in the middle of school lectures, when the clock barely moved and the teacher's voice blurred into something soft and unimportant.

But those ten seconds? They disappeared like breath in cold air—there, then gone, too quick to hold on to. All that remained was the weight of what couldn't be undone.

‘Walk me through that day, Lauren. What do you remember first?’

I tell him about Elise. About finding her that night in her bedroom.

Her body, hanging from the ceiling fan, swaying slightly—a puppet with cut strings. The air thick and wrong, like the house itself was holding its breath.

Her lavender scent still clung to the walls, to the furniture, to me. It burrowed into fabric, into skin, refusing to let go. Some days, I told myself it was just molecules trapped in the air, nothing more. Other days, it felt alive. Curling around me, pressing in. Like Elise had folded herself into the house on purpose. Like she wasn’t done haunting me yet.

‘How did it feel? Did you notice anything different—around you, in you?’ he asks, hoping the right words might pull something loose, something I haven’t quite put together yet.

I shift in my chair, press my hands together in my lap. ‘I don’t know. It’s all kind of blurred.’

He nods, like he expected that. ‘That’s okay. Just start wherever your mind goes.’

Where my mind goes? Nowhere useful. Just static and ghosts.

The soft tap of his pen matches the silence between us. He watches me with that quiet, clinical curiosity. The kind of look people give when they want to understand something they never really could.

I open my mouth, but the words get stuck, tangled between thought and sound. I already know what he’s thinking. I already feel it pressing in like an invisible weight: *crazy*.

Except psychiatrists don't say that word. They have better ones, the kind that fit neatly into medical records and treatment plans. *Major Depression. With psychotic symptoms.* That's the one he chose. Because it made sense to him.

My fingers dig into the seam of my jeans, grounding me in something real. When I finally blink and look at him, he's already watching, waiting. Like he knows I wasn't really here.

'I feel . . . distant. Like I exist, but just barely. Like the world keeps moving, and I'm stuck behind glass, watching.'

He nods, like he understands. Like this is something ordinary, something people just go through. Something I'll eventually grow out of, like an old habit.

His voice cuts through the quiet. 'Do you still see things?'

I don't answer right away. Instead, I press my thumb harder into the seam of my jeans. The air shifts. I meet his gaze, feeling something heavy settle in my chest. The truth sits between us, unsaid.

The voices never leave completely. They hum at the edges of my mind, sometimes quiet, sometimes sharp enough to make me question what's real.

Dr Gregory's pen moves, but his eyes don't. They stay locked on me, waiting.

The pills dull the edges, but they don't fix the tilt of the world—the way I still see things that aren't there. Like the woman sitting beside him, hands folded neatly in her lap, smiling like an old friend.

She raises a hand in a casual wave, like she's been waiting for me to notice.

The office carries that sharp, over-sanitized smell, like someone drowned the room in citrus cleaner. Underneath it lingers the faint bitterness of old coffee, the kind that's been sitting too long in the pot. My eyes wander to the framed degrees on the wall, their glass fronts catching the light, throwing back fractured glimpses of my face. Maybe even they aren't sure what to make of me.

They've heard it all, I'm sure. Stories worse than mine.

'We never left,' a voice murmurs, smug.

'Still mooching off your brain space,' another adds, way too pleased with itself.

I shift in my seat.

'You told me before that you're still hearing voices,' Dr Gregory says. His tone is even, unreadable. 'Are they saying anything now?'

I notice the subtle shift in his grip, the way his thumb presses a little harder against the pen. A small movement, but in the silence of the room, it feels like a sudden spike.

'No.'

The lie slips out smooth, too easy. A word dressed up in certainty, even though my pulse betrays me, thrumming like a warning.

My eyes flick to the woman beside him. She's perfectly still, but something about her feels off—a quiet challenge, daring him to make sense of her. She'd been gone for months, blurred at the edges of my mind, but now she's back, and the sight of her sends a shiver down my spine.

The sharp, impatient scratch of Dr Gregory's pen fills the quiet, marking another failed attempt, another adjustment to my meds that will only ever dull, never erase.

'What about the episodes?'

His pen hovers, waiting.

'Oh, does he mean the premium content?' one voice chimes in.

'*Would not recommend*,' another mutters.

I exhale sharply, sink deeper into the chair. 'Nothing much lately,' I say, keeping my voice light, like it doesn't matter. Like it isn't sitting heavy in my chest.

Dr Gregory doesn't react, but something shifts between us. A subtle crack in the quiet, the kind that makes me want to fill it with words, even if they aren't true. Maybe the lie will settle harmlessly between us, like dust. But I know better. He remembers every time I've sat in this chair, voice thin and frayed, listing all the ways the last pills failed me.

Instead of looking at him, I focus on the degrees on the wall and let him decide what to make of it.

'Are you still seeing her?' he asks. 'Elise?'

My stomach twists.

'Oh, great. Here we go.'

'No.'

The lie is too quick. A reflex, sharp and instinctive.

Dr Gregory doesn't call me on it, but I can feel it, the space between my answer and the truth. The part where doubt lives.

'Oh, so we're just lying now?'

I swallow hard, shift in my seat, hoping to shake her off.

Explaining Elise is impossible. She's not exactly me, but she's not separate either. More like a shadow trailing behind, always just out of reach.

I glance down at my hands, tracing the lines on my palms. 'She's just there,' I say, forcing something casual into my voice.

Elise lingers, steady and unshakable—a breath held too long.

'She's like . . . a reminder.'

'A reminder of what?'

What is she supposed to remind me of?

That I am broken in ways that don't seem fixable? That no matter how much time passes, some things don't fade? That even when a person is gone, their absence doesn't just leave—you carry it, heavy and unmoving, a weight strapped to your chest?

I exhale, staring at a spot on the floor. 'That I don't deserve a second chance,' I murmur, my voice thin, almost swallowed by the space between us. The words feel strange in the air. They'd been waiting too long to be said.

Dr Gregory sits back in his chair, considering me. 'It sounds like there's a lot you're holding onto,' he says finally. 'But the fact that you're here, talking about it, tells me that maybe—on some level—you do want that second chance, even if it doesn't feel like it right now.'

I shrug. 'Maybe.' The word barely sounds like mine. 'But it's hard to believe when everything feels . . . broken.'

Broken. Too small to hold everything I mean. I pull my sleeves over my hands, fingers curling into the fabric like it might anchor me. 'Like I keep trying to put the pieces back together, but somehow, the cracks just keep getting bigger.'

Silence stretches between us. Not empty, not comfortable. Just . . . there. Thick and unmoving, like a wall neither of us knows how to get past.

Broken wasn't the right word. It was too clean, too neat. This wasn't just a crack, something that could be sealed up, smoothed over. This was shattered. Splintered into something unrecognizable, something that slipped through my fingers no matter how tightly I tried to hold on. And even when the pieces were gone, the edges still cut, still left something behind.

I look up at him then, letting the weight of it show. 'Sometimes, I think I've been holding myself together for too long. That if I let go, even for a second, I'll fall apart completely. Maybe I already have.' I swallow hard. 'Maybe I'm just a mess of cracks, barely held together, hoping no one notices how easily I could break.'

Neither of us says anything for a while. I stare at the clock on the wall, watching the seconds drag forward, willing them to move faster.

Dr Gregory doesn't push. He just reaches for his pen, the quiet scratch of it against paper the only sound in the room. A moment later, he pulls a sheet from one of his files, skims it, and signs it with an easy stroke of his wrist.

When he reaches out to hand it to me, I hesitate before taking it. It's just a piece of paper, but it feels heavier than it should be.

The alarm on my phone buzzes. Session over. I'm reaching for my bag when Dr Gregory asks, 'Same time next week?'

I nod, muttering a quick 'thanks' before making my way to the door. My hand hovers over the handle for a second—just long enough to feel like leaving meant something bigger than just walking out of a room. Then I push it open and step into the hallway.

Clarissa is still there. Slouched in one of the stiff waiting room chairs, her head tipping forward, then snapping back up when she nearly dozes off. Her hair stuck to her lip gloss. She looks exhausted.

She could've left. No one would've blamed her. But she stayed. Just like she always does.

She stayed when Mom stopped getting out of bed, when our house turned into dim hallways and whispered conversations behind closed doors. She stayed after my sister's funeral, when I stopped talking, when I stopped sleeping, when I stopped being someone who was easy to love. She stayed through every slammed door, every silence, every moment where I made it impossible for her to keep showing up—and yet, she did.

She took me in without question. Made sure I ate, made sure I was okay, made sure I kept breathing. And Zania—her daughter, my cousin—never treated me like a guest, never made me feel like I was something to take care of. She just made space for me, like it was the most natural thing in the world.

Clarissa wasn't just my aunt. She was the person who pulled me out of bed when I couldn't move. Who learned to make my favourite pasta exactly the way Mom did, even though she always burned the garlic. Who sat outside my door for hours when I refused to let anyone in.

She is the reason I am still here.

I walk over and tap her shoulder.

She jolts, blinking hard, her glasses slipping down her nose. 'Oh,' she mumbles, rubbing her eyes. 'You're done?'

I nod. She stretches, then loops her arm through mine, leading me outside—we're making a run for it.

In the car, I toss the paper onto the dashboard. It feels wrong—the way a single sheet can declare me 'fit' to go back to school, like a permission slip for my sanity.

Clarissa glances at it, her brow furrowing. 'So . . . you're good to go?'

I shrug, keeping my voice even. 'Yeah. It says I'm "fit".'

She exhales slowly. 'That's good, right?' But her hands tighten around the wheel.

I turn towards the window. 'I'm fine, Clarissa.'

Her grip doesn't loosen. 'Dr Gregory said I should keep an eye on you.' Her voice is soft, careful. 'Not that I need a note to tell me that.'

Something in my chest twists. The car suddenly feels too small.

'I don't need you to watch me,' I mutter. But the words feel flimsy, too light to hold any real weight.

Somewhere in the back of my mind, a quieter voice disagrees. *You can't even take care of yourself. Look at you.*

Clarissa doesn't answer right away. When she finally speaks, her voice is barely above a whisper. 'I just need you to still be here.'

I look at her, something in my chest loosening. 'I am.' I swallow. 'But I'm not going to break, you know.'

She studies me for a long second, deciding whether or not to believe me. Then she nods, offering a tired, half-smile.

The drive home is quiet. Outside, the late afternoon light filters through the branches, throwing scattered shadows across the windshield. The world keeps moving, unchanged, even when mine has stopped.

When we turn onto our street, I see Clarissa's grip tighten on the wheel before she forces herself to let go. Her shoulders lift like she's bracing for something, before they drop.

She parks, but neither of us moves.

'I'll just make a few calls,' she says. 'Will you be okay?'

I nod, forcing a smile. 'Yeah. I'll be okay.'

She hesitates—she doesn't quite believe me—then pushes past it.

I step out, the evening air pressing against my skin. My feet feel heavy as I walk up the driveway, past the garden she still somehow keeps alive, past the porch light spilling onto the pavement.

I open the door—and laughter hits me. Bright, unfiltered, filling the house, making it seem like it has never known the weight of grief.

Zania is sprawled on the couch, popcorn bowl balanced on her stomach, watching something on TV. Her laugh rings out, easy, unburdened—she's never had to carry the things I did.

I don't say anything. No announcement, no grand return. Just a quiet slip through the door, the way you do when you don't want anyone to notice.

My room is exactly the way I left it—too clean, too unfamiliar, like a hotel room someone else has been living in. I step inside, let the door click shut behind me, and drop my bag on the floor. Sit on the edge of the bed, tug off my shoe, toss it to the side. The dull thud of it hitting the floor is the only sound in the room. It is nothing, but it is enough. Proof that I was here. That this isn't some in-between place where I floated instead of existed.

Then, the voices.

Not loud, not urgent—just there. A steady hum beneath the silence, a conversation I walked in on too late.

'Oh great, therapy hour's over,' the first voice sneers, dripping with amusement. *'Did you tell him about us this time, or are we still your dirty little secret?'*

A second voice, softer, almost soothing—a whisper against my ear—says, *'You don't have to listen to him, Lauren. He doesn't know you like we do.'*

'I say we ditch the meds,' another chimes in, more matter-of-fact, like she's weighing pros and cons.

A third voice hums, softer, familiar. *'Lauren.'*

I stiffen.

'We're still here,' the first voice reminds me, almost smug. *'You didn't really think we'd leave, did you?'*

I close my eyes and exhale, slow and steady. Hoping it might be enough to push them back. I should've taken the pills earlier. They wouldn't have made the voices disappear, but they'd take the edge off. Maybe turn the volume down just enough to let me breathe.

I roll onto my side, away from the voices—and there she was.

The woman from earlier.

Standing by the wall, still and silent, her dress shifting, like there is a breeze in the room. But there isn't. She tilts her head, watching me—not with urgency, but with patience. She's waiting for me to catch up.

I never gave her a name. Naming her would make her real. And I couldn't let her be real. Or worse—want her to be.

She moves without a sound, stopping in front of the painting. Lifting a finger. Pointing.

A tightness settles in my chest. I've seen that painting—Mom's painting—a hundred times, but tonight, something feels off. Maybe it's the slight tilt of the frame. Or maybe it's the flicker of a memory, just out of reach—Elise tucking things away. Notes, ticket stubs, scraps of paper filled with thoughts only she understood.

I swallow hard. It's probably nothing.

But the woman's gaze stays fixed. And so does the feeling.

I push off the bed, my legs heavier than they should be, and step towards it. The frame is rough under my fingers, dust lifting as I pull it down. Cobwebs cling to the edges—I brush them away without thinking.

Then—a shift. The frame tilts, just slightly.

A whisper of movement.

Something wedged behind the corner. A slip of paper, small and folded.

I snatch it before I can think twice.

Frowning, I turn to the woman, the question already on my lips—had she known it was there? Had she seen it before?

But the room is empty.

She's gone.

My breath catches. The ink smears under my thumb. Elise's handwriting—undeniable.

I unfold the note and read it.

2

6 August 2023

I don't see a lot of made-up people—not like the ones you hear about in those YouTube videos on psychosis. For me, it's usually just one or two at a time. Like the woman from earlier in Dr Gregory's office. Or Elise—my sister—who appears out of nowhere and just stands there, watching me. She never says a word, but her silence feels louder than anything she could've said. Loud, in the same heavy, aching way her choice to die still feels.

But most of the time, it's just the black figures.

They're not people, not really. They're shadows that forgot how to stick to the ground. No faces. No features. Just shifting outlines, like they haven't figured out where they begin or end.

At first, they terrified me. Standing in the corners of rooms. By my bed, watching. Hovering. But when your depression comes with these breaks from reality, you learn to live with it—or at least, you try. The pills they prescribe don't make them go away. They just blur the edges, make them a little harder to see.

One time, Clarissa caught me staring past her.

'What?' she asked, turning slightly.

I didn't even think before I said it. 'There's one standing right behind you.'

I wasn't trying to scare her. It was just the truth. But the way her face tightened, how her eyes flicked over her shoulder like she half-expected to see something—yeah. I regretted it instantly.

That night, I heard a soft murmur drifting through the door, and I knew without opening my eyes that it was Clarissa outside. Her whispered rosary was a familiar sound in the heavy silence of the house, a ritual she leaned on for comfort—a way to ward off the unseen forces she thought were at play.

When she finally stepped into my room after finishing her rosary prayer, I pretended to be asleep. I felt the cool droplets of holy water land on my face as Clarissa moved around my bed, murmuring her soft prayers like some sort of protective chant. It was a desperate act of faith, rooted in a past where she believed these blessings could really fight off whatever demons I was facing.

Clarissa once thought mental illness was just an excuse. Something kids made up when they didn't want to get out of bed or just wanted attention. She wasn't cruel about it—she didn't roll her eyes or call me crazy—but if someone had asked her back then, she might have said, 'It's all in your head,' or worse, 'Just think happy thoughts.' The kind of thing you'd find on an inspirational fridge magnet.

Until she saw me. *Really* saw me.

She saw me wake up screaming, clawing at my own skin, convinced something was dragging me under. She saw me go days without speaking, without eating, my body here but my mind somewhere else entirely. She saw me swallow every emotion because I knew people like her wouldn't believe me if I told the truth.

Then Dr Gregory gave it a name. Put words to the thing that had been consuming me. And suddenly, I wasn't possessed. Or dramatic. Or making it up. I was something else. Something medical. Something she could try to understand.

She didn't get it overnight. Maybe part of her still thinks a few more Sunday masses could've done the trick. But she stopped leaving rosary beads under my pillow. Stopped calling the priest every time I said I was hearing voices.

Now, when I tell her I'm having a bad day, she doesn't rush to fix it. She just nods and asks, 'Do you want to talk about it?'

I don't always answer. But the fact that she asks? That means something.

I exhale, the words blurring as I read them again, my ribs constricting like a vice.

14°34'55.37"N 120°58'51.73"E

My head spins, numbers flashing behind my eyes like a glitch I can't shake. I run through them again. And again. Searching for a pattern—anything that makes sense.

But I can't figure it out.

Elise loved puzzles, but this didn't feel like a game. The ink was pressed too hard into the page, the letters slanting like a rushed secret. She was trying to tell me something. Something that mattered.

My fingers drum against my thigh, my foot bouncing hard enough to rattle the bed frame. I can't just sit here. I have to know.

I move before I can talk myself out of it, the cold floor jolting against my feet as I cross the room. My pulse hammers in my ears as I reach Clarissa's door. It creaks open, and for a second, I hesitate.

Her laptop sits untouched on the desk, the screen black. My fingers hover over the keyboard. This is a bad idea. A really bad idea. But the need to figure it out is louder than the warning bells in my head.

I open it. Type in the numbers. Wait.

The screen refreshes, and a location blinks into view.

The National Library.

I frown. A library? That was it? Elise wouldn't leave me something this obvious. There had to be more, something I wasn't seeing yet.

I stare at the screen until the letters blur, willing them to rearrange into something that made sense. And then—

'Mom! I'm heading out with some friends!' Zania's voice carries down the hall. 'I'm stopping by the library to return some books. Be back before dinner!'

My heart skips a beat.

Was this just a coincidence? Or was I actually onto something?

I wasn't about to sit here and wonder.

Shutting the laptop, I slip out of Clarissa's room and head straight for Zania. She's by the front door, stuffing books into her bag, hair falling into her face as she zipped it up.

'Hey,' I say, trying to sound casual, even though my voice comes out tighter than I want. 'Mind if I come with you?'

Zania looks up, surprised. 'Wait—you? Outside?' Her grin widens. 'At the library? With books?'

I roll my eyes, but a smile tugs at the corner of my mouth. 'Yeah, is that so hard to believe?'

She swings her bag over her shoulder, ponytail swishing. 'No, no, not at all,' she says, obviously lying. 'Come on before you change your mind.'

Her excitement is weirdly contagious. For the first time in a while, I feel something close to momentum, like maybe this wouldn't be so bad.

We step outside. The air was cool, crisp—real. I exhale, watching my breath dissolve into the afternoon light.

The note in my pocket presses against my palm, a quiet reminder of why I was doing this. I hadn't truly left the house in months—just drifted from one room to another, hoping to go unnoticed. Inside was predictable. Outside felt too open, too vast. Like one wrong step could swallow me whole.

Doctor's appointments didn't count. Those were routine. Show up, answer their questions, pretend to care. But this—this was different. A handful of numbers scribbled on a scrap of paper pulling me forward, no explanations, no guarantees. Just the feeling that I had to go.

And somehow, that is enough.

We are nearly at the car when a familiar voice cuts through the quiet.

'Hey!'

I look up. Savannah leans against her car, lifting a hand in a half-hearted wave. There's something uneasy about it, like she isn't sure if I'd wave back. The distance between us wasn't just physical—it sat heavy in the air, a quiet reminder of everything we didn't know how to say any more.

'My mom wanted me to give you these,' she says, digging through her bag before pulling out two small, colourful boxes. Her fingers fumble slightly as she hands them over.

I open the first one and find a wooden windmill, the kind you'd see in postcards of tulip fields and slow-moving canals. The second holds Dutch liquorice. My stomach twists at the sight of it. Not my favourite, to put it mildly.

I wrinkle my nose. 'Wow. You shouldn't have.'

If I had been feeling generous, I might have shared them with her, but I mostly just hoped she wouldn't make me try one. The thought of that sticky, bitter taste was enough to make me cringe.

'Thanks,' I add, forcing a smile that probably landed more on strained than sincere. 'So . . . how was your trip to the Netherlands?'

Savannah shrugs, eyes flicking to the pavement, her mind already moving past this conversation. 'It was nice. But when I got back, I was thrown into wedding prep. My mom's getting remarried in December.'

'Oh.' The word feels small, not quite enough.

Her smile flickers—hesitant, uncertain, she isn't sure if she wanted me to believe it. The space between us stretches, weighted by things we weren't saying.

Another shrug. This one smaller, tighter, like she was trying to make herself disappear.

'So,' she murmurs, gaze sliding past me to where Zania stood by the car, arms crossed, foot tapping impatiently. 'You heading out?'

'Yeah.' The word barely makes a sound, swallowed by the distance between us.

I'm not sure why we kept standing, dragging out a conversation that didn't need to exist. She'd given me the gifts.

I'd thanked her. That should've been it. And yet, something held us in place—this thin, unravelling thread of what we used to be.

I could have asked her about what had happened between us, but I already knew how that would go. Nowhere. She wouldn't tell the truth, and I'm not sure if I was ready to hear it anyway. So, I reached for something else, something factual, hoping it might somehow fill the silence.

'You know,' I say, the words slipping out before I could stop them, 'my psychiatrist says I'm "fit" to go back to school next week.'

It feels strange saying this to her—an offering, or maybe a test. I want to believe that if I say it out loud, something would shift, that the space between us would shrink instead of stretch. But I could still feel it—the distance. The way time had worn us down into something unrecognizable.

Her eyebrows lift, a flicker of surprise—or maybe relief. 'Really?' she asks, too quick, too light. Then, tilting her head, 'And what about you? Are you "fit" to go back?'

The way she says it—*fit*—makes my stomach twist. It wasn't curiosity. It wasn't kindness. It was something else, something I couldn't quite name. Was she asking because she cared? Or was she measuring me, deciding whether I still *fit* into the version of me she used to know?

'I think so.' The words waver, unsteady even as I speak them.

She hears it. I can tell by the way she studies me, searching for something—cracks, evidence, a truth I wasn't sure how to give. And what did fit even mean?

'She doesn't believe you.'

'She's not happy to see you.'

'She hates you.'

The silence stretches between us, thick and heavy—something that could be touched, something that might wrap around my throat if I let it. She shifts her weight, uneasy. She has something to say but can't find the shape of it. She doesn't ask anything else.

'Anyway,' she says at last, stepping forward, her arms looping around me in a hug that feels more like obligation than comfort. Too quick, too careful—like she wants to pull away before either of us can realize it isn't the same.

'I mean . . . if you ever need to talk or something, I'm around,' she says, shifting her weight, already planning her exit.

The words drift between us, weightless. Hollow.

We both know the truth—if I called, the silence would answer first. If I texted, the message would sit, unseen, until time erased the need for a reply. It hadn't always been like this. Once, she'd answer before the second ring, her laughter bubbling through the speaker before I could even say hello.

But that version of us had been chipped away, little by little, until there was nothing left to hold on to.

'I guess I'll see you next week,' she says, but it sounds like a question, like she isn't sure she wants to mean it.

I nod, but the weight in my chest makes it hard to say anything back.

I watch her walk to her car, each step slow, uncertain. It makes me think—hope—she isn't sure if leaving is the right choice. She climbs in and drives off and I just stand there, feeling the distance grow between us, watching her taillights shrink into nothing.

Savannah and I haven't really talked since I stopped going to school nearly two years ago, a week after my parents died. She doesn't know about the things Dr Gregory has labelled me with, doesn't know about the things I was trying to live with.

It feels like I exist in two worlds: one built of ghosts and echoes, and another where people go about their lives, unaware of how hard it was just to get out of bed some days.

'Are you really just going to stand there all day?' Zania calls, her head poking out the car window as she honks to get my attention.

I slide into the car, and as we pull away, I dig out the Dutch liquorice candies from the bag Savannah had handed me. 'You have to try these,' I say, holding one out. Sharing food has never really been my thing, but I'm hoping she takes the bait—finishes them off so I don't have to.

With a grin, Zania pops one into her mouth. The car is filled with the sound of her chewing—loud, exaggerated.

I wince, the sound grating, each smacking noise making me want to reach over and snatch the candy back—maybe even strangle her a little. If my pet peeve took on a human form, it would definitely be Zania.

'Could you drop me off at the library first? I need to find something, and it might take a while,' I say, slipping another piece of liquorice into Zania's hand.

Zania raises an eyebrow, looking interested but not pushing for more. 'Sure, no problem,' she says, her voice a little muffled from chewing.

We drive in silence for a while, the radio humming softly in the background. Zania chews on the liquorice, popping piece after piece into her mouth. I can hear the crinkle of the wrapper as she reaches for more, her attention on the road, her fingers expertly tearing the next piece. She doesn't say much, but I can tell she's settling into the quiet, her eyes focused on the drive.

Every time she finishes a piece, I hand her another, and she takes it without question, the corners of her lips curving into that quiet, knowing smile.

Zania always eats while driving—something about it keeps her steady, helps her focus. I never ask why, but I let her do it. In a way, it feels like we are both just trying not to slip. She doesn't need to explain it, and neither do I. That's what I love about her.

She isn't the type for deep conversations where you have to explain every feeling. But she knows how to show up when it counts; on those late-night drives, music blasting, windows down, the wind filling the silence between us. Or when she'd hand me a cup of instant noodles on the rough days, acting like it was no big deal. She never tries to fix things or pull words from me. She just makes sure I know I'm not alone.

So, every time I get in the car, she'd reach into the glove compartment, grab a handful of candies, and toss them onto my lap without looking. And every time, I know what to do—because sometimes, understanding doesn't need words.

We drive in easy silence, the kind that doesn't need filling. Unspoken things sit between us, familiar but unheavy, like they've been there long enough to belong.

Outside, the city moves on—people weaving through sidewalks, neon signs flickering to life, headlights sweeping past. The world keeps turning, unaware of us, uninterested.

Then, the steady hum of the tires fade as we slow, easing to a stop in front of the National Library.

I know I shouldn't be here. Not because I don't want to be, but because I'm not sure I'm ready for whatever is waiting for me inside.

I pull the note from my pocket, pressing my thumb along the crease. This place. Why here? The building feels too big, too still, like walking through those doors would force something to the surface that I wasn't ready to deal with. But I'd come this far.

For a second, I think about telling Zania to keep driving, to turn around, to tell her this was just a wrong turn, a mistake. But then what? I'd go home, sit in my room, and spend the rest of the night thinking about what would've happened if I had just gone inside.

With a quiet sigh, I reach for the door handle and step out. The air is thick, humid, carrying the sharp scent of asphalt and something sweet, maybe caramelized peanuts from a vendor nearby. A group of students walk past, lost in their own conversation, while an old man sits on a bench, staring at the ground like he's trying to remember something important. Life keeps moving, like it always does, with or without me.

I glance at the entrance—the heavy wooden doors, the same ones I'd walked through years ago. They looked untouched, unchanged. I wished I could say the same for myself.

I don't know if I'm ready. I don't know if I'll ever be.

But I walk forward anyway.

Inside, the air is thick with the scent of old paper and something faintly musty, like rain that had dried too slowly on concrete. Shelves stretch high, packed with books that had probably been here longer than I'd been alive.

Elise's note sat crumpled in my hand, the paper slightly damp from my grip. My fingers press into the creases, as if smoothening them out would make the words clearer, easier to understand. But they only seemed to sink deeper, the weight of them settling in my chest, thick and heavy.

It has to mean something. It has to.

The librarian, a woman with round glasses slipping down her nose, barely glances up from her screen as I stop at the information desk. 'Can I help you?'

I hesitate. What if this is nothing? What if I'm chasing ghosts?

'I need to see the list of books my sister . . . Elise Sanders . . . checked out before she . . .' *Before she died.* I swallow hard, the words getting caught in my throat.

The librarian's expression shifts ever so slightly—a flicker of something before she masks it. 'I'm sorry, but those records are private.'

My stomach plummets. *No, no, no. I needed this.*

'Please,' I say, lowering my voice. 'I just—I think she has something for me here that she left behind and forgot.'

The librarian sighs, her fingers tapping against the keyboard, nails clicking like a slow-moving clock. 'I can't show you her records,' she says, hesitating. 'But I *can* tell you the kind of books she was interested in.'

It isn't much, but it's something. I nod.

'She borrowed a lot of books,' the librarian continues. 'Mostly young adult fiction.'

My shoulders sink. I picture the paperbacks Elise used to shove into my hands, swearing I'd love them if I just gave them a chance. Stories about grief and broken kids and hope that hurt to believe in. Nothing strange. Nothing that feels like a message.

The librarian hesitates, the glances back at the screen. 'There was one book,' she adds quietly. 'She checked it out several times.'

My pulse kicks up.

'What kind of book?'

'Non-fiction,' she says. 'About mental illness.'

The room feels suddenly unsteady, like the floor has shifted just enough to throw me off balance. I don't need her to say the title. I think I already know.

The Center Cannot Hold.

Elise mentioned it once, late at night, when I was half-asleep on her bed. I barely remember what she'd said, just the sound of her voice drifting through the dark.

'It's weird, you know?' she'd murmured. 'How some people survive things that should have broken them.'

I didn't think much of it then, but now . . . now, it feels like a clue. A quiet message she's left behind, daring me to figure it out.

My fingers clench around the note, my heartbeat uneven.

'Could you help me find it?' I ask the librarian, my voice tight with something close to hope. 'The book she borrowed more than once.'

The librarian nods and I follow her through the rows of shelves. The air smells like paper and dust, and the books feel too quiet, like they are holding their breath.

We stop at the psychology section. The librarian pulls out a copy of *The Center Cannot Hold: My Journey Through Madness* by Elyn Saks. The spine is cracked, and the pages worn thin in places—someone had read it too hard, too often.

'Here it is,' she says, handing it to me with a small smile.

The weight of it feels familiar somehow. Solid. Like Elise had left pieces of herself inside. I open it, and the scent of old paper fills my nose, stirring up memories I wasn't expecting. Something slips out from between the pages and flutters to the floor.

My heart stutters as I kneel to pick it up. A folded scrap of paper, soft from being handled too many times. I unfold it, and there it is—Elise's handwriting:

In a realm of my own, I shiver and sigh,
Cold and alone, beneath a vast sky.
In silence I linger, where shadows are cast,
But your voice, like a beacon, breaks through at last.
What am I, lost in the dark, yet saved by your sound,
A whisper of hope when no comfort is found?

A breathless laugh slips out of me, thin and disbelieving. The note crumpled in my hand, the edges biting into my palm. I read it again, searching for something hidden, something Elise meant just for me.

But all I find is silence.

My stomach knots. What am I even doing? Did I really believe that if I followed her breadcrumbs, I'd somehow understand why she left? Like if I solved the right riddle, it would all make sense?

My fingers twitch, the paper nearly slipping away into the breeze. For a second, I imagine letting it go—watching it drift away, feeling the weight of everything finally lift. But my grip tightens instead, knuckles white, as if some part of me refuses to surrender. To the past. To Elise. To the questions that won't stop chasing me.

Get a grip, Lauren.

I swallow hard, staring at the words again. Elise loved puzzles. Loved twisting reality into riddles only she could solve. But this . . . this doesn't feel like a game.

This feels like a door left open.

I could walk away. Pretend I never found it. Pretend it doesn't matter.

But my fingers curl tighter around the paper. If Elise had left this for me, she wanted me to find it. And I wasn't ready to let her go.

I shove the paper into my pocket, feeling its edges press into my palm. My heart thumps hard as I move through the library, my eyes flicking from shelf to shelf. I don't know what I'm looking for, but I know I have to keep looking.

The list of books is burned in my mind. I remember three titles. So, there's three chances to find another note.

I scan the shelves until my fingers land on *The Catcher in the Rye*. Elise used to say she and Holden were basically the same—both a little lost and a little angry. I trace the worn spine before pulling it free. I flip through every page, my breath catching at every crease and smudge.

Nothing. No notes. No underlined words. Not even a scribble in the margins.

Next.

Looking for Alaska. Elise always said Alaska reminded her of herself—the kind of girl who kept half her life hidden. I yank the book from the shelf, my fingers shaking as I fan through the pages. Dog-eared corners. A faint coffee stain. But no message. No clue.

I squeeze my eyes shut for half a second, swallowing down the growing knot in my chest. It has to be here. Somewhere.

Last book. *The Perks of Being a Wallflower*. Elise loved this one most of all. She used to read parts out loud to me, her voice soft and careful like she was handling something breakable.

I hurry to the fiction section and kneel in front of the shelf, legs cramping as I reach for the book. I grab the copy and flip through it, my hands aching as I scan every page like I could will something to appear.

Nothing.

My knees ache as I stand, pressing my back against the shelves. I pull the note from my pocket again, smoothing it out with shaking fingers. I trace Elise's handwriting. Maybe if I followed the curve of her letters, I'd find something I missed the first hundred times I read it.

But it was still just a note. Just a few words on paper.

I stare at it for a long time, standing there in the empty aisle, waiting for something that never comes.

3

2 August 2021

Two weeks. Fourteen sunrises that pass without meaning since Elise's death.

Every night, Mom cries—quiet at first, then louder, spilling into the stillness. I listen from my room, the sound creeping through the walls, a clock counting down to something I can't name.

Our house feels different now. It isn't haunted, but it doesn't feel like *ours* any more. It feels like we are just passing through, borrowing walls that no longer hold us the way they used to.

Everything sits too still. The air, the furniture, the light filtering through the windows—it all felt like it was waiting. Waiting for something to shift, for the weight pressing down on this place to lift. For us to wake up one morning and not feel like we were living inside a life that didn't quite fit.

I used to know this house by heart. The way the floor cooled under my feet in the early morning. The hum of the pipes when someone ran the water too long. The way the doors groaned in protest when the wind pushed too hard against them.

Now, it feels different. Like someone had reached inside and rearranged the bones of it, just enough to make everything feel unfamiliar. Just enough to make me question whether it had ever really been ours to begin with.

The basement, once filled with Mom's half-finished paintings, had turned into a graveyard of things no one wanted to deal with yet. Canvas after canvas leaned against the walls like forgotten memories. Paint jars drying up, lids sealed too tight. She'd been working on pieces for an exhibit. Now, they just sat there, unfinished. Just like her and her grief.

I know the world kept moving after Elise. The sun still rose, cars still filled the streets, people still laughed in grocery store aisles and fell asleep with the TV on. But inside this house, time stuttered. It tripped over itself, spilling into the spaces she'd left behind.

Mom was the one who stopped the most. She moved through the days waiting for something to pull her back, like any second now, the clock might rewind and undo everything.

Some days, Dad and I got stuck too. In the quiet, in the untouched things, in the way her name sat in our mouths like something heavy, something dangerous.

The days weren't moving forward, not really. They were just the same ones on repeat, looping endlessly, playing a version of life that didn't fit any more.

And I'd wake up every morning, staring at the ceiling, watching the fan blades push the air in slow circles. And I'd think—if Dad had never installed those stupid ceiling fans five summers ago, maybe Elise would still be here. It wasn't logical, wasn't fair, but the thought stayed, curling up somewhere deep, refusing to leave.

Her absence wasn't just in the obvious things—it was in the details no one else would notice. The bobby pins scattered on her nightstand, the half-empty water bottle by the couch, the way her shoes still sat by the door like she might step into them at any moment.

Her makeup pouch was still in the bathroom sink, unzipped, a lipstick stain smudged on the fabric. Like she'd left in a hurry. Like she'd be back any second to fix what she hadn't finished.

And then there was her door. Always shut. Always untouched. None of us willing to be the first to open it. Because what if the air inside still held her, frozen in time? Or worse—what if it didn't?

I force myself out of bed. The sheets tangle around my ankles, resisting like they were colluding with gravity.

The floor is cold—sharp enough to shock, but not enough to wake me up. I curl my toes against it, press down, just to feel something solid. I exhale, slow and controlled. The air moves. My chest rises. My hands aren't shaking. I am here. I am breathing. And maybe, for now, that is enough.

Walking past Elise's room feels wrong. It used to be loud—Avril Lavigne blasting from her speakers, the scent of hairspray thick in the air, Mom yelling at her to turn the volume down.

Now, it's just quiet. Too quiet.

I reach for the doorknob, fingers hovering just above it, my heartbeat steady against my ribs. I could open it. Step inside. Face whatever was waiting on the other side.

Instead, I let my hand fall to my side and turn away.

The kitchen is quiet, the kind of quiet that makes the house feel emptier than it is. Breakfast is always a hit-or-miss—

sometimes there is food on the counter, other times nothing at all.

Dad is usually gone by the time I wake up, off to work before the sun had even fully settled into the sky. I don't see him much. Not that I mind. Talking to him has never been easy.

Something on the counter catches my eye. Next to the fruit basket, a single white pill sat on a torn piece of paper: *Just in case.*

I stare at it, the words sinking into me, heavy and unmoving. The pill rests in my palm, cool and smooth—a quiet reminder of something I'm not ready to face. The psychiatrist had suggested I take the same medication as Mom. I suppose, for them, grief was something that could be measured out and swallowed. Something you could fix with a single pill.

I bring it close to my lips, pausing. Would this make the weight in my chest disappear? Or would it just make me forget I'm carrying it? The thought makes my stomach twist. Before I can think twice, I flick the pill into the trash. It lands with the softest sound—barely a whisper, barely real.

I grab my bag and leave before I can change my mind.

The bus ride to school is the same as always—too loud, too restless, too full of conversations I'm not a part of.

Kids swap stories about their weekend plans—some penthouse party in Makati on Friday night. Near the back, someone is watching a YouTube video without earphones, the sound blending with the low hum of the air-conditioning. A few seats away, two juniors argue over whether to get Starbucks or Wildflour before their first class.

I keep my head down, scrolling through my phone without actually reading anything.

Every now and then, I catch someone looking at me—soft, careful glances. They aren't sure if they should say something or pretend they don't see me at all.

I don't want their pity. It hangs in the air, thick and cloying, like perfume that wouldn't fade.

I turn to the window as the bus moves through McKinley Road, past gated villages and high-rise condos. We pass Forbes Park, where streets are lined with mansions hidden behind tall walls, then Bonifacio Global City, where glass buildings stretch towards the sky, towering over busy sidewalks.

The city doesn't care. It moves on, same as always. Like Elise had never been here.

I shove in my earphones, drowning out the noise. But the silence in my head is worse.

Elise was never the loudest in the room, but she had a way of being there without needing to take up space. She didn't demand attention—she just had this presence you felt more than heard. The kind that lingered.

Then came the rumours.

And slowly, she stopped showing up in the ways we were used to. Not in a dramatic, falling-off-the-face-of-the-earth kind of way. Just . . . quieter. Smaller. Like she was retreating inwards, inch by inch.

Things shifted after the whispers started—that Elise was flirting with every guy on the soccer team. The truth didn't matter; she wasn't. It didn't matter that she laughed less, spoke less, and shrank into herself. People don't like change, especially when they don't understand it.

And then it got worse.

Elise still sat with her friends at lunch, but no one really talked to her. She'd laugh at their jokes, and no one would laugh back. She'd ask about weekend plans, and someone would change the subject. Her voice faded—like background music no one noticed any more.

Then, one day, she wasn't sitting with them.

I walked into the cafeteria, expecting to see her at their table out of habit, but she was in the farthest corner instead—alone, head down, pushing food around on her tray like maybe, if she waited long enough, it would just disappear.

I could sit with her. I should.

But then Julia and Savannah waved me over. I hesitated—just long enough for Elise to look up and meet my eyes.

I forced a smile. Small.

Then I turned away.

And by the time she stopped trying to fit in, no one even noticed she was gone. Not until it was too late.

My friends didn't know what to say after the news broke. They tried. But 'I'm sorry' only takes you so far before silence takes over. Before people stop saying her name, like avoiding it might make everything less real.

Elise was everywhere and nowhere all at once. Her untouched locker, the photos on my phone, the posters with her face plastered across bulletin boards. As if reducing her to a lesson would change anything.

Life kept moving. The world barely noticed.

I even picked up this strange habit of watching people—I was trying to figure out how to act again.

At lunch, Julia and Savannah would chat about their weekend plans or whatever show they were watching, and I'd nod along, pretending to keep up. Most of the time, I just listened.

I blink, and the memory slips away, replaced by the buzz of the cafeteria. Julia turns to me, her expression careful, like she's testing the waters. 'Hey, we're all going to the bowling alley on Friday. You should come.'

'Yeah,' Savannah adds, her voice a little too bright. 'You can show off your gutter-ball skills.'

I almost laugh. Elise and I had always been terrible bowlers, the kind who threw the ball like it weighed a thousand pounds, watching it wobble its way into the gutter. I can almost hear her now, shouting in victory after knocking down a single pin.

A faint smile tugs at my lips. 'I'll think about it.'

Julia and Savannah share a look. They know what 'I'll think about it' really means. But they don't push.

Part of me wants to go. Wants to feel normal, or at least pretend. To sit across from my friends, listen to their conversations, and maybe even add something of my own.

But another part of me knows better. Knows I'd sit there feeling like an outsider in my own life. That I'd laugh at the right moments, nod when I was supposed to, and still, it wouldn't feel like enough. Like I was trying too hard to catch up to something that had already left without me.

After lunch, I walk to class, the air thick and unmoving. Everything around me *is* normal, but nothing *felt* normal. The hallways buzzed with life—lockers slamming, sneakers squeaking against the tile, conversations overlapping—but it all felt far away, like I was hearing it from underwater.

I adjust the strap of my bag, focusing on the weight of it against my shoulder. Something solid. Something real. But the heaviness in my chest doesn't budge.

With every step, I can almost hear Elise's voice, teasing me about my 'grumpy caterpillar' phase. I want to hold onto it, but the second I do, something else pushes it away—the reminder that she isn't here. That she isn't going to call me that again.

The thought leaves a dull, aching pull in my stomach.

As I pass the gym, I catch sight of a group of girls standing near the entrance. Their voices drop the second they notice me. I look down, but I can still feel it—the careful glances, the weight of their pity pressing into my skin like an old bruise.

It always happens like this: the soft, hesitant 'I'm so sorry,' the lingering looks, the careful way people speak to me, as if grief had made me fragile. Like they thought if they said the wrong thing, I'd break apart right in front of them.

I push through the door of my English class and sink into my seat, exhaling like I'd been holding my breath without realizing.

'Hi, Lauren!' Kelly calls, her voice too bright. I lift a hand in a half-wave, not trusting myself to match her energy. Across from me, Janice gives me a small nod. She doesn't say anything, but she doesn't need to. Somehow, that was better.

Mr Thompson walks in and sets his books down. 'All right, class. Let's talk about poetry.'

The usual shuffling of notebooks and pens fills the room, and for a moment, the air feels lighter. But my chest still feels tight in anticipation of what I knew was coming.

Elise had never been one for poetry. I was sure of that, because she preferred things that were more straightforward, less wrapped in layers of meaning.

As Mr Thompson reads aloud, I try to focus, but the words blur together, their meaning slipping through my fingers like sand.

The classroom buzzes around me—snippets of conversation, the scrape of chairs against the floor, the rustle of notebooks flipping open. But it all feels distant, like I'm hearing it through water. Like I am here, sitting in my usual seat, breathing the same air as everyone else, but somehow separate. A step removed. Present, but not really.

My pen rolls back and forth between my fingers. I will myself to write something, anything, but my brain feels empty. Everything is too much and not enough all at once.

Time drags. Every tick of the clock a reminder that life was moving forward without Elise.

When the bell rings, I stand too quickly, the legs of my chair scraping against the floor. A tap on my shoulder pulls me back.

I turn to see Kelly watching me, her expression careful.

'You okay?' she asks, her voice quieter than usual, like she was checking to see if I was still here.

I want to tell her the truth—that I'm not sure, that everything feels wrong, that I don't know how to exist in a world that had moved on without Elise.

Instead, I force a small smile. 'Yeah. Just . . . tired, I guess.'

Kelly nods, but I can see the doubt in her eyes. 'If you need to talk, I'm here, okay?'

I swallow, then nod again. 'Thanks.'

The hallway stretches ahead of me, too bright, too loud, too full of things that don't make sense any more.

At my locker, my fingers tremble, a quiet betrayal of everything I'm trying to keep steady. I'm not sure why—maybe it's the weight of the day settling in my bones.

I twist the lock open and stare at the contents. Books I wasn't sure I'd ever need again. Elise's favourite hair products, still sitting where I'd left them. I should've thrown them away weeks ago.

But I couldn't.

Memories hit me all at once—her room, a mess of clothes and books. Music playing while she curled her hair. The time she nearly set the kitchen on fire trying to make pancakes.

I can almost hear her laughing, and for a second, it feels so real that my chest aches.

A few students walk past, their eyes flickering towards me before quickly looking away. Polite. Careful. Like they aren't sure if they should say something or if silence is the kinder option.

I have no idea how the rest of the day is going to go. Hell, I don't even know how I'm supposed to do any of this.

But as I close my locker and turn down the hall, I cling to one thought, trying to make it feel true:

I am still here. And that has to mean something.

4

14 August 2023

In a realm of my own, I shiver and sigh,
Cold and alone, beneath a vast sky.
In silence I linger, where shadows are cast,
But your voice, like a beacon, breaks through the vast.
What am I, lost in the dark, yet saved by your sound,
A whisper of hope when no comfort is found?

My hand slides into my pocket before I even know what I'm doing. My fingers brush against the crumpled note, the one I'd pulled from a library book Elise borrowed.

I have the riddle memorized. Every word sat in my head, refusing to let go. And no matter how many times I turned it over, the answer stayed just out of reach, slipping through my fingers like sand.

For a moment, I let myself believe—just for a second—that Elise was right here beside me. That she had written the note for me to find, that she wanted me to figure this out. That she was leading me somewhere. Somewhere farther. Somewhere that made sense of her death and everything she left behind.

'You're zoning out again,' Zania says, her voice easy, stating the obvious.

She pops the last piece of cheese roll into her mouth, brushing crumbs off her lap. Zania always reminds me of Elise—not just because they were the same age, but because they carried the same kind of reckless brightness, like they'd never once considered dimming themselves for anyone.

Some people demand attention. Zania never has to. She just exists in a way that makes people notice. I'm not sure if I envy that or if it just makes me feel more out of place.

I glance at her, wondering—not for the first time—if she ever second-guesses herself. If she ever feels unsure about where she's going or if she just picks a direction and moves towards it.

Zania is a few weeks into her first year of college, studying business. I have no idea if she actually likes it or if she is just doing it because it made sense. And that was the thing about her—she never seemed lost. And if she was, she never let it show.

I look away, pressing my forehead against the car window. Outside, the city is already wide awake. Cars inching forward. Motorcycles slipping through gaps that barely existed. Delivery riders weaving through it all like it was second nature. Life, moving at full speed.

'I'm not,' I say, even though we both know it isn't true. I need to hold it together today. If I let my mind wander too far, I'm not sure I'll be able to pull it back. 'Just thinking about what it's like to start school all over again. In person.'

Zania hums, taking a sip from her tumbler. 'It's weird, isn't it? Summer always makes it feel like we've been gone forever.'

Except it wasn't just summer. I had been gone much longer than that.

The car slows as we pull into the school parking lot. My fingers tighten around the strap of my bag, the ridges digging into my skin. I watch students step out of their cars, moving like they belonged here, like they'd never been gone.

My hand hovers over the door handle. There will be no turning back if I step out now. My breath comes too quick, too shallow. I squeeze my eyes shut for half a second, willing my legs to move. Then I inhale—one, two, three—and force myself to push the door open.

The campus stretches out in front of me—tall buildings, open courtyards, the low hum of voices filling the air. Students spill from their cars, some waving goodbye to their drivers, others adjusting their backpacks as they head inside. Just another morning. As though it wasn't my first time back since everything changed.

'We're here,' Zania says, shifting the car into park. She glances at me, her voice steady. 'You got this, okay? I'll be back around three to pick you up.'

Her words are something solid to hold onto, something to keep me from drifting. I nod, forcing a smile even though it doesn't feel quite right.

'Thanks, Zania.'

The car door creaks open, and the Manila heat hits me immediately—thick and heavy, sticking to my skin. I take a deep breath, hoping it would settle something inside me. But the air is dense, too warm, carrying the weight of everything I was trying so hard to keep in.

Zania gives my hand a quick squeeze before I step out of the car and force myself into the swarm of students. I swallow hard, willing myself to stay steady and, for once, to *think happy thoughts*—because obviously, that would fix everything.

Inside, the hallways buzz with movement—lockers slamming, sneakers squeaking, voices blending in a dozen different accents. I force myself to focus on the rhythm of it, to slip into the flow even though it feels like I'm moving through a place that had rearranged itself in my absence.

Then I see Savannah, standing by her locker, laughing with a group of friends. Her laughter rings out—bright, sharp, effortless. Like nothing had changed. Like we were still in the same place, still the same people—just in different circles now. Like the months between us hadn't stretched and twisted everything out of shape.

A knot tightens in my stomach.

I had imagined this moment too many times—played out every scenario in my head. Maybe she'd look guilty. Maybe I'd be angry. Maybe our eyes would meet, and something unspoken would pass between us, something that said, *I miss you. I'm sorry.*

But she doesn't even notice me.

I keep my head down, moving past groups of students who barely glance my way, but somehow, I still feel exposed. Their conversations float in and out—weekend plans, test schedules, inside jokes that no longer belong to me. Things I used to understand. Things that now felt like another language.

I turn the corner just as I hear my name.

'Lauren?'

I freeze. The way it was said—so normal, so easy—felt anything but.

When I turn, I meet a pair of familiar eyes.

'Do I know you?'

He grins, stepping closer with a confidence I can't mirror. 'Aaren Legarda. We had History together in seventh grade. Remember?'

I search my memory, but I come up empty. Nothing clicks. The way he spoke—like I was supposed to remember him, like he actually remembered me—made me feel like I should.

'Sorry,' I say, shifting my weight. 'Seventh grade is kind of a blur.'

Aaren chuckles, nodding. 'Yeah, I guess it's a blur for most of us. But I remember you.'

Of course he does.

Everyone remembers me now. I used to blend in, just another body passing through the halls, unnoticed, unimportant. But ever since Elise, it's like I've been dragged to the centre of a stage I never wanted to stand on. Their eyes land on me, but they don't really see me—they see a story, a tragedy, a conversation starter. Just something to whisper about when the halls get too quiet.

'You okay?' Aaren's light-hearted tone is gone, replaced by a softer concern that crinkles the corners of his eyes. 'You look a little . . . off,' he adds, his gaze lingering with a hint of unspoken worry.

I hesitate, weighing how much of the truth to give. 'Yeah,' I say finally. 'Just . . . being back here is a lot.'

'I get that,' he says. 'This place can feel suffocating.'

I nod, but it wasn't just the school. It was everything. The hallways, the memories, the way the air felt different now—like Elise had taken something with her when she left, and I was the only one who noticed.

A group of girls pass us, laughing, their voices bright and careless. It should've been comforting, but instead, it felt like I was standing behind glass, watching a world I used to belong to.

'Hey,' Aaren says, pulling me back to the present. 'Let me know if you need anything.'

I hesitate. Maybe he means it. Maybe he is just being polite. Either way, it feels easier to keep my distance.

'Thanks,' I say lightly. 'I'll think about it.'

He nods before melting into the crowd. I watch as he disappears, blending in like it is the easiest thing in the world. Meanwhile, I'm still stuck here, feeling like an outsider in a place that used to feel like mine.

I exhale sharply, adjust my bag strap, and force myself to move.

My hands are shaking by the time I reach my locker.

I twist the lock once, twice—too many times, messing up the combination. Deep breath. Try again. The lock pops open, but the relief is short-lived.

Behind me, two girls lean against their lockers, their voices low but not low enough.

'I'm just saying, it's sad,' one of them says. 'Like, Elise always seemed so . . . normal, you know?'

'Right? You'd never guess what was going on with her. It's kinda scary.'

My hand freezes midair, gripping the locker door. I wasn't trying to listen, but their words land like stones, impossible to ignore.

Then—

'Did you hear the part about Lauren?'

A pause.

'Yeah. I mean, what do you even say to someone after all that?'

A lump forms in my throat. I pretend to dig through my bag, fingers brushing against notebooks I'm not looking for. Their words cling to me—persistent, unwanted, ink smudged on my skin.

They weren't even *trying* to be quiet.

'Do you think she knew?'

'I don't know . . . Maybe?'

A fresh wave of nausea hits me.

I slam my locker shut, harder than I mean to. Both girls snap their heads towards me. For a split second, the hallway stills.

Our eyes meet.

Then they smile—tight, polite, the way people do when they've been caught talking about you but don't want to admit it.

I smile back, stiff and fake, before turning on my heel and walking away.

I can feel their eyes on me as I move down the hall, my legs unsteady. Every step feels too loud, too deliberate. Like I'm performing for an audience, waiting for someone to call me out.

I thought I could handle this. I thought I was ready.

But now, standing here, carrying the weight of something I never asked for, it doesn't feel like I'm ready for anything.

5

25 August 2021

I haven't really seen my mom in days. Not in the way that matters.

We live in the same house, move through the same spaces, but we are careful not to collide. Two people stranded in separate lifeboats, drifting close enough to see each other but never close enough to reach. We weren't fighting, but we weren't trying either. Just existing in the same grief, Elise filling the spaces we didn't dare to close.

The walls feel thinner lately, too easy to hear through. The quiet shuffle of her footsteps. The sound of her crying when she thinks no one is listening. Sometimes Elise's name, whispered like a prayer, or maybe a curse.

For days, I told myself to check on her. And for just as many, I found reasons not to.

I'd stand outside her door, fingers hovering over the wood, heartbeat too loud in my ears. But I never knocked. Never stepped inside. Instead, I let the silence grow between us, let the distance stretch until it felt impossible to close.

Maybe it's because of last week's dinner. The way it still lingers in my head, playing on a loop like a broken record that won't let me forget.

I can still see the table, the untouched plates, the quiet scrape of a fork against porcelain. The way no one spoke, not really. Just small words stretched too thin, barely holding up the weight of everything left unsaid.

And then—Mom's voice, sharp and sudden, cutting through the quiet.

'I just don't understand how you didn't see it,' she said, and though she wasn't looking at me, I felt it. The words, the weight of them, pressing down.

Dad shifted in his seat, adjusting his glasses the way he always did when he didn't want to get involved. The room smelled like something burnt. Garlic, maybe. My plate sat in front of me, half-full, but I wasn't hungry any more.

I kept my eyes on my plate, my stomach a tight knot. If I looked up, I'd see it—her disappointment, maybe even her resentment. And if I saw that, I wasn't sure I could force another bite down.

I didn't argue. Not because I agreed, but because it wouldn't matter. It never did.

When Dad finally spoke, his voice was careful, measured—he was walking across something fragile, afraid to set off a break that couldn't be undone.

He said Mom's name softly, like that alone could bring her back. Like if he was gentle enough, she wouldn't slip further away.

But I wanted him to do more than pull.

I wanted him to fight.

To look at her the way she looked at me and say, *enough.* To tell her she was wrong. That I wasn't the villain she had rewritten me to be. That I hadn't failed Elise in all the ways she believed I had.

But he didn't.

His voice never wavered, never cracked. He held himself together with the determination of a person who knew if he let even one fracture show, the whole thing would collapse. And maybe, in a way, it already had.

His chair scraped against the floor as he stood, and just before he disappeared down the hall, he did something that nearly made me fall apart.

He apologized.

And I wanted to tell him it wasn't his fault.

Because I saw it too—the way grief had hollowed him out, made him quieter, like he was trying to disappear without actually leaving. How it settled in his bones, made a home there, pressing into his ribs until his breaths came slower, shallower—even air was too much to carry. How it weighed down his hands until they found their way to a glass of brandy, night after night, as if something at the bottom could undo everything that had already been done.

And no matter how many times I told myself it wasn't my job to fix something that had already fallen apart, I still felt like I should.

Like I owed it to him.

Like I owed it to her.

Like maybe, if I could just find the right words, the right way to make things easier, then I wouldn't have to keep carrying this feeling.

The one that had lived inside me since the day Elise died.

The one that whispered, over and over, that Mom had every reason to blame me.

So today, I stop finding ways to avoid it.

And before I can talk myself out of it, I stand outside their bedroom door.

My feet feel heavy, like they want to turn me around, lead me anywhere but here. But I press forward, nudging the door open just enough to see inside.

And then I stop breathing.

She is sitting on the edge of her bed, staring out the window. Talking to the wall.

A laugh nearly breaks free—sharp, uneasy. Because what else am I supposed to do? Cry? Walk in and ask if the wall is giving her good advice?

Something inside me curls tight, sharp and aching. I don't know whether to step forward or back away before she notices me standing there.

'Mom?' My voice barely makes it past my throat.

The word scrapes its way out, like it wasn't sure it belonged there.

She turns slowly, her eyes red and swollen, her face blotchy like she'd been rubbing at it for hours. At least she isn't crying now. That's something. But for a second, I'm not sure if I should be worried or just hand her an antihistamine.

Her gaze lands on me, flickering like a bad signal, unfocused, like she wasn't entirely convinced I was real. Like she was trying to decide if I was standing in front of her or if I was just another memory—one that hurt too much to hold onto.

Then, her lips twitch. Barely. Just a hint of something worn-out and fragile.

She lifts a hand, patting the mattress beside her.

I hesitate.

It's been a long time since she's wanted me there.

The space between us feels too wide, like something neither of us know how to cross. Still, I step forward, slow and uncertain, like I was testing the ground beneath me, waiting for it to give way. When I finally sit, I stay on the edge of the bed, careful, unsure.

For a while, neither of us speak.

She keeps staring out the window like the answers were somewhere beyond the glass. Like if she looked long enough, she'd find Elise out there, waiting for her.

I want to say something. Something that won't shatter whatever this was. Something that won't make her shut down again. But grief makes words feel sharp, dangerous. One wrong move and everything might break apart.

Then, without a sound, she leans her head against my shoulder.

I freeze.

Not because I don't want it, but because I don't know what to do with it.

How to be this for her when I'm not even sure how to be anything at all any more.

Her breath is slow. Steady. The warmth of her cheek presses into me.

I let out a shaky exhale.

And for the first time in forever, it is just us.

No blame. No grief between us like a wall we can't get past. Just something small. Something real.

And for the first time in forever, I let myself believe that maybe, she still sees me as hers.

6

14 August 2023

When the final bell rings, I move through the hall with my eyes glued to the floor, like the answers to life's biggest questions were hiding in the tile grout. Blending in had always been my thing—if disappearing were a class, I'd have a solid A+.

I spin the lock on my locker, dump my books inside, and am about to slam the door shut when I see it again.

The note.

It is crumpled, sitting in a corner of my bag, looking like it had been waiting for me to stop pretending I didn't see it. I hesitate, then pick it up, smoothing my fingers over the ink like that might make it more readable. It doesn't. The words stay exactly the same—stubborn, unreadable, and heavier than they should be.

The hallway noise fades into the background—sneakers screeching, lockers slamming, voices weaving together into a steady hum. The world keeps moving. I stay stuck.

Then, just as I'm about to crumple the note even more in frustration, a voice cuts through the noise.

'I think it means heart. But it could also mean loneliness.'

I turn and see Aaren casually leaning against the doorframe, his guitar case slung over his shoulder.

A shadow passes through his eyes, so quick I almost miss it. But it makes his words feel like something more, like he understands it in a way he isn't quite ready to admit. There is a quiet certainty about him, something I recognize—like he's holding onto something deeper, something beyond just trying to figure things out.

'And you know this because . . .?' I try to sound casual, but it comes out more like a challenge.

'Because I like riddles,' he says with a shrug, like that was a perfectly normal personality trait.

I narrow my eyes. 'That's . . . a weird hobby.'

He nods towards the note in my hand. 'I mean, it kind of spells it out for you.'

'Right. Well, good for you.'

Aaren grins, unfazed. 'So, do you have any other riddles you need help solving?' I shut my locker and start walking down the hall, but he walks backwards, matching my pace like we were in some slow-motion chase scene.

'Wow. He's like a persistent pop-up ad.'

'A very cute one.'

I roll my eyes and step to the side, but he sidesteps along with me.

'I don't know what you're trying to do, but no one asked for your help,' I mutter, stopping next to a random car, hoping Zania would appear and rescue me.

'Well, that's a heartfelt thank you,' he says, giving a dramatic bow like he was accepting an imaginary award.

I roll my eyes again. Somehow, his grin only widens.

'You're welcome, then.'

Something about the way he looks at me—expectant but not pushy, amused but not mocking—makes me grip the note tighter. He wasn't waiting for a thank you, not really. It was more like he'd already figured me out. Like he knew I'd let him in before I even knew it myself.

Aaren adjusts the strap of his guitar case. 'Anyway, I should get going.'

I hear myself say it before I can even think to hold it back.

'Wait.'

Aaren turns, one eyebrow slightly raised.

'Yeah?'

I hesitate, throat tight. I'm not used to asking for help. But there is something about the way he offered—so easy, so sure—that makes me pause.

Maybe . . . maybe I don't have to figure this out alone.

'Maybe . . . maybe I could use some help after all.'

His expression softens—not smug, not triumphant. Just . . . understanding.

'Okay,' he says.

'How about Café Verona at six?'

His eyes light up. 'Verona? The tiny place with the wooden chairs and the strawberry hot chocolate?'

'That's the one,' I say, and to my surprise, a smile sneaks out before I can stop it. 'If we're doing this, we might as well go all in—hot chocolate and everything.'

Aaren grins like I've just made his whole day.

'Sounds good.'

❀

The traffic had been heavy, and by the time we pull into the driveway, I'm still not sure about what I'm doing. But I have to say something, even if it feels wrong. 'Can you drop me off at Café Verona?' My voice barely makes it out, softer than I want it to be, like I was still trying to decide whether or not I should go—even though I was the one who'd told him to meet me there.

Zania doesn't ask why. She just gives me a look, like she's already frustrated. 'You could've told me earlier,' she says, unwrapping a piece of candy and popping it into her mouth as she turns the key in the ignition again.

The traffic is still a mess, but after what feels like another hour, we finally make it to the café.

Before I step out, Zania reminds me, 'Call me if you need a ride.'

The door shuts behind me, and I hesitate on the sidewalk, gripping the strap of my bag a little too tight. I'd been here a hundred times before, but today, it felt different. Like stepping into a memory I wasn't sure I was ready to relive.

I push the door open, and the familiar scent hits me all at once—brewed coffee, melted chocolate, toasted bread. The soft chime of the door closing behind me makes my chest tighten, pulling me back to thirteen, to sticky fingers and laughter, to Elise nudging me with her elbow while we waited for Dad to pick us up.

I exhale, shaking it off.

The café buzzes with the usual sounds—murmured conversations, the occasional burst of laughter, the clang of a spoon against ceramic. A barista weaves between tables, balancing a tray of drinks, steam curling into the air. Everything looks the same, smells the same. But nothing about it feels the same.

Then I spot him.

Aaren is impossible to miss—waving like he's stranded at sea and I'm the rescue boat. Too eager. Too much. His grin stretches wide, like he knows exactly how ridiculous he looks.

I sigh, dragging my feet towards his table.

'Wow,' I mutter as I slide into the seat across from him. 'Do you wave at all your friends like that, or am I just lucky?'

'You?' He smirks. 'Absolutely special.'

He slides a menu towards me like it's some grand offering.

I don't take it. 'I already know what I'm getting.'

'Of course,' he muses. 'A regular.'

Before I can respond, a barista in a faded Verona apron stops at our table, notepad in hand. Our eyes meet, and I know right away that she remembers me. I'm not sure of her name, but I know her face—the same one I'd seen every time I ordered here. She always got my usual right before I even said a word. And from the way her lips curve into a small, knowing smile, I could tell she hadn't forgotten.

Aaren places his order with the seriousness of someone considering a matter of life or death. 'I want an *iced* strawberry hot chocolate and a blueberry muffin, please.'

She barely looks up as she jotted it down. 'Strawberry hot chocolate and an extra hot pan-seared ube cheese roll, right?'

I smile and nod.

For a split second, Elise is there again, teasing me about ordering hot chocolate in this heat but ordering one herself anyway.

I curl my fingers into fists beneath the table.

Aaren shakes his head in mock disappointment as the waitress walks away. 'Unbelievable. I was robbed of the joy of watching you panic over what to get.'

I scoff, but a small smile slips through. Reaching into my pocket, my fingers trace the soft, creased edges of the note before I pull it out. I flatten it on the table, the paper thin and worn from being folded and unfolded too many times.

Aaren's eyes flick to it. His smirk fades, curiosity shifting into something quieter.

'You remember that riddle from earlier?' I ask.

He nods. 'Yeah.'

I hesitate, rolling the paper between my fingers, grounding myself in the texture.

'It was from my sister.'

Aaren leans in slightly, his usual playfulness slipping away.

'I found it behind the canvas of a painting in my bedroom—one my mom painted,' I explain, trying to fill in the gaps. But Aaren still looks confused.

'The first note I found had coordinates,' I go on. 'That note led me to the library. And this one—the riddle—was inside a book my sister had borrowed.'

Aaren blinks. 'Wait. Coordinates?'

I nod, letting out a slow breath.

'Okay . . . but what do you mean it was from your sister?'

'She wrote it,' I say, hesitating. 'For me to find, I think.' The last part comes out more like a whisper, uncertainty creeping in. 'It feels like she's leading me somewhere. I don't know why or what I'm supposed to find, but . . . it feels like I'm missing something. Especially about her death.'

Aaren looks at me, his eyes shifting between me and the note. He doesn't say anything, and for a second, I feel like I'm drifting away from everything I'd just said, like I could pretend I hadn't said it at all—until the sharp clang of a spoon hitting the floor snaps me back.

'You think she left them for you on purpose?' he asks.

'I do.'

I run my thumb along the edge of the paper, feeling where Elise had pressed her pen too hard, like she had been in a rush.

Aaren exhales, his face briefly clouded at the mention of my sister's name. 'Look, I'm sorry that your sister—'

I cut him off, my voice sharper than I intend. 'Please—no need.'

He raises his hands in a silent gesture of understanding. My throat tightens. 'I can't do this alone. And if I tell anyone—my cousin, my aunt—they'll just tell me to stop looking.'

Aaren's expression softens, a flicker of pain in his eyes before his lips curl into a wry smile. 'So, you need someone who speaks fluent riddle and drives a beat-up Jeep?'

'Both.'

He taps his fingers against the table, pretending to think. 'Hmm. Sounds like a lot of work.'

I roll my eyes. 'So, is that a no?'

Aaren's smirk fades slightly. He wasn't joking any more.

I clench the note, the fragile paper bending under my grip. 'I need to find them, Aaren. Not just because she left them, but because it's all I have left of her that makes sense.'

The words leave me raw but steady. 'Everyone keeps telling me to move on, to let it go—but how am I supposed to? If I do, it's like she vanishes completely, and I can't let that happen. I just need this—whatever this is—to make sense of her death.'

I meet his eyes, my chest tight. A part of me wants to take it back. But I don't.

Aaren doesn't answer right away. He just looks at me, like he's trying to figure out if helping me was a terrible idea or the only thing that made sense.

Finally, he exhales and leans back, arms draped over the seat.

'Alright, Lauren,' he says, calm and certain. 'I'll help you.'

The weight in my chest eases, just a little.

'You will?'

He nods, like it's the most obvious thing in the world. Then his gaze shifts to the window, already lost in thought, already piecing things together.

I let out a slow breath and reach for his hand, giving it a small squeeze—my way of saying *thank you* when words don't feel like enough. 'Thank you,' I say anyway, softer this time.

Aaren glances down at our hands, his lips twitching—not quite a smile, not quite a smirk. Just something real.

'So,' he says, tilting his head, 'when do we start?'

7

18 August 2023

The smell of melted candle wax and sampaguita hit me the second we step into Santuario de San Antonio. Sunlight streams through the stained-glass windows, scattering streaks of gold and blue across the polished floor.

I inhale sharply. The air here always felt heavier, thick with whispered prayers and the kind of grief that settled into wooden pews like dust.

The church is already alive with movement—older women in veils clutching their rosaries, office workers squeezing in a prayer before diving into Makati traffic, students in crisp uniforms sitting beside their overly devout mothers.

And then there's me.

Technically, I should've been at school, half-asleep in History or zoning out in another class I was supposed to be suffering through. But Clarissa had called my guidance counsellor earlier this week, asking for me to be excused for a 'special Mass'.

I didn't argue. A morning in church was better than a morning of classmates tiptoeing around me, watching for signs of an emotional breakdown like I was a walking cautionary tale. At least here, I could zone out without someone whispering my name like a tragic headline.

Still, as I step further inside, the reason I'm here settles in my chest like something heavy pressing down.

Clarissa grips the well-worn rosary beads she's always carried, setting up 'special intentions' for me. Her hope was basically a silent plea to the Virgin Mary—praying Jesus would just slap the mental illness out of me.

She dips her fingers into the holy water, crossing herself before nudging me.

I sigh but follow her example. Skipping it feels like inviting bad luck.

We slide into a pew near the back, where the scent of burning candles and old wood lingers in the air. Years of unshakable faith evident in every movement as Clarissa drops to her knees, her lips moving quickly in prayer. Each whispered word feels like a lifeline tossed towards heaven, a habit she'd built over a lifetime of turning to her faith in moments of struggle.

I stay seated, aiming for a balance between looking respectful and not looking like I was waiting for divine punishment.

Then the lector's voice rings out.

'Let us pray for those struggling with illness—physical, emotional, and mental.'

Clarissa's elbow nudges me.

I ignore her, staring up at the ceiling instead. The chandeliers sway slightly, their warm glow catching on the high arches.

'That they may find healing and strength in God's love, let us pray.'

'Lord, hear our prayer.'

The words leave my mouth automatically, like a class recitation—something I say because I am supposed to, not because I think it would actually change anything.

'Is this the part where we disappear?' a voice in my head chimes in.

Clarissa glances at me again, that same expectant look on her face. The one she's been giving me for months, like she was waiting for me to have some grand epiphany and realize prayer was the cure for literally everything.

I exhale through my nose, keeping my expression neutral as the mass continued.

I'm already itching to leave by the time communion starts but Clarissa stays kneeling long after most people have returned to their seats.

I check my watch. How many special intentions did she sign me up for? An entire novena?

Finally, she stands and turns to me.

'I really did offer special intentions for you today,' she says, adjusting her bag strap.

I force a small smile. 'Yeah, I figured.'

She ignores my sarcasm. 'I prayed for you to get better.'

And there it is.

Better.

Like I had a cold and just needed some rest and salabat to bounce back.

I swallow down the sigh threatening to escape. 'Thanks,' I mutter, because what else am I supposed to say? *Sorry, but I don't think Jesus does same-day healing services?*

Clarissa lets out a quiet breath, then reaches into her bag and pulls out a small white candle, pressing it into my palm.

'You should light this. It might help.'

The candle sits in my hand, cool and smooth, the wick still untouched. I turn it over, tracing the edges like it might reveal something if I held it long enough.

'Is this for divine intervention,' I ask, 'or are you just trying to get me to set something on fire?'

Clarissa exhales sharply through her nose, clearly debating whether smacking me in the middle of a church counted as a sin.

'Lauren, just try. It won't kill you.' Her voice softens, but not enough to hide the frustration curling at the edges. 'You don't even come to Sunday mass with me. This is the least you can do.'

The candle smells faintly of vanilla, its untouched wick waiting.

'You act like this can be fixed—with prayers, candles, holy water.'

Clarissa's hands tighten over mine. 'That's not what I'm saying.'

I exhale. 'You don't have to.'

The words come out sharper than I intended. I shove the candle into my pocket, the movement stiff and automatic.

Clarissa's eyes flicker over me, searching for the right thing to say. But the right thing doesn't exist.

Finally, she sighs. 'I just want you to be okay.'

I want to believe her. Maybe a part of me even does. But *okay* felt too far away—like light trying to break through water, only to disappear before it reached the surface.

'Yeah, because prayer totally fixes brain chemistry.'

She nudges me then, closing her eyes, hands folded in quiet prayer—a silent plea for me to keep these thoughts locked away.

I press my lips together, biting back the words bubbling in my throat. *You don't get it. You never have. This is not something you fix.*

But I swallow them down. I am too tired to fight a battle I've already lost more times than I can count.

People like to act like mental health is just a bad phase, something you can outgrow with enough positivity and devotion. Like it's as simple as flipping a switch or pressing reset.

But this isn't a broken arm that mends with time. This isn't a bad haircut you can just laugh off.

This is something that lives beneath my skin, threading itself through my bones—sometimes quiet, sometimes so loud it drowns out everything else. It doesn't heal just because I want it to. It doesn't fade with sleep, or loosen its grip just because I take deep breaths and tell myself to be stronger.

I swallow hard and glance at Clarissa, waiting for her to say something. Anything.

But when she opens her eyes and turns her head towards me, she just stares. For once, there are no words.

❀

Math class feels like a slow-motion car crash—one I can't steer away from. Every number blurs into the next, equations stacking like bricks in a wall I have no idea how to climb.

Sir Villanueva drones on about algebra like it was the greatest love story ever told, his voice flattening into a distant hum. Outside, the Manila heat presses against the windows, the sky so blue it almost feels offensive, like it's taunting me for being stuck inside.

'Does Clarissa actually think a few prayers and a mass will make us disappear?'

I roll my eyes, ignoring the voice.

'You're a lost cause, you know that?'

'Shut up,' I mutter, barely moving my lips.

'What?'

I glance sideways. Savannah is staring at me, her pencil frozen mid-air, eyebrows lifted like I'd just told her I could see dead people.

'Nothing,' I say quickly, forcing a smile. It probably makes me look even weirder.

She hesitates but lets it go. I turn back to my notebook, but I'm not in class any more. My mind has wandered off, slipping through time and distance, landing in my mom's old art studio in Quezon City. The space she rented from Bill—the quiet, balding curator who let artists like her turn his building into something alive.

Was it empty now? Had Bill packed up her canvases, handed the keys to someone new? Had he tossed out the paintings she started at home but had to move there when Dad decided the garage wasn't for art? *If you're not going to finish them, put them away. Or throw them out.* Like they were just things. Like they didn't hold pieces of her.

The bell yanks me back to reality. I shove my books into my bag and am halfway to the door when Savannah catches my wrist.

'How are you holding up?' she asks, her voice light, but her eyes too careful.

'I'm fine,' I say, the lie smooth from overuse.

It's what people expect, what keeps them from looking too closely. But 'fine' is a slippery word, one that barely holds together when your own mind feels like unsteady ground, shifting before you can find your footing.

She doesn't look convinced. But all she says is, 'All right. See you around.'

I watch her walk away, her steps easy, unburdened. She isn't carrying the weight of something she can't name. It makes me feel heavier, like I'm carrying enough for both of us.

At my locker, I yank the door open, stuffing my books inside.

'Is your mom's name Cora Cruz-Sanders?'

The voice comes from behind me, and I turn so fast I nearly smack my head against the locker.

Aaren stands there, phone in hand, expression unreadable.

My heart trips over itself. 'How do you know that?'

He tilts his screen towards me, and there it is—one of my mom's paintings. Bold strokes of gold swallowing deep, smouldering reds, colours layered so thick they almost look like they're still drying.

'That's my mom's,' I say, reaching for the phone—I had to touch it to make it real.

'I found it online,' Aaren says, like it's no big deal. 'You mentioned she was an artist, so I looked up her name. This one's in a gallery.'

I blink. 'A gallery?'

He nods. 'It's part of an exhibit.'

I don't know what hits me harder—that her work had made it into a gallery, or that someone out there still cared enough to keep it alive.

Before I can process it, the hallway erupts with movement. Laura, the cheer captain, is shrieking at her boyfriend.

'You think I didn't see you commenting "cute" on her Instagram?!'

Aaren and I exchange a look, both of us barely holding in our laughter as Laura storms off, her boyfriend trailing behind like a kid caught stealing candy from a sari-sari store.

'So,' Aaren says, still grinning. 'How about it? Road trip to Antipolo?'

8

26 August 2021

I wake up with something I haven't felt in a long time.

Hope.

It's small, almost fragile, but it's there, lingering in the quiet of my room, in the way sunlight spills through the blinds, warming the floor. It sits in my chest, light and steady, filling spaces that have been empty for too long.

Last night keeps replaying in my head—sitting next to Mom, feeling the slow rise and fall of her breath against my shoulder, existing in the same space without blame or anger pressing between us. We didn't talk, but maybe we didn't have to. Maybe just being there was enough.

Maybe things don't have to stay broken forever.

The thought feels dangerous, but I let myself hold onto it anyway.

I stretch, kicking off the covers and pull on a sweatshirt. The house is still, but not in the suffocating way it usually is. It just feels . . . quiet. Like something is settling, like something is shifting in a way that doesn't feel as heavy.

I hover outside her door, pressing my palm flat against it.

No crying. No movement. Just quiet.

Good.

Maybe she's still asleep.

A thought drifts in before I can push it away—breakfast. It's small, maybe pointless, but it's something. A piece of normal, something to hold onto. Mom always made breakfast when she wanted to pretend everything was fine, like pancakes and scrambled eggs could smooth over the cracks in our lives. Maybe I can do the same. Maybe I can fix something.

I make it halfway down the hall before I hear it.

Crying.

Not the kind you can swallow down, not the kind that stays pressed into a pillow. It's wrecked, open, spilling out of her like it's been locked inside too long.

I stop.

The hope that had been quietly growing inside me, soft and cautious, vanishes.

I should leave. I should go downstairs, keep moving, let her have this moment alone. But then—

A crash.

Something slamming against the wall, hard enough to shake the floor beneath my feet.

I freeze. My pulse stumbles, trips over itself.

Another crash.

Then her voice—raw, shaking, falling apart midair.

'It should've been her.'

The air shifts, thickens, presses down on my chest.

Something heavy hits the porcelain floor with a dull, final thud.

'It should've been Lauren.'

The world tilts, slips out from under me.

I don't move. I don't blink. I don't breathe.

I don't know if she's talking to herself, if she thinks Elise is in the room with her, if she even realizes I'm standing here, catching every word like they're meant for me.

I just know I need to leave.

One step back. Then another. And another.

Like if I get far enough, the words won't stick. Like if I move fast enough, they won't settle under my skin, won't crawl into the cracks I thought were finally closing.

My hands won't stop shaking. My nails dig into my palms, hard enough to ground myself, hard enough to hold something real.

She didn't mean it.

She didn't mean it.

She didn't mean it.

But the words are already there, already settling in, already carving themselves into a place I can't reach.

I don't go downstairs.

I don't make breakfast.

I don't even try.

I go back to my room, pull the covers over my head, and let the quiet take me under.

Maybe I was stupid to believe anything could be different.

9

18 August 2023

Aaren taps his fingers against the steering wheel, exhaling sharply as he fiddles with the AC.

'Whose genius idea was it to drive through Manila during rush hour?'

I peel the plastic lid off my iced coffee, letting condensation drip onto my fingers. 'Yours. Pretty sure the universe is just humbling you right now.'

He snorts, shifting gears as we crawl forward. 'Yeah, well. Message received.'

The car smells like coffee, sun-warmed leather, and the faint trace of Aaren's cologne—musky, clean, something that sticks around long after he's gone. His guitar case sits in the backseat, half-hidden under his hoodie, like it's unsure whether it belongs there.

My phone buzzes against my thigh, Zania's name flashing on the screen, her texts popping up one after another.

> Where are you?

I sigh, already typing.

I have a project to do with a classmate

A few seconds later, another message.

School just started. What kind of teacher gives out projects already?

I hesitate, trying to come up with a lie that doesn't sound like one, but before I can send anything, another text pops up.

Anyway, I'll tell Mom you'll be out. Call me when you're done.

I stare at my screen, my fingers hovering over the keyboard.

Might take a few more weeks for this project to end.

A pause. Then—

So does that mean I won't have to wait for you anymore? No more driving to your school to pick you up?

I swallow.

Yeah . . .

My classmate will drive me home.

Another pause. Then—

If it's a boy and you like him, you can just tell me. I won't tell Mom.

I roll my eyes, shoving my phone into my lap.

Beside me, Aaren lets out a slow breath, his hair falling into his eyes as he shakes his head at the unmoving sea of cars ahead.

For some reason, I laugh.

It's not like that.

I put my phone down and watch the city move around us. Or at least, try to.

Manila is never still. Even in gridlock, it hums with life—the endless beeping of horns, the distant clang of construction, the murmur of street vendors calling out their goods. Billboards stacked high above us flashed ads for whitening soaps and fast food, for politicians promising change with rehearsed smiles. On the sidewalks below, students in oversized uniforms clutch their backpacks, office workers dodge puddles left over from last night's rain, tricycle drivers lean lazily against their bikes, waiting for passengers.

A jeepney swerves into our lane without warning, the conductor hanging off the side, slapping the roof with an open palm.

'Cubao! Cubao!'

His voice cuts through the thick, humid air, barely louder than the symphony of car horns.

Traffic wasn't just slow—it was stubborn, the kind that stretched seconds into lifetimes. Aaren flicks on his turn signal like it means something, like anyone would actually let us in. The light turns green. No one moves.

A motorcycle weaves through the tight space between two cars, knocking against a side mirror without so much as a glance back.

We inch past Aurora Boulevard, hemmed in by traffic and concrete. The road widens as we move onto Marcos Highway, stretching straight ahead through haze and glass. At the end, we turn right, the city thinning as the road begins to climb.

By the time we reach Sumulong Highway, we're already in Antipolo.

The road slopes upwards, the city shrinking in the rearview mirror. No more traffic. No more horns. Just the steady incline of the highway, winding higher and higher, pulling us away from the city's endless hum. The air feels lighter, even if the roads don't—steep climbs, sharp turns, tricycles dragging themselves uphill like they were questioning every decision that led them here.

I eye the narrow road ahead, the sharp curves hugging the mountain like a dare.

'Does this GPS even know there's an actual road up there?' I mutter.

'Nope,' Aaren deadpans. 'We might have to hike the rest of the way.'

I shoot him a glare as he effortlessly weaves past a slow-moving truck.

'I just wanted to say thanks again,' I say, fingers tightening around my cup. 'I know you've got a lot going on.'

He shrugs, the easy curve of his smile faltering for a split second. 'Not that much. I mean, I have things to do, but nothing I can't handle.'

I glance at the guitar case. It feels different somehow, like it has shifted slightly in the last four days, like it was taking up more space than before.

'So, you still lug that thing around?' I ask, tapping my fingers against the plastic lid of my drink.

Aaren shoots a quick look at the rearview mirror. 'Yeah. Had to borrow it from my bandmate. Mine's still in the shop.'

'Ah.' I try to picture him with a guitar, standing on a stage somewhere, fingers brushing over strings like it was second nature. 'So, you're, like, in a band or something?'

He smirks. 'Or something.'

I raise an eyebrow. 'Wow. Mysterious.'

'It's not a big deal. We're not trying to get famous or anything. We just play for ourselves. It's . . . a way to get out of my head for a while.'

Something about the way he says it makes me pause. 'Get out of your head?'

Aaren runs a hand through his hair, gaze flicking towards the window before settling back on the road. 'Yeah. Life gets . . . heavy sometimes. Music helps me make sense of it.'

I nod slowly, letting his words settle. 'Yeah, I get that. Everyone needs something that makes things feel a little less . . . complicated.'

His eyes flick to me, just for a second, like he was seeing if I actually meant it.

'So, what about you?' he asks. 'What do you do when you're not staring dramatically into the void?'

I let out a short laugh. 'That makes it sound like I have hobbies.'

'Well, do you?' His smirk deepens. 'Or are you one of those people who stares out of windows while sad music plays and pretends they're in a music video?'

I roll my eyes. 'I used to paint. A little sketching, too.' I hesitate, fingers drumming against my cup. 'But I haven't really done much of either lately.'

Aaren just nods, waiting.

'It's just . . . after everything that happened, it's been hard to pick up a brush.' Saying it out loud felt strange, like setting something fragile on a table and hoping it wouldn't break.

He doesn't say anything right away. Just grips the steering wheel a little tighter. 'Yeah. I get that.'

Silence settles between us, but it isn't awkward. Just there.

Then, after a beat, Aaren clicks his tongue. 'Well, if you ever feel like getting back into it, I'd be happy to judge your work.'

I shoot him a flat look. 'Wow. Encouraging.'

He grins. 'Hey, someone's gotta keep you humble.'

I shake my head, and before I can stop myself, the words are already out of my mouth. 'How long have you been at our school, anyway?'

Aaren quirks an eyebrow. 'You really don't remember seventh grade, do you?'

I search my memory, trying to place him in the blur of that year, but nothing clicks. 'Nope.'

He lets out a dramatic sigh. 'That's cold.'

I smirk. 'Not my fault you weren't memorable.'

He clutches his chest like I've physically wounded him. 'Wow. That hurt.' Then, after a pause, he says, 'I was a new student in seventh grade. Scholarship kid.'

That catches my attention. 'Scholarship?'

'Yeah. My dad works at the British Embassy. He found out the school was offering a partial scholarship and told my mom about it. She thought it was a good idea.'

I frown. 'Why?'

Aaren keeps his eyes on the road. 'She went through a lot growing up. Didn't have much, had to fight her way into the business world. One thing she always believed in was connections. She figured if I went to school with the right people, I'd have a head start.'

It makes sense, in a way. His mom had to build something from the ground up, and he was just . . . placed into it.

'And what do you think?' I ask.

Aaren taps his fingers against the steering wheel. 'I think she meant well.'

The most neutral answer I've ever heard.

'You don't feel weird about it?'

He lets out a quiet laugh. 'Of course I do. Most of the kids at our school are loaded. I've been to some of their houses—insane, by the way. Some of them have pools bigger than a public resort.'

I chuckle. 'That's accurate.'

Aaren shoots me a look. 'And you? You're there because . . .?'

'My mom,' I say, rolling my cup between my palms. 'She wanted me to have a good education. Something that would open doors.' I exhale slowly, my gaze drifting to the trees lining the road. 'She was kind of a big deal in the art world. Built a reputation, knew the right people.' I pause. 'And my dad—he's American. He wanted me to have the same kind of education he had. The plan was to move back to the US once Elise and I graduated.' My fingers tighten around my drink. 'But . . . things happened.'

Aaren nods, not pushing for more.

The road stretches ahead, winding through the mountains. The city has faded in the rearview mirror, replaced by stretches of green, the afternoon sun slanting through the trees, painting the pavement in shifting light.

The only sounds are the quiet hum of the car, the occasional buzz of a passing tricycle, and a song playing low from Aaren's phone—indie, something soft, something that fit the slow stretch of road curling ahead of us.

And then, I see it.

The sign stands just off the main road, bold white letters against a deep blue background: Studio Bazaar Gallery.

'There!' I point, nearly knocking over my drink.

Aaren flinches, jerking the wheel slightly as he pulls over and parks the car. 'Jesus, give a guy some warning next time.'

But I'm already unbuckling my seatbelt, fingers fumbling with the door handle.

'Lauren, for the love of—'

Too late.

The evening air hits me first—warm, carrying the scent of damp earth and the distant charcoal of street food grilling nearby. The sky had begun shifting to burnt orange and purple, casting long shadows over the gallery's sleek exterior.

By the time Aaren catches up, I'm already standing in front of the window, staring inside.

Paintings line the walls in neat rows—cityscapes drenched in neon, delicate portraits frozen in time, abstract pieces that don't make sense but still make you feel something.

Behind the counter stands a woman, her name tag glinting in the light: Emily.

'Hello!' she greets us, her voice smooth, polite, practised.

Before I can say a word, Aaren steps forward like he owns the place.

'We're here to check out some paintings!' he announces, way too cheerfully.

I shoot him a look that screams, *What the hell are you doing?* but he just grins, like this is all part of a plan.

Emily lifts an eyebrow, perfectly arched, like she already knows something we don't. 'Looking to buy?'

'Yep!' Aaren says, way too fast.

'Not really,' I mutter at the same time, cutting him off. The words come out sharper than I mean, and Emily's expression flickers—so fast I almost miss it.

'And we'd rather browse on our own.'

A pause.

She holds our gaze for a second longer, then gives a slow nod. 'All right. Let me know if you need anything.' She turns, stepping away, but not too far.

I exhale, turning on my heel, my pulse hammering. I scan the walls, my eyes darting over each painting, but none of them were right.

Aaren lingers just behind me, hands shoved in his pockets, his voice low. 'Relax, Sherlock. The painting isn't gonna sprout legs and make a run for it.'

I try to ignore Aaren's murmured reassurances, my breath catching in my throat as I scan the rows of paintings. The landscapes melt into a blur of colours, and the abstract swirls seem to mock my focused search. Then, in the far corner, partly hidden by a velvet rope, I see it.

My mom's painting.

'There,' I whisper.

Aaren's teasing disappears. 'It looked so big in the photo.'

I nod, stepping closer, heart in my throat. It's there at the bottom right corner—her signature. Small and neat, the same way she signed grocery lists, birthday cards, permission slips.

Aaren shifts his weight, a small grin tugging at the corner of his lips. 'Mission accomplished,' he says, his voice light.

But as the words hang between us, I feel the air thicken, like something's just out of reach—unfinished.

He catches my expression, his smile faltering. 'What?' he asks, his tone softening, the question more than just words.

I don't answer. Instead, I crouch slightly, pretending to study the painting. That's when I see it—just barely peeking out from behind the frame. A thin, folded piece of paper. Taped to the back.

Aaren's voice drops. 'Lauren. No.'

I don't listen.

I reach out, barely brushing the edge before my eyes land on the 'DO NOT TOUCH' sign bolted to the wall.

Aaren makes a strangled noise. 'I swear to God, if you get us arrested—'

'I'm not gonna get us arrested,' I whisper, even though my pulse was a drumbeat in my ears.

The gallery is quiet, the only sounds the occasional shuffle of footsteps on polished floors. I glance at Emily—still at the counter.

I swallow hard, faking nonchalance as I run my fingertips along the frame. Then, in one quick motion, I peel the note loose.

The tape rips, loud in the silence.

Aaren inhales sharply. 'Oh, dear heavens.'

I brace myself. Alarms. A hand on my wrist. Emily's voice demanding to know what the hell I was doing.

But nothing happens. The gallery remains still. Oblivious.

I reach for the note, hands shaking. The tape resists, peeling off slow, too loud.

A flash of movement in the reflection.

I shove the note into my pocket just as—

'Did you find what you were looking for?'

I spin around, pulse slamming against my ribs.

Emily stands in front of us, hands clasped, expression unreadable.

My fingers curl around the note like it's something dangerous. Something burning.

'Just . . . browsing,' Aaren says, forcing a grin that clearly screams, *We're definitely lying*. 'I think we're good, though. Don't you?'

I nod as he continues to pretend to study the painting, clearly deciding against buying it.

Emily's gaze flicks between us. A beat. Then another.

'All right,' she says finally, voice smooth as glass. 'Enjoy the rest of your day.'

We don't move until she turns and walks back to the counter.

Aaren lets out a breath first. 'We should go.'

I don't argue.

We walk—too fast—towards the exit. My hands shake as I press my pocket, reassuring myself the note is still there, my heart still rattling against my ribs.

The second we step outside, the humid air hits, thick and suffocating after the sharp chill inside.

On the sidewalk, neither of us speak at first.

Then Aaren turns to me, still catching his breath. 'Okay, Sherlock,' he mutters, glancing over his shoulder like Emily might march out and demand we submit to a full-body search. 'What's next? Steal a painting?'

I pull the note from my pocket, unfolding it carefully. The ink is smudged in the places where my fingers had pressed too hard.

'First,' I say, looking up at him. 'We figure out where this leads.'

10

17 October 2021

Dad's grip tightens around my wrist as we step into Dr Gregory's clinic, his fingers firm but not rough. He wasn't dragging me, but he also wasn't giving me a chance to change my mind.

The air-conditioning hits first, a sharp contrast to the humid afternoon outside. It settles on my skin, making the sweat on the back of my neck feel cold. The room smells like antiseptic, clean but suffocating, with a faint trace of stale coffee from the receptionist's desk.

I sink into a stiff vinyl chair, the material creaking beneath me. Dad sits beside me, his leg bouncing—a steady rhythm I'd never noticed before. His eyes stay fixed on the wall, like if he stares hard enough, he can pretend we aren't here.

A man across from us flips through a tattered *Reader's Digest*, his fingers smoothing down the corners of each page before turning them. A few seats away, a mother whispers something to her son, her hand resting gently on his back as he kicks his feet against the chair, leaving faint black scuff marks on the floor.

I catch sight of my reflection in the darkened window—hollow eyes, skin stretched thin over exhaustion. A version of me that feels out of place even in my own body.

A door creaks open. A nurse in navy scrubs steps out, clipboard in hand.

'Lauren Sanders?'

Dad nudges me gently.

'I'll wait here,' he says.

Something inside me twists.

You're not coming in?

The words stick in my throat, but I swallow them down and stand. The nurse leads me down a narrow hallway that smells like rubbing alcohol and something stale—like old paper left too long in a damp room.

Dr Gregory's nameplate catches the fluorescent light: 'Dr Gregory Stone, M.D. Child and Adolescent Psychiatry'.

I hesitate, then push the door open.

Dr Gregory's office isn't what I expected. No cold sterility, no intimidating degrees framed on the wall like warnings. Bookshelves line one side of the room, filled with thick psychology textbooks and random novels with cracked spines. A corkboard is pinned with children's drawings—stick figures, lopsided hearts, a bright yellow sun. A potted plant sits on the windowsill, its leaves curling slightly at the edges.

The couch across from his desk looks too soft, too inviting, like if I sit down, I might sink into it and disappear. So, I take the chair—the one that feels like I'm supposed to sit there and be studied.

Dr Gregory, mid-forties, glasses perched on the bridge of his nose, flips through a folder before setting it down. He has the kind of presence that makes you feel like lying is pointless.

'How are you feeling today?' he asks.

I stare at the buttons on my sleeve, pretending to think about it.

'I'm okay,' I say eventually.

He doesn't look surprised. Just nods like it's a perfectly acceptable answer.

'Okay's a start,' Dr Gregory replies calmly, his gaze steady but gentle. 'Walk me through what that feels like for you, Lauren.'

I rub the worn edge of my sleeve between my fingers. 'Like I'm moving through water. I can still get from one place to another, but everything feels slower, heavier . . . like I have to work twice as hard just to keep up.'

He taps his pen softly against his notebook. 'That sounds tiring.'

I let out a breathy laugh. 'Yeah. It is.'

There is a pause, the kind that makes you wish you could disappear into your chair. Then he says, 'Your dad mentioned you've been hearing Elise.'

My stomach twists. I nod, forcing the lump in my throat down. 'Yeah.'

'When did it start?'

I take a deep breath—if only I could hold it long enough to feel steady. 'A few weeks ago,' I say, voice quieter now. 'It's just . . . my name. From her room.'

Dr Gregory leans forward slightly, like he's giving me space to say more if I want to.

'Do you ever answer?' Dr Gregory's question breaks the silence, making me flinch.

My fingers curl into the worn wool of my sweater, the familiar texture offering a bit of comfort.

'No,' I admit, my eyes glued to the stubborn stain on his desk—something from the past, scrubbed at but never fully erased. 'Part of me . . . doesn't want to know.'

'Do you think it's real?'

I keep my eyes on the stain near the leg of his desk—a faint smudge of something dark that has been scrubbed but never fully erased.

'I don't know,' I say finally.

He doesn't push. Just waits, like he knows there's more but isn't going to pull it out of me before I'm ready.

I swallow hard. 'It *feels* real. But I know it's not. I just—sometimes, for a second, I forget. And I turn my head, expecting to see her.'

His expression doesn't shift into pity. No rehearsed lines about grief. Just a simple, steady, 'How does it make you feel when you hear her?'

I clench my hands in my lap. 'Like she's waiting for me to do something. I just don't know what.'

Dr Gregory gazes at me steadily. 'Do you think there's a part of you that blames yourself?'

A sharp ache presses against my ribs, like something heavy settling in. I swallow. 'Doesn't everyone?'

He doesn't flinch. 'Maybe. But I'm asking you.'

The lump in my throat tightens. My vision blurs at the edges. I exhale through my nose, slow and careful—if I'm not careful, it might come out as a sob. 'Yeah,' I whisper. 'I do.'

He lets the words settle between us, giving me space to hear them out loud before he speaks. 'Guilt convinces us we have control over things we don't.'

I pick at the edge of my sleeve. 'Then why does it feel like I should have done something?'

Dr Gregory doesn't answer right away. He lets my words sit, turning them over in his mind before he says, 'Because feeling helpless is worse than feeling responsible.'

I nod, biting the inside of my cheek.

He shifts in his chair. 'Have you been sleeping?'

I shrug. 'Sometimes.'

'Nightmares?'

I hesitate. 'Not nightmares exactly. Just—' I search for the right words. '—I wake up feeling like someone was just in my room. Like I missed something, but I don't know what.'

Dr Gregory tilts his head slightly. 'Someone?'

I press my lips together. 'Elise,' I say. 'But it's just a feeling.'

He lets the silence stretch, waiting.

I exhale. 'Sometimes I hear my name. Like she's calling me from the hallway. Or I'll see a shadow move in the corner of my eye, but when I turn—' I stop, shaking my head.

'But when you turn, no one's there,' he finishes gently.

I nod. My fingers trace the seam of my sleeve, following its uneven path over my wrist. 'It's worse when it's quiet. Like I can feel her watching me.'

Dr Gregory taps his pen against his notebook. 'Does she ever appear?'

A shiver crawls up my spine. 'Not exactly. Just glimpses. The edge of her hair when I pass a mirror. A reflection in a window that disappears when I blink.' I shift in my chair, arms tightening around myself. 'It never lasts, but it's enough.'

A knock on the door interrupts us.

Dr Gregory presses a button on his desk, and the nurse pokes her head in. 'Should I let Mr Sanders in?'

'Yes, bring him in.'

Dad steps inside, looking more tired than he had this morning. His shoulders are stiff, hands clasped together like he's bracing for impact.

Dr Gregory leans back in his chair. 'Lauren, I want to talk about next steps.'

A cold weight settles in my stomach.

'We're going to start you on a low dose of risperidone,' he said. 'Half a tablet for two weeks. It should help with the auditory hallucinations and any paranoia.'

The words land heavy. Medication.

Dad clears his throat. 'Side effects?'

'Some drowsiness, maybe dizziness at first.'

Dr Gregory slides a small notebook across the desk, tapping the cover lightly. 'I know this might seem pointless, but I want you to use this. Not just to write down feelings—this is about recognizing patterns.'

I hesitate, my fingers hovering over the edge of the notebook.

'When you start the medication, you might not notice the changes right away. But if you write down even small things—how you're sleeping, what your mood is like, if you feel restless or numb—it gives us something to work with.'

I flip the cover open, staring at the blank pages. They feel too clean, too expectant.

'And it's not just for me,' Dr Gregory adds. 'It's for you, too. Sometimes we don't see how far we've come until we look back.'

I let out a slow breath, running my thumb along the spine. 'So . . . it's homework?'

Dr Gregory smiles slightly. 'More like a map. You don't have to write paragraphs. Even one-word entries help. It's not about making sense of everything all at once. It's about noticing.'

Noticing. Right.

I snap the notebook shut and stuff it into my bag. Let Dr Gregory think I'll use it. Doesn't mean I actually will.

11

25 August 2023

In me, secrets often hide,
Where dreams are born and hopes collide.
The place you once called home holds a piece of what's gone,
A trace of shadows, lost and drawn.

My walls can whisper, soft and clear,
I cradle time, your joy, your fear.
A quiet space where hearts align,
What am I? Seek, and you'll find.

We park a few streets away, wedging the car between a rusting tricycle and a silver SUV that had probably been sitting there for days. It was close enough to walk but far enough to keep us from looking suspicious—not that we were doing anything outright illegal. But sneaking into a house that hadn't been ours for years wasn't exactly something the homeowners' association would encourage.

Getting past the guardhouse was easier than I thought. Aaren had used his childhood friend, Alexander, as an excuse to get in, which, apparently, was good enough for the guards.

Aaren shuts off the engine and leans back in his seat, tapping his fingers against the wheel. 'Remind me again why this isn't a bad idea?'

I don't answer right away, just stare through the windshield at the familiar streets ahead. The tree-lined sidewalks, the perfectly spaced lamp posts, the faint hum of a gardener's radio playing somewhere in the distance. It's all the same, yet it doesn't feel like it belongs to me any more.

My fingers curled tighter around the strap of my bag. 'It *is* a terrible idea,' I admit, my voice even. 'But I . . . I just have to see it. I'm pretty sure it's leading us here.'

Aaren sighs like he's about to risk his entire life savings on this decision. 'You know, when I imagined sneaking into a gated village, I thought there'd be more action. A secret tunnel. Maybe a dramatic car chase.'

I snort, pushing the car door open. 'Sorry to disappoint. Next time, I'll make sure we have a getaway motorcycle.'

He grins. 'Ooh, can we get matching helmets?'

I ignore him, stepping out onto the pavement. The heat clings to my skin instantly, the afternoon sun making the air thick and heavy. We move quickly, keeping to the side of the street, avoiding eye contact with the occasional passerby.

Every step feels like walking through the past, each corner pulling up an old memory I hadn't meant to revisit. The narrow alley I used to take when I needed a quick run to the nearest convenience store. The house with the towering *kamias* tree, where Elise and I would sneak a few sour fruits, wincing and laughing as we popped them into our mouths.

The cracked pavement near the corner, where I'd once fallen off a bike I barely knew how to ride, leaving a scar on my knee that never quite faded.

Aaren must have sensed the shift in my mood because he keeps quiet as we walk. No more jokes, no dramatic sighs. Just the steady sound of our footsteps against the pavement, the weight of what we are about to do settling between us.

Then we turn the last corner, and my breath catches in my throat.

The house stands at the end of the street, tucked between two neatly kept lawns that looked like they were trying to pretend it didn't exist. It wasn't just empty. It was *abandoned.*

It looked smaller than I remembered, like time had shrunk it down to something unrecognizable. The paint—once warm and inviting—had dulled into a lifeless grey, peeling in jagged strips like old wounds left to fester. The wooden porch sagged under its own weight, warped from years of neglect, as if exhausted from waiting for someone to come back.

No one ever did.

The windows—some boarded up, others streaked with thick layers of dust—reflected nothing but the dull afternoon light. A faded strip of police tape still clung stubbornly to the railing, its edges frayed from years of being ignored.

They never sold it. Not for lack of trying.

After my parents died, we had no choice but to put the house on the market. But no one—not even the most desperate buyers—wanted it. Maybe it was the history attached to it, the tragedy that sat in its walls like a stain that wouldn't wash out. Maybe it was something else.

People in Verenna Heights Village had a way of keeping stories alive, twisting facts into whispers that slithered from one house to the next. I remember the last rumour I'd heard before I left for good—that if you passed by the street around 6 p.m., you'd hear voices. Whispers crawling through the cracks in the walls. Some swore they saw figures moving behind the windows.

Most dismissed it as gossip. Some believed it. But no one, it seemed, wanted to test it.

I swallow hard.

'This isn't it,' I mutter, crossing my arms. 'The note's probably wrong.'

Aaren shoots me a look. 'Lauren.'

I lift my chin, defensive. 'It could mean anything. Maybe "home" is just a metaphor.'

'For what?' He smirks. 'Your childhood trauma?'

I glare at him.

'Look, the note literally says, "The place you once called home holds a piece of what's gone." Unless you spent your formative years living in a Jollibee play area, I'm pretty sure it means this house.'

I clench my jaw, looking away. The truth sits heavy in my chest. I know he's right. I just don't want to be.

Aaren claps his hands together. 'All right, let's break in.'

'Break in?' I hiss. 'I have the keys!'

'Oh,' he says, deflating slightly. 'That's . . . less exciting.'

I shoot him a glare as I pull the old key from my pocket. It's heavier than I remembered, cold despite the warmth of my fingers. For a moment, I hesitate, thumb running over its worn edges.

Then, with a deep breath, I push it into the lock.

The door groans open, the sound stretching through the empty halls like the house was waking from a long, uneasy sleep.

The air inside hits me first—thick with dust and something metallic, like rusted nails left to rot. The light filtering through the boarded-up windows cast long, slanted streaks across the furniture, all covered in white sheets like forgotten ghosts.

Everything was exactly as Clarissa and I had left it. Frozen in time. Holding its breath.

Aaren steps inside behind me, his sneakers scuffing against the dusty tiles. 'This place is straight out of a horror movie,' he mutters.

'No kidding.' I swallow and square my shoulders. 'Okay. Quick search. You check the basement. I'll take upstairs.'

'Why do I have to take the basement?'

'Because you're taller. And it's dark. If something jumps at you, you'll see it first.'

'That's the worst reasoning I've ever heard.'

I shove him towards the stairs leading down. 'Just go.'

With a heavy sigh, he disappears into the basement. I turn towards what used to be my mom's art room.

The door is stuck. I shove my shoulder against it, forcing it open, and dust explodes into the air, making me cough. The room smells of old paint and turpentine, like the ghosts of unfinished canvases still lingered here. Sunlight filters through the dusty curtains, making the covered easels cast long, eerie shadows.

Then—*tap. Tap. Tap.*

I freeze.

The sound comes from upstairs. Slow, deliberate.

'Elise?' I whisper, my breath catching in my throat, the scent of dust and old paint suddenly heavy with a desperate hope that she might somehow answer.

Silence.

I turn towards the staircase, heart pounding. The concrete steps stretch ahead, worn smooth by time, each one daring me to climb. I swallow, forcing my feet to move. The higher I go, the louder the tapping grew, echoing against the walls like it was leading me somewhere.

The door to Elise's room stood slightly open, just enough to show a sliver of darkness inside.

I hesitate.

The tapping stops.

I take a shaky breath and step inside. The air is colder here, sharper. Dust clings to the old curtains, the scent of faded perfume barely lingering beneath it. The voices—quiet at first—urge me towards the dresser. My hands tremble as I yank open the top drawer, like I have no choice but to obey.

Nothing.

The second. Empty.

The third—

A folded piece of paper sits on top of a stack of old photos. My breath catches as I pick it up, the handwriting instantly familiar.

I capture time but never change,
In vivid hues and endless range.
From winter's chill to summer's heat,
Four worlds collide where colours meet.

Aaren's footsteps pound up the stairs, and he bursts into the room, slightly breathless. 'Did you find something?'

I hold up the note, my fingers trembling. 'Another riddle.'

Aaren snatches it from my hands, scanning the words. His face lights up like he's just cracked a code. 'It's a clue.'

'No kidding, Sherlock.' I fold my arms, keeping my voice steady even though my pulse is anything but. 'Do you even know what it means?'

Aaren taps his temple like some genius detective. 'Give me a second.'

I barely have time to roll my eyes before the sound cuts through the silence.

A low, drawn-out groan.

Not the wind. Not the house settling.

Or was it?

My pulse slams against my ribs. The air thickens, pressing down on me. Then—footsteps. Slow, deliberate. Too real to ignore.

Unless they aren't real at all.

My breath catches. The shadows at the edges of my vision twist, flickering like they were alive.

My name. I swear I heard my name. Elise's voice—soft, pleading—

'Who's up there?'

A flashlight beam slashes across the wall downstairs.

Aaren and I snap our heads towards the staircase. The air between us thickens, heavy with unspoken panic.

His grip tightens around my wrist. 'Lauren, we need to leave. Now.'

I can't move. My legs feel welded to the floor, my heartbeat slamming against my ribs. The air in my lungs turn solid, refusing to let me breathe.

The footsteps get louder. *Faster.*

Aaren grabs my wrist, his grip firm and urgent. 'On three,' he hisses. 'Okay?'

I manage the smallest nod, my throat too tight to speak.

One. The footsteps grow louder.

Two. The light creeps up the steps.

'Wait, is this a one-two-three or a three-two-one situation?'

'Three!'

Aaren's fingers clamp around my wrist, yanking me towards the hallway.

We run—fast, reckless—blurring past the guard like nothing more than a passing gust of wind.

'Hoy!'

Our feet pound against the tiled stairs, each step sending vibrations through the hollow space. The house seems to tremble around us, the walls closing in. Up ahead, the front door stands wide open, sunlight streaming in, a sharp contrast to the suffocating dimness inside.

We bolt down the street, sprinting so fast it feels like the pavement is trying to pull us back. The car is still a few blocks away—a decision that now feels incredibly stupid. My lungs burn, my legs scream, but stopping isn't an option.

Aaren runs ahead, glancing back only to make sure I'm still behind him. 'Remind me,' he huffs, 'whose genius idea was it to park this far?'

'Yours,' I shoot back, breathless.

The moment we reach the car, Aaren yanks the door open and practically dives into the driver's seat, hands scrambling for the keys. I barely have time to slam my door shut before the engine roars to life.

He revs the engine and speeds out of the compound, tires screeching against the asphalt as we accelerate towards the exit. The guard lifts the boom gate without a word, and we shoot through, leaving the neighbourhood behind. My pulse pounds in my ears, matching the rapid thud of my heartbeat. I twist in my seat, watching the street, where our old house was, disappear in the rearview mirror. The farther we go, the less real it feels. But the tightness in my chest doesn't fade.

Aaren lets out a breathless, slightly manic laugh. 'Well. That was—'

I punch his arm. Hard.

'You're insane,' I snap.

'Maybe.' He grins, rubbing his arm. 'But we got the note, didn't we?'

I let out a deep sigh and roll my eyes.

12

29 October 2021

'Why does this guy act like he knew Elise better than her own family?'

The voice cuts through the air—sharp, bitter, and impossible to ignore. But I'm too tired to care.

I sit in the stiff plastic chair of the principal's office, my hands curled into fists in my lap. Across from me, Principal Caldwell folds his hands over his desk like he's about to deliver a eulogy instead of some canned speech he's probably rehearsed five times in front of a mirror. About two and a half months after Elise's death, he's finally decided it was time to talk about bullying and mental health.

The timing couldn't have been worse.

Because that's how it always goes, isn't it? They only start caring when it's too late. When the damage is done, when someone like Elise is gone, that's when they scramble to play the part of the concerned adult. Suddenly the same people who whispered about her, laughed at her, and shut her out were posting condolences online—calling her an angel, acting like they gave a damn.

They didn't listen when she was alive. But now they wanted to 'raise awareness'.

I can practically hear Elise's voice in my head—dry and unimpressed. *Oh, so now they care?* She would've rolled her eyes. *Bet they're using the same Canva templates from the Homecoming posters.*

And she wouldn't have been wrong. I can see her in my mind, sitting at the back of the classroom, tapping her pen against her notebook as Caldwell droned on about 'mental health awareness'. She'd have shot me a look, whispered something sarcastic, then gone back to doodling in the margins of her paper.

But she wasn't here to be annoyed. Or angry. Or say any of it.

And that makes me furious.

The school had organized a memorial—without asking me. Not my dad. Not our relatives. They just decided on their own, like slapping Elise's name onto a school event would erase the fact that they let her slip away. Like a line-up of candles and some borrowed words could undo everything.

And they want me to stand on stage and talk about her. Like I'm supposed to turn her life into a cautionary tale.

Principal Caldwell had called me in earlier this week. It had been a boring, expected conversation where he wanted to 'check in' with me. But when I walk in today, and see him sitting there, hands neatly folded like he was about to sell me something, I knew what was coming.

'We'd like you to speak before the memorial starts,' he says, all smooth and practised. 'It'll help raise awareness.'

Ms Wilson, the school counsellor, is sitting off to the side, her head tilted in this forced sympathy that didn't do her any favours. She gives me this look—half hopeful, half like she expected me to fall apart right there.

Neither of them knew Elise. Neither of them were there for her when she needed someone. But now they want me to tell her story—*their* version of her story—to make themselves feel better.

'I see where Principal Caldwell is coming from,' Ms Wilson adds, reaching across the desk to squeeze my hand like that was supposed to fix something. 'Think about how powerful your voice could be. You could help someone feel less alone. You might even save a life.'

I almost laugh. Not because it's funny, but because it's so incredibly ridiculous.

A speech wasn't going to save anyone. Elise wasn't some lesson they could use to scare people into being better. She was a person. A person they ignored, dismissed, and ridiculed—until it was too late.

And then Ms Wilson says it.

That word.

You.

Like it's on me. Like I could've saved her.

And maybe that's what hurts the most—because some part of me believes it.

'No,' I say flatly.

My voice comes out sharper than I mean it to, but I don't care. I cross my arms and lean back in my chair, making it clear I was done.

Principal Caldwell lets out this long, heavy sigh, clearly annoyed. His fingers twitch like he wants to argue, but Ms Wilson jumps in first.

'You don't have to share everything,' she says gently. 'Just . . . something meaningful.'

I look at her, and for a second, I think maybe she actually believes what she was saying.

But the truth is, if they'd cared about something meaningful, they would've cared about *her*—not the version they could use to make themselves feel less guilty.

'I'm sorry,' I say, my voice low but steady. 'I'm not doing that.'

Principal Caldwell leans back in his chair, his face hard to read. I could tell he'd been expecting some emotional speech—some brave, grieving sister standing on stage, voice shaking but strong, urging everyone to be kind.

I wasn't going to give him that.

'No,' I say again as I stand up. 'I'm not doing this. And I'm definitely not making this about them.'

I walk out before either of them can stop me.

By the time I reach my locker, my hands are already moving on autopilot—yanking the door open, shoving books inside, fingers curling too tightly around the edge of the metal shelf. Like if I grip it hard enough, it might steady something in me.

Then my eyes land on the photo taped inside—me and Elise, grinning like idiots. She has a smear of chocolate on her cheek from the milkshake we'd been sharing, but I never told her. I'd just taken the picture and let her laugh.

Now I stare at it like it belongs to someone else.

The muffled chatter of students drifts down the hallway—too casual, too normal. Like they were lining up for a pep rally instead of a memorial.

I start towards the auditorium but stop short. Through the small window in the door, I spot the framed portrait they'd set up of Elise—her yearbook photo, blown up too big. Her smile was too polite, her hair too neat. It didn't feel like her at all.

Ms Reel stands at the podium, shuffling her notes. She glances up, sees me, and gives me this look—soft, like she was about to say something.

I turn and walk out.

Outside the school gates, I pull out my phone and book a Grab. Six minutes.

The late afternoon rush swallows the streets whole—students spilling onto sidewalks, cars honking impatiently, cyclists weaving through gaps too small for anything but recklessness.

Somewhere near High Street, a street performer strums a guitar, his melody swallowed by the hum of engines and the murmur of strangers. The air is thick with the scent of coffee and gasoline, a combination I used to love. Now, it just makes my stomach twist.

I make my way to the pickup spot, standing beneath the waiting shed. My phone buzzes. Probably Zania checking in. I ignore it. Another notification pops up.

'Your driver has arrived'.

A silver sedan eases up to the curb, headlights blinking in recognition. I adjust my bag on my shoulder, exhaling before slipping into the backseat.

The door clicks shut, and the cold from the air conditioning hits me instantly, leaving goosebumps in its wake.

The city blurs—towering glass buildings reflecting the last streaks of sunlight, LED billboards flashing advertisements for things I don't care about, crowds shifting at crosswalks like restless waves. I turn my face towards the window, watching everything pass by, but not really seeing.

I close my eyes and try to breathe, try to let the steady hum of the engine calm me. But grief doesn't work like that. It doesn't settle—it lingers, clings to every breath, every heartbeat. And with it, the memories rise, uninvited and razor-sharp.

The café near the mall where Elise dared me to dip my fries into her strawberry milkshake, grinning when I gagged but reached for another anyway. The bookstore where she could spend hours, pulling random novels from the shelves and making up ridiculous plots just to make me laugh. The scent of her perfume—too much lavender, too much everything—still lingering in the hoodie she used to lend me, still hanging in the back of my closet like a ghost that refused to leave.

I suck in a breath, curl my hands into fists. *Don't do this now. Not here.*

But the memories aren't just thoughts. They are voices, echoes, fragments of a life that used to be mine.

Elise laughing. Elise nudging my shoulder. Elise standing beside me, as real as the breath in my lungs.

I turn towards the window, pressing my forehead against the glass, willing the cold to seep into my bones, to quiet the ache rising in my chest.

The driver doesn't speak. No small talk. No radio. Just the robotic voice of Waze map app, directing us down unfamiliar roads.

I breathe in. Count.

Five seconds in. Five seconds out.

It doesn't help.

Grief swells in my throat, thick and suffocating. I dig my nails into my palms, chasing the sting, needing something tangible, something real.

By the time we reach my stop, the sky has deepened into burnt orange, shadows stretching long across the pavement.

I unbuckle my seatbelt with stiff fingers, exhaling before stepping out.

The house looks the same. But it isn't. It hasn't been since Elise. She isn't behind the door. She isn't anywhere but in the spaces she left behind.

I hesitate at the foot of the steps, adjusting my bag like it would fix something. Like it would fix me.

I step inside.

And immediately, I feel it.

The air was wrong. Tension pressed against the walls, curling into the corners. And then—

Voices.

Raised. Sharp. Familiar.

'I don't need a psychiatrist!' My mom's voice, raw with anger. 'I'm not crazy! I lost my daughter!'

My body locks.

'Stop pretending this isn't serious, Cora!' My dad, lower, restrained, but unravelling at the edges. 'You need help.'

The words echo through the house, through me.

'I'm not going back there!'

'Cora—'

'She didn't do anything, Jack!' My mother's voice cracks. 'She just stood there. If she had helped Elise instead of just—just watching—maybe . . . maybe we wouldn't be in this mess.'

The guilt hits like a fist to the ribs.

I tell myself there's nothing I could've done. That I hadn't known.

But maybe I had.

Maybe I should have.

I press my back against the wall, fingers curling tight around the strap of my bag. The air is thick, heavy with words that had nowhere to go. My chest aches. My eyes burn. But I swallow it all down—every tear, every sharp edge of grief—burying it beneath the weight of silence.

Loss isn't just something that lives here. It's built into the walls.

And no matter how far I run, no matter how long I stay away—

I am always going to drown in it.

13

2 September 2023

My brain is glitching again.

It started in math class, just after 9 a.m. At first, it was barely there—a hum blending with the fluorescent lights and the steady whir of the air conditioner. I almost ignored it. But then it shifted, each sound stretching, warping into something almost like words, too clear to be my imagination.

The classroom pulsed. The words on the whiteboard slid sideways—smearing like wet ink, rearranging into something I couldn't read. The air was too thick, pressing against my chest.

'You shouldn't be here.'

The voices don't come from anyone in the room. They *shouldn't* have come from anywhere.

My breath stutters. The fluorescent lights drill into my skull, too loud, too bright, like they were inside me. My pencil hovers uselessly over my notes, the letters flickering—blurring, shifting—

'Look behind you.'

I squeeze my eyes shut.

I take a deep breath and press my forehead against the desk for a second, trying to ground myself. When I look up, Sasha Harding is standing next to me.

'Hey, Lauren. About the literature project? It's due in two weeks. Have you thought about how you want to divide the work?'

I open my mouth to respond, but the words get tangled up in my throat like a knot. My brain is screaming, the voices overlapping now:

'She knows.'

'Don't answer her.'

Sasha gives me a weird look, like she's trying to figure out if I'm about to pass out or do something insane. 'Uh . . . okay. I'll catch up with you tomorrow.'

She walks off, and I grab my bag, pushing through the door like I could outrun my own thoughts. My pulse pounds in my ears, my breath too shallow, too fast. The hallway feels too tight, like the walls are pressing in, like I need to get out now before my brain swallows me whole.

And then I see him.

Aaren is leaning against the wall, hands in his pockets, like he's been waiting for me this whole time. Like he knew.

'Hey,' he says. 'You good?'

The noise in my head is still there—but suddenly, Aaren is louder. Sharper. Real in a way the rest of it isn't.

For a second, everything settles. The fluorescent lights don't buzz. The floor does not shift beneath me. The posters on the walls stop melting into unreadable messes. All I can hear are the soft sounds of lockers clicking shut, footsteps echoing somewhere down the corridor, and the steady weight of Aaren's gaze.

'You good?' he asks again, quieter this time.

I blink at him, savouring the stillness. 'Uh . . . yeah. Totally.'

Aaren raises an eyebrow, and I can tell he doesn't buy it. Not even a little.

'Right. Totally.'

He studies me like he's waiting for me to crack, but I don't. Not yet.

Instead, he shoves his hands deeper into his pockets and tilts his head towards the hall. 'Come on. I want to show you something.'

I hesitate, my pulse still trying to figure out if we're panicking or not. 'Now?'

'Now.'

I don't ask why. I just follow him. Because when everything feels off-balance, Aaren has a way of making things feel a little less impossible.

The hallways blur past as we walk. I focus on the rhythm of my footsteps matching his, the steady sound keeping me from spiralling. Before I know it, we are in the library, where the air smells like old books, stale coffee, and something vaguely dusty but familiar.

Aaren leads me to a computer in the back, typing something into the search bar without explaining. The screen lights up with an article, a grainy photo of my mom standing in front of one of her paintings staring back at me.

LOCAL ARTIST HINTS AT SECRETS HIDDEN IN HER WORK.

A slow, sinking feeling settles in my stomach.

I skim the first few lines, my fingers curling slightly at my sides.

> Rumours swirl that Cora Cruz-Sanders, known for her abstract pieces, drew inspiration from her personal life—most notably her rumoured affair with Bill Harper, a well-known art curator in town.

My jaw clenches. Heat rises up my neck, sharp and all-consuming.

'What does this have to do with the notes?'

Aaren leans back in his chair, scrolling like this isn't setting my entire world on fire. 'It's a clue,' he says, pointing at the screen. 'Apparently, Bill Harper's in New York now, curating for celebrities.'

My pulse pounds in my ears. 'And?'

Aaren glances at me, too calm. Not nearly as excited as he should be. 'It's possible . . . that he has some of your mom's paintings. And those paintings could have notes in them.'

'Possible?' I shoot him a look. 'If there's even a chance, we have to find out.'

My voice comes out sharper than I mean for it to, and the librarian peers over her desk, frowning. I force myself to lower my voice.

'We need to figure out how to get to him.'

Aaren sighs, crossing his arms. 'Lauren, be realistic. He's in New York. We're here. It's not like we can just hop on a plane and track him down.'

I clench my teeth, staring at the photo of Bill Harper standing in front of a row of paintings that look way too familiar.

'But what if he does have them?' I murmur. 'What if we're missing something huge?'

'You're jumping too far ahead,' Aaren says, steady as ever. 'We need more information first.'

'I can't just sit around waiting for more information,' I shoot back. 'We're wasting time. These notes could be anywhere. If we don't act fast, I might lose them forever.'

Aaren tilts his head, watching me the way people watch thunderstorms from a distance—fascinated, a little wary, like they know something's about to break loose.

'I get it,' he says, but the words don't sit right. The hesitation is too thick, like he was trying to talk himself into believing it more than telling me the truth. 'You want answers. But we can't rush this. We have to be smart.'

I shake my head, frustration tightening around my chest. He doesn't get it. Not really. He can't know what it feels like to chase after fragments of something broken, always falling short, always reaching for something that seems just out of reach.

'I'm sorry,' he says, softer now, like he's trying to hold onto something that keeps slipping away. A flicker of something—maybe regret or pain—passes through his eyes, something I can't name but know well enough. 'I just thought . . . maybe it's worth thinking about where all this note-hunting could take us,' he finishes, his voice trailing off as his gaze wanders, distant and lost.

For a moment, I see it—the quiet weight of his own search, the way it had led him nowhere, only deeper into emptiness. A road he'd already walked, one I was afraid I was on, too.

I exhale hard through my nose. 'It's fine,' I say, even though it isn't.

I stare at the article again, my chest tightening. 'You're right. It's not like we can just hop on a flight to New York if the next note sends us there or something.'

Silence stretches between us—of words thick and unspoken.

Aaren shifts in his chair, hesitating before he speaks again. 'Yeah. And . . . sorry about the article. That writer's an idiot.'

I shrug, my brain too busy replaying all the possibilities, all the unknowns.

Then, out of nowhere: 'Hey, did you ever talk about your sister?'

It hits me like a punch to the stomach. My fingers curl slightly. 'What do you mean?' My voice comes out flat. 'Why are you asking?'

Aaren hesitates. 'I didn't know her well. But . . . there were rumours. You know how people are.'

My stomach twists. The way it does when you're blindsided, and you don't know if you want to scream or disappear.

He doesn't say more, but something in his face tells me there's more to it.

'You know what, never mind,' he says quickly, forcing a grin. Like he's trying to shove the words back down. 'Forget I asked.'

Aaren leans back, drumming his fingers against the desk. 'Do you ever think about what you'd be doing if things were different?'

I frown. 'What do you mean? Different how?'

He shrugs, gaze flicking towards me before settling on the empty library. 'If Elise never left. If none of this ever happened. Who would you be?'

I open my mouth, then hesitate. The question catches me off guard, like stepping onto a stair that isn't there. I'd spent so long reacting—chasing, searching, holding on—that I hadn't really stopped to think about who I was outside of it all.

'I don't know,' I admit. 'I don't think I've had time to figure that out.'

Aaren studies me for a second, then says, 'Maybe that's the problem.'

I exhale, rubbing a hand over my face. 'Well, what else am I supposed to do?'

'Live,' he says simply.

I let out something between a scoff and a laugh. 'Right. I'll pencil that in.'

'I'm serious,' he says, his voice cutting through the quiet. 'If you weren't stuck in all this, what would you be doing?'

I hesitate, running my fingers along the edge of the desk, feeling the rough grain beneath my skin. 'Probably trying to pass as a normal high school student. Pretending I've got it together. Hoping no one sees the cracks.'

Aaren doesn't answer right away. He just watches me, his usual sharpness softening into something quieter.

'That sounds exhausting,' he says finally.

I let out a breath, shaky but steady. 'It is.'

'Honestly?' He leans forward, resting his arms on the desk. 'I think "normal" is just something people chase when they're too scared to admit they're barely holding on like everyone else.'

I let out a quiet laugh, the kind that isn't really laughter at all. 'Maybe. But sometimes, the idea of predictable—boring, even—feels like relief.'

Aaren tilts his head, considering that. 'Maybe. But you?' He shakes his head like he already knows the answer. 'You're anything but boring.'

I feel the corners of my mouth twitch. I'm smiling.

14

19 September 2023

Aaren sits cross-legged on the worn carpet near the last bookshelf, surrounded by a mess of open yearbooks—2015, 2016, 2017, all the way up to 2019. He flips through the 2017 edition with the kind of focus that makes it seem like the answer is just a page away, like he's this close to cracking some invisible code.

'It's gotta be a photograph,' he mutters, turning another page. 'It makes the most sense.'

I lean against the bookshelf, phone in hand, scrolling aimlessly. My fingers are moving over the screen, but I'm not really seeing anything. The glow of it feels like a distraction, a way to keep myself from thinking too hard.

Aaren looks up, something flickering in his expression—understanding, maybe, or just curiosity. His gaze drops back to the yearbook in front of him, and then his mouth twitches like he's just pieced something together.

'The yearbook,' he says, shutting the 2017 edition with a soft thud and reaching for the next one. 'What if it's here?'

I raise an eyebrow, but he's already flipping through the pages like he can feel the answer waiting for him.

'I don't think she would've left clues in a school yearbook.'

The library is nearly empty—three hours past dismissal, long enough for the fluorescent lights to feel too bright, for the quiet to settle in a way that made the whole place feel forgotten. The librarian had disappeared into her office ages ago, probably counting down the minutes until she could lock up and leave.

Aaren taps the 2019 yearbook, his finger landing just beneath Elise's photo. A familiar weight pulls at my chest.

Beneath her headshot, bold and impossible to ignore, was her quote:

'Sometimes the best moment to sing a victory song is in THE middle of your BATTLE.'

Aaren leans in, close enough that I catch the faint trace of peppermint gum. His eyes are narrowed, scanning the words like they hold a secret only he can see.

'Look at the capitalized words,' he says. 'That's gotta be the next clue.' He presses his finger against the page, leaving a soft crease in the corner.

I stare at the quote. The letters blur together for a second, then snap into focus. My stomach twists, something between realization and the kind of ache that never really goes away.

She left this here on purpose.

'My sister,' I say, my voice coming out stronger than I expect it to. 'She was on the volleyball team in 2018. Barely played, but she was still on the roster.'

Aaren nods, slow and thoughtful, like he's connecting invisible dots. Then his gaze flicks back to me, and I can see it—the excitement catching, like the first spark before a flame.

'What if this is about her?' he asks, sitting up straighter. 'What if the note—the one we found at your old house—is literally connected to your sister?'

I let out a sharp breath, crossing my arms. 'Obviously.'

Aaren smirks at that—amused—but his eyes stay serious, flicking between the quote and whatever theories were spinning in his head. His mind was already racing ahead, faster than the conversation.

I shift, clearing my throat. The words are out before I can second-guess them.

'I remember she used to hide things in her gym locker.' The memory slides into place so easily it was like it had never left. 'I'm pretty sure it's in the old gym at the far end of the building.'

Aaren lifts an eyebrow. 'You're saying that the next note's been sitting in an old gym locker for, what, five or six years? Without anyone noticing?'

I hesitate, then nod. 'Yeah. Pretty sure no one's touched that locker since . . . well, you know.'

His smirk fades. He gets it.

'Some people started saying it was cursed or unlucky after she died,' I say, keeping my voice even, but my fingers curl into my sleeve. 'Dumb stuff like that.'

Aaren sits back, rubbing a hand through his hair. 'All right. So, we just . . . stroll into the old gym, go through the lockers, and hope no one catches us?'

I glance at the clock on the wall. 5.47 p.m.

'Not yet,' I say, pulling my bag over my shoulder. 'We wait until seven. By then, everyone'll be gone, and we can check it out without any interruptions.'

Aaren doesn't argue. Maybe he knows better than to tell me to wait.

❀

The school library feels different at night. Not just quiet, but abandoned. The kind of silence that makes you feel like you've stepped into a place that has forgotten how to be alive.

Aaren and I take over a table in the farthest corner, where the shelves stretch higher and the books look like they haven't been touched in ages. He leans back in his chair, spinning a pen he'd picked up off the floor between his fingers, while I trace invisible shapes with my finger along the edge of my notebook, pretending not to be bothered by the heavy awareness of how still everything is.

We let the silence sit between us. Not exactly comfortable but not suffocating either.

Then Aaren speaks.

'So,' he says, voice low but clear. 'What's the endgame here? You find all the notes, and then what? Do they add up to something big? Lead to buried treasure? Or do they just . . . stop?'

I hesitate, clicking my pen against the table, pretending I have an answer. I don't.

'Honestly?' I exhale. 'I don't know.'

His eyebrow lifts. 'So, you're chasing these things down without knowing how many there are?'

'There's no instruction manual for this, okay?' I say, the words sharper than I intend them to be. 'I just—' I sigh, pressing my thumb into the paper like, hard enough to believe I can ground myself with it. 'I feel like I'm supposed to find them. Like maybe they'll explain something.'

'Explain what?' His gaze stays steady, waiting.

I could've dodged the question. Almost do. But the words escape before I can reel them back in.

'Everything,' I say quietly. 'Everything she never got to say. To me. To us. To anyone who wasn't there when she needed someone.'

Aaren doesn't answer right away. He just watches me, his fingers tapping out a slow rhythm on the table. I can feel it—the way he's studying me, like he's trying to figure out if I was about to cry or just completely unravel.

It's too much. Too raw.

So, I do what I've always done when things get too serious. I change the subject.

'You know,' I say, leaning back, 'for someone who spends a lot of time reading other people's secrets, you don't share much about yourself.'

Aaren smiles. 'What do you want to know?'

'Something unexpected. Like, what's your biggest fear? Or the weirdest thing you believed as a kid?'

He tilts his head, considering. 'Okay, weird childhood belief. When I was five, I thought if you swallowed a watermelon seed, it'd grow into a full-on watermelon inside you. Like, I was convinced I'd wake up one day with vines sprouting out of my ears.'

I laugh. 'Classic kid logic. Did you ever test it out?'

'No way. I avoided watermelon for three years just to be safe.'

'Tragic,' I tease. 'So, what finally convinced you it wouldn't happen?'

'My lola. She told me she ate seeds all the time and never turned into a fruit.'

'Grandmas are the ultimate fact-checkers,' I say, grinning. 'Okay, your turn. Ask me something.'

He leans forward, resting his chin on his hand. 'All right . . . what's the strangest thing you've ever done just to prove a point?'

I think for a second. 'In sixth grade, I wanted to prove I could win the school spelling bee without studying. Pure arrogance, really.'

'And did you win?'

'Second place.'

'Ouch.'

'Yeah, it haunts me to this day. The word was "repertoire". I spelled it with an "i" instead of an "e".'

Aaren winces. 'That's rough. But also, very on-brand for you to go into something like that unprepared and still almost win.'

I shrug. 'What can I say? I thrive on impulse decisions and questionable life choices.'

'You don't say,' he deadpans, glancing around the dark library.

I nudge him with my foot. 'Come on, you're here too. Clearly, we're both thriving on impulse right now.'

'Touché,' he says, shaking his head, but I catch the hint of a smile.

For the next hour, we whisper back and forth, careful to keep our voices low. I ask him random things, point out weird book titles, do whatever I can to keep things light. But Aaren is restless. His foot taps against the carpet, his fingers drum against the table, his whole body buzzing with something unspoken.

And I'm not doing much better.

Because no matter how many distractions I throw at him, my mind keeps circling back. To the notes. To her.

Because what if I stop?

What if I give up?

If I stop, would Elise disappear? Would all I have left be old yearbooks and fading memories? Were these notes the only thing keeping her real?

The thought presses against my ribs, heavy and unforgiving.

I can't let that happen.

Because as long as I keep searching—as long as there's still something left to find—then she is still here.

I tap my pen against the table, staring at the open yearbook in front of me. The words blur together, unreadable. My chest feels tight, like something heavy had settled there and refused to budge.

Aaren must have noticed because, for once, he doesn't fill the silence. He just flips through pages, letting the quiet stretch between us, a kind of understanding that doesn't need words.

Overhead, the speakers crackle.

'The library is now closed.'

I exhale slowly, fingers tightening around the edge of my notebook. We don't move. Just sit there, waiting, listening.

Then comes the distant click of the front doors.

'All right,' I whisper, pulse kicking up. 'Let's go.'

We move from our hiding spot, slipping down the empty hallway towards the old gym at the far end of the building. The school at night feels different—too still, too hollow, every footstep ricocheting off the lockers like a warning. The floors creaks beneath us, too loud, too obvious, like the whole place is holding its breath.

When we reach the gym doors, I wrap my fingers around the handle and pull. Locked. No surprise.

'Figures,' I mutter, shooting a look at Aaren. 'Got a hairpin?'

He gives me a flat look. 'Do I look like the kind of guy who carries hairpins? And those don't actually work, you know.'

'Fine. Plan B,' I say, sweeping my phone's flashlight across the entrance until the beam lands on a window cracked just enough to climb through. 'There. Give me a boost.'

Aaren stares at the window like it's personally offended him. 'You've got to be kidding.'

'Do I look like I'm kidding?'

With a sigh, he crouches and laces his fingers together. 'Try not to kick me in the face.'

His hands wobble slightly as I step onto them, and I grab the window frame, hoisting myself up with more effort than I want to admit. My sneakers scrape against the bricks, and I wiggle through the narrow opening, landing hard on the gym floor. A thud echoes through the space, loud enough to make my heart jump.

I stumble but catch myself, brushing dust off my jeans. The air inside is thick, stale, tinged with sweat and wood polish. The bleachers loom in the shadows, metal seats creaking faintly as the night breeze ghosts through the open window.

The overhead lights stay dead, leaving the space swallowed in dim, uneven light.

I hurry to the door and unlock it with a sharp click, pulling it open. 'Welcome to the world's creepiest gym. Enjoy your stay.'

Aaren steps inside, glancing around. 'Charming.'

We make our way deeper into the gym, our footsteps bouncing off the walls. The silence presses in, the kind that makes you feel like you weren't alone, even when you knew better.

I aim my flashlight at the row of lockers tucked behind the bleachers. 'Over there. Third from the left. That was hers.'

We walk towards it, no longer bothering to stay quiet. I tug at the lock. It doesn't budge.

'It's stuck,' I grumble, yanking harder.

'Move,' Aaren says, pulling a metal ruler from his backpack—because of course he has one—and wedging it into the gap. A little jiggling, a pop, and the door swings open.

The inside is a disaster—crumpled paper, an old water bottle, sneakers that smell like death itself. I push past the mess, fingers brushing against something smooth and solid. A folded piece of paper, edges yellowed with time.

'This is it,' I whisper, barely breathing as I reach for it—

A shadow flickers at the edge of my vision. Too tall. Too still.

I turn my head sharply. Nothing.

But something was wrong.

BANG.

The gym door slams shut, rattling against its frame.

I flinch, the note slipping from my grasp.

'Who's in here?'

A gruff voice. Footsteps, fast and closing in.

Panic punches through my chest.

'Shit,' Aaren mutters. 'We need to go.'

'You didn't close the door behind you?'

'How was I supposed to know if I should? What if the lock's busted, and we got trapped?'

Footsteps, louder now.

We run.

We're almost to the window when a sharp beam of light slices through the dark, pinning us in place.

'Hey!'

We skid to a stop, blinking against the sudden brightness. Footsteps come faster, heavier, until a figure emerges from the shadows.

Not the janitor.

Worse.

'Well, well. Lauren Sanders,' she says, arms crossed, flashlight aimed straight at my face like she was catching a criminal in the act.

My stomach drops. Of course, she knows who I am. My sister's name was still stamped all over this school, and my last name had been on too many honour rolls to go unnoticed. And now here I was, breaking into the gym like I had no business being here.

'H-hi,' I stammer.

Her gaze flicks to Aaren. 'And your partner in crime?'

'Aaren Legarda,' he says, jaw tight. His voice doesn't waver, but his hands curl into fists at his sides.

Coach Ramirez sighs, looking between us. 'All right, Legarda and Sanders. Here's what's going to happen. Tomorrow. 8.30 a.m. Principal's office. Don't make me come looking for you.'

I nod quickly. 'Yes, ma'am.'

Aaren stays silent, staring past her like he was already somewhere else.

She points towards the door. 'Go home. And maybe next time, think before you sneak into school after hours.'

We don't argue. We slip out, the door slamming behind us. Outside, the night air feels colder, sharper. We walk in silence, our footsteps too loud, the weight of what just happened settling between us.

At the edge of the street, Aaren finally stops, his face unreadable.

'That was a disaster,' he says, voice low.

I swallow. 'Could've been worse.'

He lets out a sharp, humourless laugh. 'We got caught, Lauren. Tomorrow, we'll be sitting in the principal's office, probably getting suspended—or worse. This whole thing is blowing up in our faces.'

I try to speak, but the words get tangled, too heavy to push out. Because he isn't wrong.

He exhales hard, dragging a hand through his hair. 'I've got too much to lose for this.'

The words hang there, cutting through the quiet. He glances at me, then away, like he was already pulling back.

A beat passes. Then he sighs. 'Come on. I'll drive you home.'

He doesn't wait for me to answer. Just turns and walks towards the parking lot, shoulders tense, steps quicker than usual.

And for some reason, that hurts more than getting caught.

15

19 May 2014

The voices cut through the walls, sharp and jagged, slicing into the quiet I'd been holding onto.

I turn over, pressing my pillow against my ears, but it doesn't help. The tension in their voices isn't just noise—it's something I can feel, creeping under my skin, settling in my chest like a weight I can't shake.

I shove my blankets aside and slip into the hallway, my bare feet light against the floor. I'm not even sure why I'm moving towards the stairs. Maybe I just need to know if it's as bad as it sounds.

Elise is already at the top of the staircase, knees tucked to her chest, her head tilted slightly like she was trying to make sense of it all.

She looks up when I sit beside her, her expression unreadable but her eyes saying enough.

'You can hear them?' I keep my voice low.

She nods. 'It's about Bill.'

The name lands heavy between us.

Below, the argument presses on.

'Bill's not doing anything wrong, Jack!' Mom's voice was thin, fraying at the edges. 'This is business. You have to trust me.'

Dad doesn't even wait a second. 'Trust? He walks in here like he owns the place. Goes straight to the basement without so much as a hello.'

Elise stiffens beside me. Neither of us speaks. We just listen.

'He's here to see my work. That's it,' Mom shoots back. 'You're making this into something it's not.'

Dad's voice comes fast, clipped. 'He's not supposed to be down there, and you know it. What if he's up to something? What if you are? You're not telling me everything, Cora.'

Something about his words make my stomach turn.

Mom lets out a breath, sharp and exhausted. 'How many times do I have to tell you? I'm not cheating on you with Bill. This is ridiculous.'

I glance at Elise. Her fingers are curled around the hem of her pyjama pants, knuckles pale. Her face mirrors mine—torn between wanting to hear more and wishing we hadn't heard anything at all.

Dad's voice cracks on the next part. 'It's not just about trust, Cora. It's about feeling safe in my own home.'

Mom lets out a bitter laugh. 'You're being paranoid.'

Elise grabs my wrist.

'Come on,' she whispers, pulling me up.

I hesitate, still half-turned towards the staircase, still listening.

But Elise's grip tightens. 'We're not doing this,' she mutters. 'Let's go.'

She doesn't let go until we're back in our room. The door clicks shut behind us, muffling the argument but not erasing it. Elise drops onto her bed, sprawling out, staring at the ceiling like it had answers.

She pats the space beside her. 'Sit.'

I stay where I am, arms crossed, their voices still pressing at the edges of my mind.

Elise sighs, sitting up. 'Lauren.' Her voice is softer now, careful. 'We can't keep listening to them. It's not good for us.'

'I just—' I run a hand over my face, exhaling. 'I want to know what they're saying.'

'You already know.' She rubs her forehead, eyes closing for a second. 'It's always about Bill.'

I swallow. She's right. His name has been lingering in this house for months, sitting in the background of every tense silence, every sharp exchange.

Elise lays back down with a sigh, then stretches her arms over her head, her body sinking deeper into the mattress. 'You need to stop worrying about them, okay?'

I don't answer. Because I don't know what to say.

She watches me for a second, then suddenly sits up again, something lighter flashing across her face. In one quick motion, she moves closer and covers my ears with her hands.

'Hold still,' she says, half-serious, half-smiling. 'Let's pretend we're somewhere else. Like a beach. Can you hear the waves?'

I close my eyes, breathing in. The sound of water rushing over sand, the pull of the tide, the muffled laughter of people in the distance. It's almost real. Almost.

Elise holds her hands there for a second longer, letting the silence settle between us. Then, finally, she pulls away.

'See?' she says. 'No more arguing. Just us.'

I blink at her, the smallest smile tugging at the corner of my mouth.

She grins. 'And let's make a pact. No more listening to their mess. We have better things to focus on.'

'Like what?'

She smirks. 'Like what flavour ice cream we're getting next time we go out.'

That startles an actual laugh out of me. The kind that feels easy.

'Mint chocolate chip,' I say.

'Always mint chocolate chip,' Elise agrees, flopping back onto her pillows.

16

20 September 2023

We sit outside the principal's office, the silence stretching between us—a wall neither of us wants to break. Aaren taps his foot against the linoleum, the steady rhythm almost too calm compared to the way his arms are crossed and the neutral expression he wears. But I could tell—there was that almost imperceptible knot in his jaw, one that gave away how tense he was.

I curl my hands into fists in my lap, stealing glances at him between breaths. I want to say something—anything—but my throat feels like it has been stuffed with cotton. My mind flickers between gratitude and regret, between apology and excuse. Nothing comes out.

The door swings open, and Coach Ramirez steps into the hallway.

'Inside. Now.' Her voice is clipped, her expression unreadable.

My legs feet stiff as I stand, like they belong to someone else. Aaren follows, silent, the door clicking shut behind him.

Principal Caldwell sits behind his desk, adjusting his glasses. He doesn't look angry. Just tired. Like he had seen this exact scene play out too many times before.

He drums his fingers against the desk, then leans back. 'I'd love to hear what the two of you were doing at the old gym lockers last night.'

My heart slams against my ribs, my stomach dropping like I had just stepped off a ledge. I glanced at Aaren, hoping for some kind of signal, but his face is a blank slate. My mind scrambles for an explanation that won't sound completely ridiculous, but nothing feels right.

Principal Caldwell waits, his gaze steady. Beside him, Coach Ramirez crosses her arms, eyebrows raised.

I should tell the truth, I think. Maybe they'd understand. Or maybe they'd just decide I was a lost cause all over again.

Principal Caldwell's voice dips lower, steadier. 'I expected better from you, Ms Sanders. Especially now that you're back. But this? This isn't like you.'

My throat tightens. I open my mouth, but before I can get a word out, Aaren speaks.

'Lauren just needed my help.' His voice is calm, too calm, like he has already worked this out in his head. 'She wanted to grab some of her sister's old stuff from the lockers. Her sister played volleyball here, and Lauren thought she'd bring her things home. You know, since she wasn't exactly able to come back to school for the past two years.'

He glances at me, just for a second. A silent cue. Don't screw this up.

'Yeah,' I murmur. 'That's it.'

Principal Caldwell sighs, rubbing the bridge of his nose. 'Lauren, I understand why you'd want to retrieve your sister's things. Given everything, I get why you couldn't do it before now. But that doesn't give you the right to sneak around after hours. Those lockers are still school property. You could have been charged with trespassing—or worse.'

I nod, pressing my nails into my palms.

His voice turns firmer. 'Here's what's going to happen. You're both getting detention. If anything like this happens again, you'll be suspended. And that means no school activities.' His eyes lock onto Aaren. 'Especially school activities.'

Aaren's jaw tightens, but he says nothing.

'You're dismissed.'

The hallway feels longer than it did before, stretching endlessly in front of us. Aaren shoves his hands in his pockets, his expression unreadable.

'At least we didn't get expelled,' I try, offering a weak smile.

He doesn't smile back. He doesn't even look at me. When he speaks, his voice is low, tight. 'Lauren, we need to be more careful. I mean it. I'm not just risking detention here—I could lose my scholarship.'

I open my mouth to interrupt, but he keeps going.

'Do you get what that means?' His words sharpen. 'That's my entire shot at staying here. At keeping my place. At—' He exhales sharply, shaking his head. 'And if I get suspended, I'm banned from performing with my band too.'

'I know,' I say quickly, trying to fix it before it unravels any further. 'We just got unlucky—'

'No.' His voice cuts through mine, final and unyielding. 'You don't get it.'

The words hit harder than I expect them to. My stomach twists. I want to defend myself, to tell him this isn't just some reckless game for me. But the words stick.

'Some of us actually have something to lose,' he adds, voice flat.

His words land like a slap.

Some of us actually have something to lose.

And what, I don't?

The thought sinks into my ribs, twisting there, ugly and undeniable. I want to snap back, to tell him I was losing something too—but the truth is, I wasn't even sure what that *something* was any more.

Maybe he's right.

And maybe I'm just ruining things.

Aaren exhales through his nose, running a hand through his hair.

'I'll see you at detention,' he mutters before walking off, leaving me standing there with my stomach in knots and my chest too tight, wondering how the hell I'm supposed to fix this.

17

13 November 2023

Aaren sits at the far end of the cafeteria, laughing at something one of his bandmates said, his body angled slightly away, like he wasn't expecting to be interrupted. Like he wasn't expecting me.

He's been avoiding me for weeks. Not in a dramatic, storm-out-of-the-room kind of way, but in a way that stings more—like he's just too busy, too distracted, too something. The kind of avoiding where you check your phone at just the right moment to miss eye contact. Where you suddenly have somewhere to be when you were standing still just a second ago.

And maybe it wouldn't bother me so much if I hadn't gotten used to him being around. If I hadn't started looking for him in a room without meaning to.

I push my food around on my tray, the shepherd's pie turning into a sad, lumpy mess. Across the room, Aaren is deep in conversation with Cody, Jax, and Brandon, their heads pressed together like whatever they're talking about actually matters. Like nothing else does.

Like I don't.

I grip my tray, my pulse hammering against my ribs. I should wait. Maybe later. Maybe after school. But no—I've been waiting. Days, weeks. And every time I tell myself to let it go, to give him space, it only leaves me feeling like I'm disappearing. Like I'd become a background character in my own life.

Screw waiting.

I stand abruptly, nearly knocking over my drink. His friends glance up, their expressions shifting just slightly—like they know something's about to happen. Aaren still hasn't noticed me.

Good.

I cross the cafeteria, my heartbeat in my ears. Doubt creeps in for half a second. What if I'm overreacting? What if this is all in my head? But then I remember what it feels like to be ignored. To be erased. And I keep walking.

I set my tray down with just enough force to make Aaren glance up. His easy smile falters, then disappears completely.

Cody pauses mid-bite, his fork hovering. 'Uh, hey?'

'I need to talk to you.' My voice wobbles, but I point at Aaren like he's personally wronged me. Like he ran over my cat or stole my WiFi password.

Aaren raises an eyebrow. 'Oh, really?'

'Yes. Really.' My face is on fire.

Confidence, Lauren. Confidence.

'Look, I'm sorry for what happened . . . seven weeks ago. I'll be careful from now on, I swear. No more breaking into gym lockers unless it's, like, a life-or-death situation.' My words come out too fast, tumbling over each other. 'But I can't do this without you. I'm terrible at riddles. I've tried—

seriously, I have—but my brain doesn't work that way. You're the smart one. You should be leading this whole thing, and I'll just follow you around like . . . I don't know, a backup dancer or something.'

Aaren blinks at me, still wearing that smug expression that makes me want to punch him and also maybe high-five him.

'Okay, okay,' he says, holding up his hands. 'I get it. You can't live without me.'

His bandmates burst out laughing. Cody gives me a slow, approving nod.

But something in Aaren's expression flickers—like he's not convinced yet.

I swallow. 'I mean it, Aaren.'

A beat of silence.

Then he sighs, running a hand through his hair. 'Fine. But if we get caught again, you're taking the blame.'

He stands, grabbing his tray with one hand and my wrist with the other. 'Catch you guys at practise tomorrow,' he calls over his shoulder.

I stumble after him as he weaves through the cafeteria, my face still burning. He leads me to a table at the far end, away from everyone else, and drops into a seat. He doesn't let go of my wrist right away. His fingers are steady, warm. My pulse jumps.

Then, just as quickly, he pulls back.

'Okay,' he says, leaning back in his chair. 'Talk.'

I drop my tray and sit across from him, my earlier confidence shrinking. But I push forward anyway.

'I can't solve the riddle.'

Aaren tilts his head, interest flickering in his eyes. 'Riddle?'

'Yeah. I've been trying for days . . . weeks. My brain is fried.'

'Let me see it.'

I dig into my bag and slide the folded paper across the table. Aaren picks it up, his eyes scanning the words.

He reads aloud, voice low enough that no one else can hear:

'I change my face but never leave, Dress in green, then gold, then weave. I'm cold, then warm, then hot, then chill—You know my name, you always will. What am I?'

He looks up, one eyebrow raised. 'Cryptic as usual.'

'Tell me about it,' I mutter. 'I've read it a hundred times, and it still makes zero sense. How can something be cold, warm, then hot, and still be the same thing? I even Googled it, and you know what I got? A bunch of dating advice on how red flags are just misunderstood green ones.'

Aaren smirks. 'Well, I hate to break it to you, but I don't think your sister was sending you an inspirational quote.'

'No kidding.'

He leans back, tapping the paper thoughtfully. 'This was from her old gym locker?'

'Yeah.'

'Huh.' He folds the paper carefully, slipping it into his pocket like it's something worth keeping secret. 'Could be a mural. Or something about the seasons.'

He says it like it's obvious, like it isn't a jumbled mess of words and frustration. For a second, I just stare at him, wondering how his brain even works.

'Oh,' I say, nodding as if I understand. 'Yeah. Totally. Makes sense.'

Aaren shrugs, a half-smile tugging at his lips.

The cafeteria stretches out around me. Laughter bounces off the walls, trays slammed onto tables, voices tangled together into a low hum that fills the spaces between my ribs. Every so often, I catch someone looking, their eyes flitting away too fast, like they don't want to be caught staring.

It isn't a big deal. Not really. But it still manages to shake me; it makes my skin crawl, the way people watch without watching. Like they know me but don't. Like I was some story they'd half-read and abandoned before the ending.

I keep my gaze on my tray, hyperaware of everything—the way I sat, the way I gripped my fork, the way my shirt pressed against my shoulders. It all felt wrong, like I was trying too hard to seem normal. Like I was trying at all.

Aaren must've noticed. He always does.

'They're not looking at you,' he says, voice just low enough that it doesn't get lost in the noise. 'It just feels like they are.'

'Easy for you to say.' I stab my shepherd's pie, reducing it to a mess of mashed potatoes and regret. 'People actually like you. Besides, you weren't the one running your mouth five minutes ago.'

He smiles, easy and unconcerned. 'Trust me, they don't like me that much.'

I don't believe him. Not really.

My stomach tightens. It still feels strange, sitting here, surrounded by kids whose biggest problems were pop quizzes and breakups. Kids who didn't know what it was like to become a headline.

I knew what they were thinking. I'd seen it before—the recognition in their eyes, the hesitation, the way they'd glance at me like I was breakable. Like I was tragic. The girl whose sister—

And then they'd stop. They always stopped. Because saying it out loud made it real, and people like to keep tragedy at arm's length.

'Hey.' Aaren nudges me lightly, grounding me before I could spiral. 'Don't let them get to you.'

As if it were that easy. As if I could just shrug it off, brush past the weight of knowing that no matter how many times I started over, I would always be the girl with the sister who didn't make it.

'They're just curious,' he says, softer now.

'Curious people are the worst,' I mutter, but the corner of my mouth twitches despite myself.

Aaren grins. 'No kidding.'

And just like that, the weight in my chest loosens, just a little. He wasn't looking at me like the others did. He wasn't trying to figure me out. He was just there, letting me exist. And maybe that was enough.

'So,' he says, tilting his head towards his pocket. 'Where do you think this note leads?'

I blink, the moment slipping away as the puzzle in front of us came back into focus. 'Right. The note.'

Aaren taps his phone screen, scanning through something. 'Let's try Google first. Might save us some trouble.'

Grateful for something else to think about, I pull out my phone and type: 'Cora Sanders mural painting'. The screen fills with links, but the images are small, pixelated, never quite right. Nothing clicks.

'Wait.' My fingers hover over the keyboard, my heart picking up speed. 'Seasons. It has to be.'

Aaren glances at me, curious.

'Elise used to talk about it all the time,' I murmur, mostly to myself. 'She had this dumb theory that people have seasons. Some are a summer, some are a winter, some last forever.' My throat tightens. 'She wrote it down once.'

I type: 'Four Seasons'.

A painting fills my screen, divided into four panels—winter in muted greys, spring in soft pinks and greens, summer burning in reds and oranges, autumn fading into golds and browns.

My chest constricts. 'That's it.'

Aaren nods, eyes locked on the screen. 'Okay, where is it?'

I scroll through the search results, skimming articles and art blogs. Nothing useful. Nothing that told me where to go.

'Great,' I mutter. 'We have a painting, but no clue where it actually is.'

Aaren leans back, rubbing his chin. 'Maybe it's in a gallery. Somewhere familiar?'

I chew my lip, thinking. 'Maybe.'

I start typing again, but the ring of the bell echoes through the cafeteria, sharp and sudden. Around us, chairs scrape against the floor, voices rise, backpacks slung over shoulders. Lunch is over.

'Guess that's our cue,' Aaren says, stretching as he stands.

I hesitate before getting up, the weight of everything pressing in again. The looks, the whispers, the way the world tilts when too many people knew your story.

'Come on, I'll walk you to class.' Aaren's voice is casual, like it isn't a big deal.

I slip my phone into my pocket and pick up my tray. I freeze, my grip tightening on it. 'Are we . . . good?'

Aaren looks at me, his expression unreadable for a second before something in it softens. 'Lauren, I wouldn't still be here helping you if we weren't.'

I bite the inside of my cheek, fighting a smile. He notices—of course he does—and his mouth twitches like he's amused by the effort.

We drop off our trays and step into the crowded hallway. The thought of walking through it, side by side, makes my stomach twist. The looks, the whispers—I could already feel them.

'You don't have to walk me,' I say, trying to sound indifferent.

'Yeah, I know.' He slings his bag over one shoulder. 'Still gonna.'

Aaren shrugs like it isn't a big deal.

And maybe it isn't.

But somehow, it feels like it is.

18

7 November 2021

Lying would be easy. A simple 'I'm fine' or 'nothing's changed', and we'd move on. But Dr Gregory knows better. He waits, letting the quiet stretch between us, steady and patient, until it feels heavier than the truth I don't want to say.

So, I give in. Because the silence doesn't budge, and because the words always come eventually.

At first, I keep it neat. Manageable. Just enough to make it seem like I have control over it. But then it starts slipping, spilling into places I don't mean for it to go.

I tell him about the figures. How they're not always people—not really. Sometimes they're just shapes at the edge of my vision, vague as smudges on glass that won't wipe away. Other times, they're too real. Sitting on benches. Standing at crosswalks. Walking through crowds like they have somewhere to be. They never speak, never look at me. But they don't seem to know they're not supposed to be here either.

And then there are the moments when I don't see them at all—I just feel them. The way you know someone's watching before you turn around. A weight pressing against the air.

A shift that shouldn't be there. I catch glimpses, just for a second—but when I turn to look, there's nothing.

Dr Gregory nods, jots something down, nods again.

I wonder if he believes me. I wonder if it even matters.

I've learned how to say it in a way that doesn't make it sound like too much. I trim it down, keep it tidy. I don't tell him about the ones that linger, the ones that watch, like they're waiting for something. I don't mention how, every so often, I see one where it shouldn't be—too close, staring at me from the glass like it belongs in my reflection.

I don't tell him how much I doubt myself.

'Are you sure they're not just thoughts?' he asks.

I could say yes. Let him explain it away, call it stress, trauma, a mix of things I'll never fully understand. But I know what I see.

So, I just say, 'No. They're real.'

He doesn't argue. Just nods again, filing my answer away for later. Maybe to study. Maybe to forget.

And for a second, I almost wish he'd tell me I'm wrong. Because some days, I almost believe it myself.

But then there are the other days. The ones where they're so sharp, so real, that I can't understand how anyone could tell me they're not.

Like the man I saw last week, standing at the edge of my bed. He looked like someone I should know but didn't. And the way he stared—it wasn't blank. It wasn't neutral. It was the kind of look that saw too much. That made me want to disappear.

Those are the worst days. Because it's not just about seeing them, it's about wondering if they can see me, too.

There was this one day—maybe a few days ago, maybe longer, but it won't leave me alone. It's stuck in my head like a bad song, the kind you hate but still hum under your breath. I was at my cousin Zania's house because my dad thought fixing things was how you mended people, too. Not the small things, like leaky faucets and squeaky doors, as if tightening a few bolts could keep the whole house from falling apart. And I knew when he said fixing things, he meant trying to fix Mom.

And when he said I needed a change of scenery, what he really meant was, *You need to get out of here before you start talking to Elise, too. Before you start believing she's still here, the way your mom does.* Elise has been dead for three months. But that doesn't stop Mom. And Dad doesn't want me around for that—like I haven't already seen it more times than I could count.

Staying over at Aunt Clarissa's is its own kind of awful. Zania is fine, but the house feels . . . off. Like it had either been lived in for too long or not long enough—like it couldn't decide what it was supposed to be. Zania's room sits at the end of a dim hallway, where the air carries the weight of old books and dust that had settled into the walls. The only window has thick, stubborn curtains that swallow what little daylight tries to get in. No matter how hard you pull, the room stays trapped in its own kind of gloom. Most of the time, I just lay on her bed, staring at the ceiling, waiting—for what, I don't know.

That day starts like all the others. I'm flipping through a magazine, not reading it, just letting the pages turn so I look busy. Zania is downstairs, laughing on the phone with her friends. I'm not listening. I'm not paying attention to anything, really.

And then I see it.

At first, it's just a dot on the wall. So small I almost don't notice it. I think maybe my eyes are playing tricks on me. But then it moves. Slow at first, like it's testing me. Then faster. Skittering across the wall like it had a plan.

My breath snags. My hands clench. My whole body locks up.

It isn't just any spider. It's huge. The kind you only see in nightmares. Bloated body, too many legs, moving like a glitch in reality. But the worst part? Its eyes. Tiny, gleaming. Watching.

It knows I've seen it.

I can't breathe. Can't blink. Can't move.

For one awful second, I think, *This is it. This is how I die.*

And then something in me snaps. My hand shoots out, grabs the first thing I can reach—a can of hair spray. I don't think. I just aim and spray, finger locked on the nozzle like my life depends on it.

'Lauren!'

Zania's voice hits me like a slap.

I turn, still clutching the can. She's in the doorway, staring, her mouth open.

'What the hell are you doing?!'

I whip back around, but there's nothing on the wall.

The spider's gone.

My stomach turns over. I feel lightheaded, like I've suddenly been untethered from my own body.

'I—I thought there was a spider,' I say, my voice barely there. My face burns, shame crawling up my spine.

Zania rubs her arm, her expression shifting from annoyance to something worse. Understanding.

'Do I look like a spider? You sprayed me!'

I want to explain. To tell her that sometimes my mind does this. That sometimes, it's voices. Sometimes, it's people. And sometimes, it's things like this—a spider so real I swear I could feel it crawling across my skin.

But how do you say that out loud? How do you say it without sounding completely broken?

So, I just say, 'Sorry.'

Zania lets out a slow breath. 'It's fine,' she says, but she doesn't sound convinced. 'Just . . . don't do it again, okay?'

I nod, but we both know I can't promise that.

She leaves, and I sit there, staring at the wall, my pulse still hammering. I try to shake it off, but my brain wouldn't let go.

What if you just missed it? What if it's still here? What if it's waiting?

I don't sleep that night.

A few days later, Dr Gregory mentions switching my meds. He's been hinting at it for weeks, but I guess the whole Zania-spider-attack thing gives him the push he needs.

The medicine I'm on is supposed to quiet the hallucinations. It doesn't. I'm still seeing, still hearing, still feeling stuck in a world that doesn't match up with everyone else's.

It's like living in a half-lit room, where everything is almost what it should be, but not quite. Elise lingers in the echoes, her voice tangled up with the ones I know aren't real. And the worst part? Sometimes, I can't tell the difference.

So, we switch.

Dr Gregory suggests another pill. He says it might help more. Might make the voices, the sounds, the spiders—everything—fade a little.

I want to believe him. I really do. But another pill means another promise. Another round of 'maybe this will fix it'.

But what if it doesn't? What if it's always going to be like this?

He hands me the prescription, and I take it.

Because what else am I supposed to do?

❀

I start the new meds because I want something to change. I want the voices to leave me alone. I want the walls to stop shifting, the shadows to stay still. I want to feel like my own mind isn't working against me.

It's been a few weeks now, and I don't know if it's working.

But some days are better. The world feels a little softer. The noise in my head isn't as loud. Other days, it's the same as it's always been.

Maybe it's too soon to tell.

Or maybe I'm just hoping for too much.

19

14 November 2023

Tagaytay wasn't exactly a road trip to the edge of the earth, but the way Aaren gripped the wheel like it had personally offended him made it seem like we were crossing continents.

'We could've picked literally any other day,' he mutters, fingers drumming out his frustration against the steering wheel. We inch forward—if you could even call it that.

'But no,' he continues, voice thick with sarcasm. 'Let's do this when half of Metro Manila decides they also want a bowl of bulalo and a view.'

Outside, the rain drums against the windshield, turning the roads into a slow-moving river of brake lights and frustration. The scent of wet pavement and exhaust fill the air, mixing with the occasional whiff of roasting corn from roadside vendors trying to make the best of the weather.

I watch the last of my iced coffee swirl in its plastic cup, ice melting into something too weak to even call a drink anymore. 'You're the one who said we should check out another gallery.'

'I did not say, "Let's spend two hours breathing in jeepney exhaust while uncles in SUVs cut us off like traffic laws are just rumours."'

'You're so dramatic.' I stretch my legs as much as the cramped space allows. 'And it's not my fault your car decided air conditioning was optional today.'

Aaren exhales through his nose, slow and measured, the way someone does right before they consider whether launching themselves out of a moving vehicle is worth it.

By the time we pull up in front of Prism Atelier, my patience is hanging by a thread, my legs stiff, my stomach a tangled knot of nerves.

The gallery is perched on the hillside, sleek and cold, like it had been designed to keep people like us out. Too much glass. Too much silence. The kind of place where the walls don't just hold art, they hold expectation.

Inside, the air shifts. Cool and crisp, laced with the scent of polished wood and wealth. Not the flashy kind, but the kind that never has to announce itself. The kind that whispers in perfectly pressed blazers and quiet, knowing glances.

Aaren walks in like he belongs. Like he wasn't just swearing at traffic an hour ago. Meanwhile, I'm painfully aware of every step I take, my sneakers squeaking against the marble floors like an unwanted guest announcing their presence.

A woman in pearls glances at me, gaze lingering for just a beat too long, as if she can tell I don't belong here.

A lady with a sharp bob and a dress that probably costs more than my entire life approaches, all polite efficiency. 'May I help you?'

Aaren doesn't hesitate. 'We're looking for a specific painting—Four Seasons by Cora Sanders.'

A pause. Barely anything. A flicker of something crosses her face before she smooths it away. 'This way.'

She leads us through a maze of colour—oversized canvases and price tags that probably had too many zeroes to count. And then—we were there.

The painting isn't the biggest in the gallery. It doesn't demand attention, doesn't reach out and shake you by the shoulders, doesn't need to. It's just there—steady, certain, like it had always belonged. And the second my eyes land on it, I know.

Not in the way you recognize a famous painting from a textbook or the way you appreciate brushstrokes and colour palettes. It's deeper than that. It's the way you recognize a voice in a crowd before you even see the face it belongs to. The way you notice the shift in someone's laughter, the way you just know when your mother's voice is off, even when she swears she's fine.

I don't have to step closer to know every shade, every stroke, every intention behind it. Because I'd already memorized it long before this moment—before it ever found a place on this gallery wall.

This is hers. This is *my* mom's.

I barely notice Aaren move closer. He isn't looking at the painting the way I am, though. His gaze traces the edges, searching for something. And then—I see it too.

A sliver of yellowed paper, peeking from behind the frame. Small, curled at the edges. The kind of thing you'd never notice unless you were looking for it.

My breath catches. My pulse kicks up. I can feel the panic-fuelled adrenaline spike before I even reach for it—whatever it was, it mattered.

Aaren's voice is steady, but I know him well enough to hear the tension underneath. 'Would it be possible to inspect the frame?'

Dani, the curator, smiles. A polite, practised kind of smile. 'I'm afraid that's not allowed.'

This is the moment I should have let go. The moment I should have said, 'Okay,' and walked away. But my fingers move before my brain catches up.

Explaining myself would mean explaining my mother, and I've learned how quickly people decide who you are once they have a reason.

I lift the painting from the wall, careful, but not careful enough.

A hand grabs my wrist, fast and firm.

'Hey!' The guard's voice is sharp, slicing through the stillness of the room.

My stomach drops. The sound of his radio crackling makes my throat tighten.

Aaren mutters something under his breath that I'm pretty sure isn't a compliment.

'I wasn't stealing it!' The words tumble out of me too fast, too loud.

'Step away from the artwork.'

I let go like the painting has burned me. But Aaren—Aaren moves before anyone can stop him. A quick motion, so smooth it's like second nature, and suddenly the paper is gone, tucked safely in his pocket. Nobody sees. Nobody notices. Except me.

The guard doesn't care. His attention's on me. 'Ma'am, you need to come with me.'

My limbs won't move. I'm stuck, my brain trying to process how exactly I let things spiral this fast. Aaren shifts, positioning himself between me and the guard, his voice unnervingly calm. 'Look, this is just a misunderstanding—'

'Sir, step aside,' another guard orders, approaching from behind and stepping in front of Aaren to block his path.

Dani approaches me, her expression unreadable. 'Ma'am, I'm afraid—'

Before she can finish, Aaren cuts in, quick and deliberate. 'Wait. Look—we're just stupid, reckless kids, okay?' His voice is steady, persuasive, the kind that could talk a teacher out of marking him late. 'We weren't trying to steal anything. We got carried away, and it won't happen again.'

Dani stands there, phone in hand, her eyes scanning the room. She doesn't lower her phone. The guard beside her shifts, his gaze flicking between us, looking like he was trying to decide what the easiest way to drag us out was.

Aaren presses on. 'You can put us on a list. A banned-for-life list. Hell, print our faces out and stick them at the entrance. Just—please, let us leave. No cops. No charges.'

I barely breathe. Dani's lips press together. Her gaze flicks to the guard, then back to Aaren, calculating.

The silence stretches.

Then—she exhales sharply. 'If I ever see either of you here again,' she says, voice cool, 'there won't be any second chances.'

Aaren nods, already pulling me towards the exit. 'Understood.'

The guards usher us out with the kind of cold efficiency that told me this wasn't the first time they'd done this. The gallery doors shut behind us with a finality that echoes in my chest.

Aaren grabs my wrist, pulling me towards the car. 'Get in.'

I don't argue. I barely register the motion of climbing into the passenger seat. My hands tremble in my lap.

The car peels out of the parking lot, the tires screeching just a little too loud against the pavement. For a moment, the only sound is the hum of the engine, the wind rushing past, the shallow pull of my breath.

Three minutes pass before Aaren finally speaks.

'Lauren.'

The weight in his voice makes my fingers tighten around my sleeves. I keep my eyes on the road, forcing my breathing to steady.

'I panicked,' I admit. My voice comes out smaller than I want it to. 'I promise, next time, I won't—'

Aaren lets out a breath, one hand gripping the steering wheel harder. 'There shouldn't be a next time.'

His voice is steady, but there's weight behind it. I can feel it in the silence between us, his frustration tightening like a knot. He was probably tired of helping me, tired of digging through these notes—of me putting ourselves at risk.

His grip on the wheel loosens just a little. 'If you pull something like that again, it'll be the last time I help you.'

He doesn't wait for me to respond.

He just grips the wheel tighter, eyes locked on the road.

And for the first time, I wonder if I've finally pushed him too far.

20

22 November 2023

The lunch bell rings, sharp and loud. The sound of a locker slamming shut makes me jump. The sound echoes, and a few people glance around, but I keep my focus. My backpack feels heavier than usual, pulling down on my shoulder, or maybe it's just me. One of those days where even breathing feels like extra work.

I dig into my front pocket, fingers closing around a granola bar. I tear the wrapper open halfway without thinking and take a bite, chewing without tasting. My eyes flick to the inside of my locker, to the photo taped there—Elise and me at the festival, arms slung around each other like we'll never let go. Like we'll always be the same girls in that picture, laughing at something neither of us can remember now.

Except we didn't stay the same.

And she's not here any more.

The photo is worn now—edges curling, colours fading, time pressing into the paper. I found it tucked inside her notebook months after she was gone, like she left it there on purpose, like she wanted me to find it.

Every day, my eyes go back to it, drawn like a needle to a magnet. I should take it down. I should stop waiting for her face to move, for her lips to twitch into a real smile instead of the one frozen in ink. But my fingers hover over her image anyway, the way they once hovered over her hand, the way I used to hesitate before reaching for her. If I let go of this, what else will slip through my fingers?

But I know I can't.

Because some part of me still believes that if I hold on to enough of her—her notes, the scraps of paper with her handwriting, the memories—maybe she won't feel so far away.

But that's not how this works.

'Lauren.'

It's been a while since anyone's said my name like that. Like it still belongs to me.

I turn, bracing for the usual rush of unwanted attention, and there she is—Savannah. A few feet away, arms crossed, but it isn't just a defensive stance.

There's something delicate about her posture, like she isn't sure whether to stay or walk away, her head tilted down just enough to show hesitation.

Her hair, longer now, frames a face that seems quieter somehow, a little thinner. And in her eyes, there's a flash of something—a mix of longing and resignation—that hits me harder than I expect. It's a sharp reminder of the distance between us now, a distance I hadn't noticed until it was too late.

'Savannah?' My voice comes out more confused than anything. 'What's up?'

She doesn't answer right away. Just looks at me.

My stomach twists. I don't like the way she's looking at me, like she's about to drop something heavy between us and walk away before it lands. And now she's here, standing in front of me like she never left, like she still has the right to come into my life and rearrange things.

'We need to talk,' she says finally, voice low, serious.

I blink at her. 'Okay . . . what happened to hello?'

She doesn't laugh. Doesn't even crack a smile.

'It's important.'

I cross my arms. 'What?'

She hesitates. I can see it in her face—this flicker of doubt, like maybe she's about to change her mind and walk away. Maybe I should let her. Maybe I should say, *whatever it is, I don't care* and keep moving.

But then she leans in, voice lowering.

'It's about someone you've been hanging out with,' she says. 'I think his name is Jare . . . Jam . . . I don't know, but—'

The words barely register before something inside me snaps.

'You're joking.'

Savannah shifts her weight, pressing her lips together. 'Janice told me—'

'Janice?' The name hits the air like a slap. My pulse picks up, heat rising under my skin.

Savannah doesn't flinch, but she also doesn't say anything. Maybe she wasn't expecting me to push back. Maybe she thought I'd just take it.

I take a step forward. 'You're seriously basing this on *Janice*? The same Janice who will say anything if it means people will look at her for five more seconds? Janice, who once told half the school I was locked in a psych ward after Elise died? Janice, who has never gotten a single thing right about me?'

Savannah doesn't answer.

And that silence? That heavy, stretching silence? It makes me want to scream.

I let out a short, bitter laugh. 'Why do you even believe her?'

Her jaw tightens. 'I just thought you should know.'

'That's it?' My voice comes out flatter now, emptier. 'You *thought* I should know? And what exactly am I supposed to do with this, Savannah? Drop everything because Janice decided to stir up more shit?'

For the first time, her expression flickers—like maybe she's realizing this isn't playing out the way she thought it would.

I don't know what she expected. I don't know what I expected either. But I know I don't want this.

'Well, thanks, I guess,' I say, and even I can hear the emptiness in my voice. 'But I don't need this from you. Especially if you're so quick to believe the same people who spent years turning me into a joke.'

Savannah's mouth opens like she has something to say—maybe an apology, maybe a way to soften the edges of this conversation before it cuts too deep. But she doesn't.

Instead, she exhales, slow and sharp. 'Look, Lauren, I don't know. Janice said something about him, but . . . you know how she is.'

I bark out a dry laugh, rubbing a hand over my face. 'Exactly. She makes up half the shit she says.'

Savannah hesitates. 'Yeah, sometimes. But . . . not always.'

Something in my stomach turns over, uneasy and sour. Heat crawls up my spine, my pulse hammering behind my ribs. 'What are you saying?' My voice is sharper than I mean it to be, but I don't care. 'That you actually believe her? That you believe them over me?'

Savannah doesn't flinch, doesn't look away. She just stares at me, and when she finally speaks, her voice is quiet but solid, like she's dropping something heavy between us.

'Yeah.'

The word lands like a punch.

I don't know if she means it, or if she just wants to hurt me back. But either way, it does.

She folds her arms tightly, like she's holding herself together. 'Look, I don't even know you any more.'

The words hit harder than they should. Like a slow, sinking realization that something is already gone.

My stomach knots, my mind scrambling for something to say, something that can fix this before it unravels completely. 'What do you mean?' I ask, trying to steady my voice, but it wobbles at the edges. 'Where is this coming from?'

She exhales sharply, shaking her head. 'You've changed, Lauren. You used to care. About everything. About me.'

Something inside me recoils. Used to. The phrase hangs in the air like an unfinished thought, like a door left open just wide enough to remind me of everything on the other side.

'I'm still here,' I say, but the words taste hollow even as I say them.

She looks at me then, and there's no softness in her face. Only exhaustion. Only hurt.

'No, you're not.'

The silence between us isn't just silence. It's every unanswered text, every moment she reached for me and found nothing.

Savannah swallows hard, her throat working around the words like they physically hurt. 'You stopped coming to school. You dropped out. And then you just . . . disappeared. And I waited. I waited for you to come back, to answer my texts, to look at me and actually see me again, but you never did.'

My chest tightens, guilt curling inside me like something sharp. 'What's your point?' I ask, the words coming out too sharp, too defensive. A shield I don't even mean to hold up.

She flinches, but her voice doesn't waver. 'My point is, I lost you too.'

She says it so simply, like it's something she's known for a long time. Something she's been carrying alone.

'I needed you, Lauren,' she says, her voice breaking in the middle, splintering apart. 'But you didn't see it. You didn't see that I was falling apart too. My parents split up, and while that was happening, I was losing you.'

She blinks fast, her breath shaky, and suddenly, it's not just about her parents. It's about us. About what I didn't see.

'I know it's not the same as what you've been through,' she continues, her voice smaller now. 'But I thought maybe I could lean on you. That we could help each other. But you . . . you were too lost in your own world to even notice I was slipping too.'

A lump rises in my throat. The worst part isn't the words. It's how true they are. I was drowning. And I didn't see that she was right beside me, sinking too.

'I didn't—' The words tangle in my throat, coming out thin, broken. 'I didn't know what to do, Savannah. I didn't know how to—'

'What?' she cuts in, her voice raw. 'How to be a friend?'

I flinch.

'I don't know how to fix me,' I whisper, the words unravelling before I can stop them.

Savannah just stares at me, shaking her head. 'That's the thing, Lauren. I don't think you want to.'

I open my mouth, but no words come out.

She swallows hard. 'You keep carrying this grief around like it's the only thing keeping you together. Like if you let go of it, even for a second, you'll lose yourself completely. But the truth is, you're not holding onto it because you can't let go. You're holding onto it because you don't want to.'

Her voice softens, but the words are still heavy. 'And I get it. I do. Because if you let it go, if you start living your life again, it means she's really gone. It means you have to face everything you've lost. And that's terrifying.'

She exhales shakily, eyes shining. 'But Lauren . . . you're losing people anyway.'

The air between us shifts.

'You're losing me.'

It's the quietest thing she's said all, but it feels the loudest.

I shake my head before I even realize I'm doing it. 'No,' I say, voice uneven. 'Savannah, I—'

She wipes at her eyes, fast, like she doesn't want me to see. 'I don't know what to do any more,' she admits, and I don't know if she's talking about this conversation or about everything else.

The silence stretches. And then, she blinks, a tear slipping down her cheek.

She swipes at it quickly, shaking her head. 'Never mind,' she says, voice barely above a whisper. 'Why do I even bother? You don't care. You never did.'

The words carve into me.

'Savannah—'

But she's already stepping back.

She looks at me one last time, something fragile in her expression—something that might've been hope, once. But it's gone now.

'Forget it,' she says, voice thin and tired. 'I told you what you needed to hear. If I'm right about that guy you've been hanging out with, don't come running to me.'

Her words are final.

And then she's gone, her footsteps fading down the hallway, leaving nothing but silence in her place.

I stand there, staring at the space where she was, feeling like the ground has been ripped out from under me.

And I do nothing.

I just watch her go. Knowing I should stop her. Knowing I won't.

21

24 November 2023

I watch Aaren across the table, hoping the answers to all the questions spinning in my head will just show up—written on his face, maybe, or floating above his head like a flashing neon sign that says, *Figure it out already.*

But nothing appears, and my mind keeps circling back to Savannah. Two days have passed, and her words still won't leave me alone. She said I was too caught up in my own world to notice she was slipping too. And maybe she's right. Maybe I was so busy chasing the pieces of Elise, trying to hold my grief and guilt at the same time, that I forgot to look around—to see who was still here.

And maybe I should've let Savannah finish what she was saying about Janice and Aaren. Maybe then I'd know if I'm overthinking or if there's actually something I should be worried about.

Aaren catches me staring, and I immediately look down at my plate, suddenly fascinated by the sad excuse for a salad. The lettuce is wilting, the dressing is pooling in the corner of the tray, and my sloppy joe looks like it lost a fight with a blender.

'Do you want to say something?' His voice pulls me back, and I force myself to look at him.

I shake my head. Because even if I did, I wouldn't know where to start. I don't even know what I'm supposed to be asking.

Aaren studies me for a second before saying, 'Have you read the note yet?'

Another shake of my head.

His brows knit together as he tilts his head, like he's trying to figure out what's going on in my brain. 'Are you okay? Is something wrong?'

Yes. Something is definitely wrong.

But I don't know how to explain it. I don't even know what *it* is—I just know something feels *off*. So, I shake my head again and let the silence speak for me.

Aaren watches me a moment longer, like he's waiting for me to crack, to spill whatever I'm not saying. But when I don't, he just nods and picks at his plate, like he's accepted that whatever's going on with me is a mystery he won't solve today.

I hate that I'm acting weird, and I hate even more that I can't explain why. Maybe I *could* if I tried hard enough. But that would mean admitting that Savannah's words are still messing with my head, making me second-guess everything.

I push my fork through my food, dragging it in slow circles.

Aaren clears his throat. 'So, uh . . . I know you haven't read the note, but . . . do you want to talk about it? Or talk about anything?'

His voice is so careful, so *genuine*, that for a second, I almost tell him everything. Almost let it all spill out right here, in the middle of the cafeteria. But where would I even start?

'Hey, Aaren, Savannah told me weird things about you, and now I don't know if I even know who you are any more.'

That sounds ridiculous. Even just thinking it makes my stomach twist. But part of me still wonders—*if* there's something to know, *if* there's something he's not telling me.

'I . . .' My fingers tighten around my fork. 'I guess I'm just feeling off today.'

Aaren doesn't look convinced.

'Off how?' he asks, leaning forward slightly. His eyes are locked on mine, like he's not letting me off the hook.

I exhale slowly. 'Off like . . . when you're in a room, and you know you're forgetting something important, but no matter how hard you try, you can't figure out what it is.'

I force a small smile, but it's not convincing, and Aaren knows it.

He laughs anyway, shaking his head. 'That happens to me all the time.' But his eyes stay on me, searching, waiting. 'Still feels like there's something you're not saying.'

He's right. There is.

Before I can figure out what to do with that, his phone buzzes on the table. He glances at it, then back at me with an apologetic look. 'Hold that thought for later. I gotta go—urgent band meeting. Student council wants us to play at the Christmas Festival next month, and we haven't practised in *forever.*'

I blink, caught off guard. The Christmas Festival. I'd almost forgotten about it.

Elise used to go *all out* for it—talking about it for weeks, insisting it was the highlight of the year.

And everyone else seems to love it too. Once December hits, it's like a countdown to break. But this year? It just feels . . . different. Like maybe I *should* be excited, but I'm not.

'Oh . . . right,' I say, trying to sound normal. 'I forgot about that.'

Aaren raises an eyebrow. 'Forgot? Isn't that, like, *the* thing people look forward to in December?' His grin is easy, teasing. 'But I guess you've got other things on your mind.'

'Yeah . . . I guess so.' I nod, relieved for the shift in conversation.

He picks up his tray. 'Don't stress about whatever's bugging you, okay? And if you do,' he pauses, giving me a look—part question, part reassurance. 'You know I'm here.'

And then he's gone, disappearing into the crowd, leaving me alone at the table with a hundred unsaid things still sitting in my throat.

I stare at my tray, wishing I could make sense of all of this. But I don't.

So instead, I sit there, lost in thoughts I can't untangle, wondering if I ever will.

❀

I step out of the cafeteria, moving before I even realize it. My body leads, my brain follows. The hallway stretches ahead, a straight shot to the bathroom. My feet know the way. They've done this before.

The second I push open the door, the noise cuts off. No trays clattering, no voices overlapping, no bursts of laughter that feel too sharp, like they might slice through skin. Just silence. Thin, uneasy.

I slip into a stall, lock it. Press my palms flat against the cold metal door. My breath comes in short, uneven bursts. Inhale, exhale. Try again. Get it right this time.

The bathroom door swings open.

Footsteps. Rubber soles scuffing against tile. Voices.

Janice.

I know it's her before she even speaks.

'Yeah, I don't even know why she's back here. If I were her, I'd just leave.'

I lower my hands from the door, fingers curling against the waistband of my jeans, nails pressing into denim. I don't move. I barely breathe.

'And her sister—Elise—was such a mess,' Janice says, her voice light, like this is nothing. Just words. Just noise. 'Honestly, I think her dying was kind of a relief. She was always so . . . desperate, throwing herself at every guy who looked at her.'

The air shifts, pressing down on my chest, forcing itself into my throat. I squeeze my eyes shut. Focus on the pressure of my hands against the denim, the ridges of the stall lock pressing against my back.

'She was so out of control,' Janice continues, her tone laced with something that almost sounds like sympathy. Almost. 'Guess the attention wasn't enough, so she decided to kill herself instead.'

Something caves inside me. The floor tilts. My breath snags.

'Lauren just watched. Can you imagine? Standing there while your own sister kills herself?'

A sharp, splintering inhale. My ribs strain, barely holding me together.

'Maybe you wanted her dead.'

'Maybe you were fine with it.'

The words scrape against my skull, burrow into the spaces I've tried to keep empty. The stall walls press closer, close enough that my shoulders might brush them if I move even an inch.

I clutch my stomach, nails digging deep, hard. But then—

A shadow.

A figure standing just beyond the door.

She tilts her head, watching me.

Dark, damp strands of hair cling to pale skin. Hollow eyes fix on mine, unblinking.

Elise.

A pulse of cold sweeps through me. My body locks up, muscles screaming to run, to move, to do something, but I can't.

Her lips never part, but the words reach me anyway.

Why didn't you save me?

A tremor starts at my fingertips, spreads up my arms, through my chest.

I squeeze my eyes shut. Count to three. Try to breathe. Try to remind myself that she isn't here. That she can't be here.

But when I open them again, she's still there.

The lights buzz overhead, flickering slightly, and for a second, it feels like the whole world wobbles around her. Like everything else is shifting, but she's staying perfectly, impossibly still.

'You wanted her gone.'

'You watched her die, and you did nothing.'

'It's your fault she's dead.'

The voices twist together, some mine, some not. A low ringing starts in my ears. My chest tightens. My body curls inwards.

I press my hands against my temples, fingers digging in, but it doesn't help.

She's still there.

Staring. Waiting.

The air is too thick. The walls too close. My skin too tight.

I can't move.

I can't breathe.

I just sit there, trapped in the space between then and now.

22

25 December 2018

The Christmas tree stands tall, dripping in gold and red, its lights blinking like they're trying to fill the silence. The scent of pine and cinnamon clings to the air, thick and sweet, like a secret wrapped too tightly.

Dad's in the kitchen, elbow-deep in seasoning, his hands moving with the kind of focus he only ever gives to food. The sizzle of oil and the clatter of trays blend with the low hum of Christmas music from the radio. Mom's at the counter, rolling out cinnamon roll dough with slow, deliberate movements. A tray of bibingka sits by the window, the cheese already melting into the soft, golden tops. Everything smells warm, but there's something else beneath it. Something I can't name.

Elise and I sprawl on the couch, still in our pyjamas, the fabric wrinkled from sleep. The pile of presents sits untouched beneath the tree, their ribbons curled at the edges, like they've been waiting too long. Elise leans forward, fingers grazing a box wrapped in glossy red paper, the gold ribbon tied in a careful bow.

'That one's mine,' I say, reaching for it.

Elise snatches it up before I can touch it. 'No, it's not.' She clutches it close, her fingers digging into the edges. 'Dad got it for me.'

My stomach twists. 'What are you talking about? My name's on it.'

She doesn't even check. Just grins, wide and unbothered. 'Doesn't matter. I want it more.'

I wait for Mom to say something, to tell her to give it back. But Mom just steps into the room, wiping her hands on a dish towel. Her eyes flick to the gift in Elise's hands—just for a second, so quick I almost miss it. Then she smiles, the kind that stretches too far.

'Lauren, just let her have it,' she says lightly. 'She likes it better.'

Something inside me folds in on itself. Elise's grin sharpens, and I wonder if Mom sees it. If she cares.

I don't argue. I don't ask why. I reach for the next closest box, one with my name on it, though it suddenly feels like a consolation prize. Elise hums under her breath as she runs her fingers along the ribbon of the red package, like she's already won.

The morning passes the way it always does—ripped wrapping paper, scattered bows, the hum of carols playing in the background. The same routine, the same traditions.

But something about it feels different.

At dinner, Dad carves the prime rib, his voice warm as he asks about our plans for the break. Elise chatters away, her words spilling over each other, while Mom nods along, laughing at all the right moments. But her smile is careful, placed on her face like an afterthought.

'What about you, Lauren?' Dad asks, glancing at me between bites.

I poke at the mashed potatoes, my fork sinking into the smooth surface. 'I don't know.' The words come out quieter than I mean to, but I don't bother fixing them.

Elise fills the space I leave behind, and Dad turns his attention back to her, nodding along to her stories. I let the conversation drift around me, the laughter too bright, the air too thick. It's like watching a play I forgot the lines to.

When dinner ends, I slip upstairs, away from the noise, away from the feeling that I don't quite fit in the picture we're painting. My room is quiet, but not the peaceful kind. I sit on my bed, staring out the window, the sky stretching into a deep, endless grey.

Downstairs, the house starts winding down. Dishes clink in the sink. Dad's voice hums low, and then—Mom's.

It's different. Softer. Strained.

I creep down the stairs, moving slow, careful. The hallway is dim, the glow from the living room casting long shadows. I don't mean to listen. Not really. But then—

'I'm not telling them.'

Mom's voice is steady, but there's something caught in the edges. A pause. Then, softer, like she's holding something fragile in her hands:

'Not yet. Not until they understand.'

A chill runs through me.

The words don't make sense, but the feeling does.

She knows I'm there before I can move. Her head turns, and our eyes meet across the dim hallway.

For a moment, everything stills.

Then, her smile.

The kind that's too quick, too smooth. But now I know what to look for—the way her eyes don't match, the way she's too careful, too polished.

I bolt upstairs before she can say anything, before she can weave another lie into something that sounds like the truth.

But the words don't leave me.

Not yet. Not until they understand.

Understand *what?*

The question follows me, curling around my ribs, refusing to let go.

I don't stop at my room. I slip into Elise's instead. She's already asleep, her breathing slow and even. I climb into bed beside her, curling up on the edge of the mattress.

She stirs slightly. 'Lauren?' Her voice is thick with sleep.

'I just want to sleep here tonight,' I whisper.

She doesn't question it, doesn't push. 'Okay, whatever.' And then she's gone again, lost in sleep.

Elise shifts beside me, her breath slow, steady—unbothered. I tell myself it doesn't matter, that I don't need her to ask why I'm here. But the silence settles too easily between us, and somehow, that stings more.

I stare at the ceiling, tracing the cracks I can't see in the dark. The house is still, wrapped in a quiet that doesn't feel gentle. It presses in, thick and heavy, like a truth no one wants to say out loud.

I squeeze my eyes shut, reaching for sleep, but all I find is the echo of Mom's voice—soft, uncertain, careful in a way that makes my stomach twist. I see the way she turned her back, the way her words lingered too long in the air, like they weren't meant to be heard.

Maybe I'm overthinking it. Maybe I'm making something out of nothing.

But deep down, I know better.

Nothing about this has felt right in a long time.

23

26 November 2023

The room is exactly the same as it always was. Beige walls, a chair too soft to sit in properly, the air conditioner humming like it had something to say. It is familiar, but not in a way that makes you feel safe. More like the kind of place you end up in when you have nowhere else to go.

I can hear everything—the slow tick of the clock, the quiet scratch of pen against paper, the shifting of my own weight as I try to sit still. But none of it feels like it's coming from inside me.

My hands rest in my lap, fingers curling in on themselves, tight and nervous. I don't want to be here. More than that, I don't want to look at him. Dr Gregory sits across from me, pen poised, waiting with a patience that feels too steady. Like he has all the time in the world.

'So, Lauren,' he said finally, his voice soft, careful. 'How have things been since our last session?'

I open my mouth, but nothing comes out. Not because I don't have anything to say—because I don't know where to start. The words sit heavy in my throat, unwilling to move.

I focus on my hands, the way my nails dug into my skin. 'Two days ago . . .' My voice sounds distant, like it wasn't even mine. 'I had an anxiety attack.' I swallowed. 'In the bathroom.'

The words barely made it out before the voice in my head turned sharp. *Pathetic.*

Dr Gregory doesn't push, doesn't fill the silence with anything unnecessary. He just nods and jots something down, like he's giving me space to breathe, to gather the words I'm not sure I want to say.

I let them come anyway. 'I was in the stall, and I heard Janice talking with someone else. They were talking about Elise.' My stomach twists. 'About her death.'

The pen in Dr Gregory's hand stills, but he doesn't say anything. Just listens.

'Of course, they were talking about her,' I mutter. 'Everyone's always talking about her.'

The voice in my head agrees. *No one cares how you feel, Lauren.*

I force myself to keep going. 'They said it was a relief. That it was better this way.' My breath catches in my throat. 'Then they said I wanted her dead. That I just watched her die.'

My chest burns, heat crawling up my ribs, but I keep my eyes locked on the floor. If I let myself look up, I'm not sure I'll be able to hold it together.

'Lauren.' Dr Gregory's voice is steady, but his gaze sharpens. 'Tell me what you felt in that moment. Not what you *think* you should've felt. What was *really* there.'

I swallow, the words trapped in my throat. He waits. He doesn't let me run from it.

'. . . Angry,' I admit. The word feels like a weight. 'And hurt.' My fingers clench. 'It felt like they took something from me. Like they erased her. Like they erased *me*.'

The voice inside me whispers, '*They're right, you know.*'

'*You didn't save her.*'

I can feel the pressure in my chest, too much, too tight, but I swallow it down. Force it into something smaller. Something I can pretend isn't there.

Dr Gregory nods, slow, measured. 'Grief isn't simple. It never is. Especially not when it's sudden, like it was with Elise.'

I barely hear him. It doesn't feel like enough.

'When I heard them talking,' I whisper, 'it was like I couldn't breathe. Everything just—' I exhale sharply. 'It felt like the walls were closing in. And then I blacked out.'

The silence stretches between us, pressing in around me.

'Do you remember what happened after that?' he asks. His voice is gentle but firm, like he's guiding me back to myself.

I nod, but I don't feel steady. 'I woke up in the nurse's office. They said I fainted. A friend found me.' The memory feels blurry, like something I'd only half lived through. 'I don't even know how long I was out.'

My fingers find the cold edge of the chair, running over it again and again, trying to anchor myself to something real. 'It's embarrassing,' I admit, my voice barely above a whisper. 'I didn't even tell Clarissa what happened. Maybe I didn't want her to know.'

Dr Gregory is watching me, quiet, like he sees something I'm not ready to show.

'Lauren,' he says finally, steady but soft. 'It sounds like you were overwhelmed. That's not something you have to apologize for. It's okay to react when you're triggered—especially when it's something as painful as losing Elise.'

I nod, but I'm not sure I believe him. His words don't make it go away. They don't make it hurt less.

'I just . . .' I hesitate, the words thick in my throat. 'I don't want to feel like that. Like I couldn't handle it. Like I was falling apart.' My jaw tightens. 'Maybe I am.'

You are unfixable. This is who you are now.

The space between us grows heavier, the quiet stretching, filling every inch of the room.

I can hear my own breathing—shallow, uneven, like I've just run up a flight of stairs I don't remember climbing. My fingers curl into the fabric of my jeans, nails pressing hard enough to leave little crescent moons on my skin.

Dr Gregory sits across from me, quiet, steady. Watching, but not in a way that makes my skin itch. It isn't pity, isn't some over-practised therapist stare that told me he already had me figured out. He just waits.

'Maybe I'm not okay,' I say, the words falling out before I can stop them. 'Maybe I'll never be okay. Maybe I'll always be like this.'

I brace myself for some rehearsed reassurance. Something soft and meaningless, like *you'll get through this* or *you're stronger than you think.* But Dr Gregory doesn't say anything right away. He lets the silence sit between us, not awkward, not heavy. Just there.

Then, finally: 'You don't have to have everything together, Lauren.' His voice is even, careful. 'But I want you to think about something. What happens when you stop waiting to feel better? Sometimes, the only way forward is to take a step, even if you're not sure where it'll take you. It won't fix everything, but it might make the next moment a little easier to hold.'

I stare at the floor, at the scuffed linoleum, the way my shoe taps against it like I'm not in control of my own foot. 'I don't want to feel like this any more.' The words barely make it out. 'I don't want to feel like I'm coming apart all the time.'

Dr Gregory doesn't rush to answer. He just watches me with that same careful patience, like he knows anything too quick, too soft, would slip right off me.

'Grief doesn't move in a straight line,' he says eventually. 'It doesn't go away just because you want it to. But it won't always feel this way. You can keep moving through it, even if it's slow.'

I nod, but it's just for show. I don't believe it. The weight in my chest, the way my brain keeps running in circles—it feels permanent, like something I'll have to carry forever. I can't imagine a time when it wouldn't hurt.

'Tell me about your parents,' Dr Gregory says, his voice calm, careful. The kind of voice that's meant to be reassuring but still has the power to cut straight through you. 'You've told me about Elise, but not them. How do they fit into all of this? Do they bring up the same kind of emotions?'

The question lands harder than I thought it would. Elise? I could talk about her. I could rip myself open, bleed it all out, let the pain take over because it was familiar. But my parents? That was different. That was a mess I didn't know how to untangle.

I stare at my hands, at the chipped nail polish and the tiny scar on my thumb from a broken bottle last summer. My mind searches for words, but nothing feels right. The room presses in, too small, too still. I can feel Dr Gregory waiting, giving me space to answer, but all I can think about is how much I don't want to.

'They're not like Elise,' I say finally, my voice quieter than I mean it to be. 'I don't hear them the way I hear her.'

Dr Gregory doesn't push. He just lets the silence settle between us, patient in a way that makes my chest tighten.

'They're just . . . gone.' The words barely make it past my throat. 'But not like she is. With her, I know what I feel. But with them? It's like they were never really here. I try to remember, but it's all empty space. I can't even picture them any more.'

I swallow, my hands curling into fists. 'They were just people I used to know. And now . . . now, I don't even know what to call them. Every time I try to remember, all I get is the hurt.'

The air in the room feels thick, pressing against my ribs, making it harder to breathe. But I keep talking. Maybe because stopping would mean sitting in the silence, and that's worse.

'I don't want to think about them. Not after everything. Not when it feels like if I start, I won't be able to stop.'

Dr Gregory doesn't rush to fill the silence. He just sits there, steady, like he knows there was more. Like he knows I was holding something back.

I look away. 'It's not just the pain,' I whisper. 'It's knowing I should've mattered to them. That I should've been enough for them to stay.'

I can feel the tears burning at the edges of my eyes, but I blink them away. There is too much between us—too much left unsaid. And it isn't just anger. It's something else, something heavier, something I don't know how to name.

I don't tell him about the dreams.

The same one, over and over.

I'm back in my old room, before everything. The walls are still blue, chipped at the edges, the colour I picked when I was ten because it reminded me of the ocean. Everything looks the same, but it isn't. The air feels wrong, thick and unmoving. The posters on the wall—the bands I don't even listen to any more—seem faded, like they were tired of waiting for me to come back.

The hallway stretches longer than it should. Too long. At the end of it, my parents' bedroom door is cracked open, just enough to make my stomach twist. I tell myself not to go in, but I do anyway. The air is thick—stale, unmoving. The scent of something sweet, almost rotten, clings to the walls. My bare feet barely make a sound on the floor, but with each step, a ringing starts in my ears.

Inside, everything is still. The kind of stillness that doesn't belong in a room that is supposed to be lived in. My mom's book sits open on the nightstand. The laundry basket in the corner is full. The soft yellow glow from the lamp makes everything look normal, but it isn't.

Because they are there. On the bed. Eyes open, staring at the ceiling. Their mouths slightly parted, caught mid-sentence in words they'd never get to finish.

My hands shake. My feet refuse to move. My brain screams at me to wake up.

Then, my mom's fingers twitch.

Once. Twice.

Her eyes flick to mine, locking in place for the briefest moment. Just long enough to steal the air from my lungs. Just long enough to make my pulse hammer in my ears.

And then I jerk awake, gasping.

Every single time, I check my hands for blood, but there's never anything there.

Just a dream, I tell myself. Just a stupid dream.

Except it never feels that way. It feels real. Real enough that I avoid looking Clarissa or Zania in the eye at breakfast, just in case they somehow know. Real enough that I check my hands every time I wake up, searching for something that doesn't exist.

But Elise—her death—was real. I saw it. I felt it. There is no waking up from that. No 'just a dream' to make it go away.

And even though she's gone, she is also still here. In the quiet moments, in the spaces between thoughts. I can feel her, like she's waiting for me to notice her, to reach out and find her again.

But my mom and dad? They feel like ghosts. Not the kind that haunt you, but the kind that slip away before you even realize they're gone. I try reaching for them sometimes, in old memories or in the quiet moments before sleep, but there's nothing solid to hold on to. Just vague outlines, like faded photos left out in the sun too long.

I used to think Mom and Dad were solid, like nothing could ever shake them. But maybe I was wrong. Maybe I had idealized them, turning them into something softer in my mind than they really were. Maybe I convinced myself they would have stayed if they could. But in the end, they didn't.

They saw her. The daughter they lost. The one frozen in time, forever perfect in a way I'll never be. The one I couldn't save.

And when they looked at me—if they even bothered—I knew what they saw. Not their daughter. Not someone worth holding on to. Just the girl who stood there, useless, while the world caved in.

Maybe that's why their faces don't come back to me. Maybe I've erased them the way they erased me. Or maybe they left long before I even had the chance to lose them.

24

30 November 2023

The café hums with life—voices overlapping, the hiss of steamed milk, the quiet clatter of spoons against porcelain. It's a little too loud, the kind of noise that fills up the space in your head when you need it to. I keep my hands wrapped around my coffee cup, feeling the warmth seep into my fingers, but I don't take a sip. It's too hot. Or maybe I just like having something to hold on to.

Across from me, Aaren keeps flipping the paper I gave him earlier—the one with the riddle—like the answer might magically show up if he turns it over enough times. He squints at it, brow furrowed, like it's the most confusing thing he's ever seen.

'Okay,' he starts, his voice laced with frustration. 'What is this supposed to mean?'

I don't answer him immediately. I'm focused on the moment, the way the light from the overhead bulbs glimmers off the polished wooden table. It's almost like time slows down here, allowing me to forget about everything else. But the feeling doesn't last long. I can't escape the noise, the thoughts swirling in my mind, constantly fighting for attention.

It's been six days since everything fell apart. Six days since I was curled up on the bathroom floor, barely breathing, thinking I was dying. My body didn't feel like mine then, everything was numb and yet too much at once. Dr Gregory has a word for it, but naming it doesn't make it any less terrifying.

'Lauren?' Aaren's voice breaks through the haze, pulling me back. I glance up at him, and he's watching me carefully, his eyes searching.

'Are you okay?' he asks, quieter now, like he's treading carefully, not wanting to make things worse.

'I'm fine,' I say, my voice betraying me. It comes out stiff, like a lie I've told too many times.

'Sure?'

His gaze sharpens, and I feel the weight of it. He sees right through me, the way he always does. It's like he knows more than I'm willing to admit. It's irritating how easily he figures me out, like I'm wearing my thoughts on my face.

'I'm just . . .' I pause, shaking my head. I crumple the napkin on the table into a little ball, then roll it between my fingers. 'Thinking about stuff. Elise. My parents. You know.'

Aaren doesn't push for more. Instead, the silence hangs in the air, awkward but familiar. Neither of us speaks, but the space between us feels strangely comfortable, like an old habit we both know too well.

'Do you ever feel like you're carrying something that you can't shake off?' I ask, the words slipping out before I can stop them.

Aaren blinks, clearly caught off guard. 'What do you mean?'

I press my palms flat against the table, grounding myself, trying to steady my thoughts. 'The kind of feeling that makes you wonder if you missed something. Like, if you didn't see something coming, or if you had done something differently, would things have turned out better? The kind that eats at you and makes you second-guess everything.' I stop, realizing how tangled the thought is. 'It's the feeling that leaves you asking, "What if I could've done more?"'

Aaren's expression softens, and I can tell he's thinking it through, maybe more closely than I intended. He taps his fingers against the table, the rhythm steady and calming. 'Yeah,' he says, his voice low, thoughtful. 'I've felt that. A lot.'

I'm surprised. 'And it doesn't mess with you?'

'It used to,' he admits. 'I'd replay everything in my head—every little thing I could've done differently. But then I realized . . .' His voice quiets as he shifts in his seat. 'It doesn't change anything. No matter how much you wish it did.'

There's something in the way he says it, calm but practised, like he's been through this before and found a way to live with it. It feels like he's learned how to make peace with things that won't change.

'How do you stop it from taking over?' I ask, my voice barely above a whisper.

Aaren exhales, rubbing his thumb over a scar on his knuckle, like he's remembering something. 'It doesn't really stop,' he says, voice soft. 'It just fades into the background.'

He shifts again, his gaze distant. 'I used to replay everything a hundred times, wondering if I could've done something different. But . . .' He stops, like he's trying to put words to something he's never said aloud. 'Eventually, you realize no matter how much you play it over in your mind, you can't change it. You can't fix what's already been done.'

His words hit hard. It's like he's talking about more than just regrets—he's talking about accepting the things you can't change.

'Does that make it any easier?' I ask, the question slipping out before I can stop it.

Aaren meets my eyes, and for a moment, it feels like he sees right through me. He shakes his head slowly.

'No,' he says quietly. 'It doesn't. But you figure out how to live with it. You learn to forgive yourself, even when you don't feel like you deserve to, because in the end, you're the only one who can decide how to carry it.'

His words hang there between us, thick with truth, and I finally exhale a breath I didn't know I was holding. Maybe it's not a solution, but it feels like a small shift, like someone cracked a door open just enough to let in some air.

Aaren looks at the riddle again, flipping it back and forth in his hands. 'All right, I've been reading this for the tenth time, and it's still not making sense. What is this even supposed to mean?'

I glance at the paper he's holding, still crumpled in his hand. Honestly, it looks like nonsense to me, too.

He reads it aloud, each word dripping with more confusion. 'In a place where colours dance and secrets lie, walls hold whispers, both low and high. Painted stories linger, both bold and bright, only two pairs of eyes can reveal their light. Who am I, where art and mystery play, a wall of visions, where shadows sway?'

I shrug, my mind too foggy to think. 'I don't know,' I admit, rubbing my temples. 'That's why I gave it to you.'

'I thought I was good at riddles,' Aaren mutters, his voice dripping with frustration. He twists the paper sideways as though it will somehow make more sense. 'This one's . . . it's like it's trying too hard to sound deep.'

'Yeah, welcome to my life,' I mutter, leaning back in my chair, feeling the weight of the conversation still lingering.

Aaren stares at the paper, tapping it against the table. 'Okay, let's break it down. "Colours dance", "walls hold whispers". That sounds like something to do with art, right? Like a gallery?'

I nod, but the words still feel slippery. 'Maybe. But what does "only two pairs of eyes" mean?'

Aaren frowns, turning the note over like a different angle might change the meaning. 'Something hidden. Something only certain people can see.'

I press my fingers against my forehead, the weight of everything settling behind my eyes. 'Maybe we're overthinking it. It could be something simple.'

Aaren watches me, something shifting in his expression. 'Could be. But where do we start?'

I open my mouth, then close it again. The thought is barely formed, but it's there, pressing at the edge of my memory. 'Bill's studio,' I whisper.

Aaren's head snaps up. 'Bill?'

'Yeah,' I say, the words coming out faster now. 'My mom's art curator. She keeps her unsold paintings there. It's in Quezon City, not far from here.'

He leans forward, interest flickering across his face. 'Wait—what's the name of the studio?'

I hesitate. 'I don't know. I don't even remember the last time I was there. Or the first, really. It's just . . . Bill's place.'

Aaren studies me, head tilted slightly. 'And you never went back?'

I shake my head. 'Nope,' I answer with forced nonchalance—the word lighter than how I feel. I press my fingernail into the table's surface, following an invisible line. 'It always felt like my mom wanted it to be just her and Bill. Something about needing to focus. Needing the space to be theirs.'

The words sit between us, heavier than I mean them to be. I didn't plan to say that out loud. Aaren doesn't push. He doesn't offer some neat, easy response that's supposed to make it better. He just listens.

I glance down at the note again, my fingers brushing over the uneven paper. Something about it sticks, like a word on the tip of my tongue that refuses to come out.

And then it clicks.

I look up. 'What if the note means it's a secret?' My voice is quieter now, like saying it too loud might make it disappear.

Aaren's eyes sharpen. 'Go on.'

'The "two pairs of eyes"—' I swallow, my throat suddenly dry. 'It could be my mom's and Bill's.'

Aaren doesn't speak right away. He just watches me, thinking, waiting. Then, finally: 'That's weird.'

I let out a breath, pressing my palm flat against the cool table, grounding myself. 'Maybe it is.'

Aaren pulls out his phone and starts scrolling. 'If it's in Quezon City, there's gotta be something about it online.'

I nod, but my mind is already slipping elsewhere. Back to that place between past and present, between what I know and what I don't. Ice shifts in my untouched drink, melting into something watered down and unrecognizable.

'So, you think the riddle's pointing us there?' Aaren asks, tucking the note into his pocket.

I swallow. 'Yeah. It has to be.'

He leans back in his chair, the legs creaking against the floor.

'I guess we'll find out soon,' Aaren says, his voice steady.

I nod, but it's instinct more than intention, like my body is on autopilot while my mind lags behind. Aaren offers a small, hesitant smile. I try to mirror it, but it slips before it can fully form.

Because the truth is, I don't even know what I'm hoping to find. And maybe that's the part that unsettles me most—realizing I might not recognize it, even if it's right in front of me.

25

10 November 2021

The shrill beep of my alarm drags me from sleep, sharp and jarring, its sound grating against my nerves. It's not Elise singing, not the off-key version of 'Happy Birthday' that used to make me roll my eyes and pretend I was still asleep. It's just noise, the kind that makes your teeth grind before you even have a chance to open your eyes.

I slam my hand down on the clock, cutting off the shriek, and the silence that follows feels too heavy, like the room is holding its breath, waiting for me to notice what's missing.

Elise should be here. She should have already burst in, jumping on my bed, messing up the blankets, shaking me awake whether I wanted to be or not. But she's not.

I stare at the ceiling, letting the quiet sink in, letting the truth settle into me like a stone in my chest.

This is my first birthday without her. And I don't even know if it counts as a birthday without her.

When I finally drag myself out of bed, everything feels off—empty, almost like I've lost something important but can't figure out where I left it. I skip breakfast, not even thinking about it. I grab my bag and head for the door. But then my feet hesitate, turning me towards Elise's room, and I don't even know why I'm doing it. It's like my body knows what my mind can't admit.

My hand hovers over the doorknob, and before I can stop myself, I push it open.

Mom's asleep on Elise's bed, curled up with one of her sweatshirts, clutching the stuffed penguin Elise and I fought over last Christmas. It was supposed to be mine, but Mom made me give it to her. And now she's holding it like it's the last thing that matters, like it belongs to her more than it ever did to me.

I don't say anything. I just stand there, frozen in the doorway, my fingers tightening around the strap of my backpack. There's this sharp, tangled knot in my chest—anger, maybe, or something close to it. Mom used to go all out for Elise's birthdays. Cakes, decorations, everything. Mine? She always forgot. Elise had to remind her every year. That was just how it was.

And now Elise isn't here to remind her, so I guess it's not worth remembering.

By the time I get to school, I'm already exhausted. Like I'm moving out of sync with the rest of the world. I walk through the halls, past people laughing and talking, like it's just another day, like nothing's different. But everything feels different.

No one knows it's my birthday. No one knows anything.

I get to my locker, twist the combination lock, and pop the door open, ready to grab my books and just get through the first period. But then I see it.

Sitting on top of my stuff, a little squished but still intact—a cupcake. There's a note stuck to it, the handwriting shaky, like the person who wrote it wasn't sure if they should.

I stare at it for a long moment, my fingers hovering over the paper, my throat tight. I don't know what to feel.

Happy Birthday.

Savannah's standing a few lockers down, watching me like she's bracing for something, like she's not sure if I'm going to smile or break. When I pick up the cupcake, her face brightens, and she gives me a little nudge.

'Make a wish!' she says, trying to sound cheerful, like this moment is supposed to mean something.

I swallow hard, pushing back the lump in my throat, and close my eyes. But I don't think about wishes, or candles, or anything that might feel normal. Instead, I think about Mom—how I wish she'd notice me, see me, like I'm more than just someone to forget about when the important things come around.

I open my eyes and force a smile. 'Wish made.' Then I take a bite of the cupcake, even though I'm not hungry.

Savannah grins, launching into some story about a movie she saw, her voice filling the space between us, easy and unbothered. I nod along, pretending to listen, pretending the cupcake doesn't taste like cardboard in my mouth.

We start walking to class, and then I see it.

Elise's locker.

I freeze.

It's covered in sticky notes.

From a distance, they look harmless—bright colours against the grey metal, like little memorials left behind. But when I get closer, I see the words. The ugly ones.

Slut. Bitch. Liar.

As if someone thought this was funny. As if Elise deserves this.

'Who did this?' I ask, my voice sharper than I mean it to be. A few people turn, their eyes flicking away like they don't want to hear, don't want to be involved.

No one answers. No one stops. They just keep walking, looking at anything but me.

My fists clench so tight my nails dig into my palms. My breath catches, and something hot and ugly builds in my chest. The hallway tilts, like the ground isn't steady beneath me.

And then I see her.

Elise.

She's standing a few feet away, in the middle of the crowded hallway, like she belongs here, like nothing's changed.

My breath catches in my throat. She's watching me, her face unreadable, like she's waiting for me to figure it out.

I blink, hard. But she's still there.

She's not real. I know that. I know it. But she feels real. So real that if I just reach out, if I take one step forward, maybe—

'Elise?' I whisper, the word slipping out before I can stop it.

She doesn't move.

And then the whispers start. Soft at first, like the rustle of paper, but then louder, sharper, until they're piercing, cutting through me.

'It's your fault.'

'You're a freak.'

'You're the reason why she's gone.'

The words tangle together, bouncing off the walls, filling the space around me until I can't breathe, until I can't think.

The hallway shifts. My legs feel like they're made of stone, and I grab Elise's locker to steady myself. But the floor keeps tilting, the world stretching and warping, like it's not real, like nothing is.

And then—

Nothing.

❀

The first thing I notice when I open my eyes is the sharp, sterile light above me. It's so bright, it feels like it's digging into my skull. I blink, trying to clear the fuzziness in my head, but it only makes my headache worse. The air smells like rubbing alcohol and something faintly metallic—like the remnants of a place too clean to feel like it's really lived in.

I'm on a cot, one that's uncomfortable enough to remind you it's not meant for comfort, just for getting through the moment. It feels like the mattress is holding me hostage, keeping me locked in a place I don't want to be.

Savannah is sitting beside me, her hands twisted in her lap like she's trying to keep them from shaking. She looks pale, her eyes wide, scanning me like she's trying to figure out if I'm really here or not. 'You okay?' Her voice is soft, barely above a whisper, as if the words might break if they're spoken too loudly.

'You were breathing weird,' she adds, her voice catching. 'Then you just . . . you just collapsed.' She swallows, looking away. 'I didn't know what to do.'

I should say something. Reassure her, tell her it's nothing. I should laugh or shrug it off—anything to make her feel better. But the words don't come. How do you explain to someone that you saw your dead sister standing in the hallway, looking just as real as anyone else? How do you say that, for a brief moment, she was more present than the walls around you?

You don't.

Instead, I stare at the scratchy blue blanket covering me, the edges worn, like it's seen a thousand others before me. I don't shake my head, but I feel it all over again—the hollow ache in my chest, the tightness in my throat, the way everything still feels too loud and too still at the same time.

The door creaks open, and Dad steps in. He looks at me like he's checking for damage—like there's something about me he needs to be sure hasn't broken. His face softens when he sees me awake, but the relief in his eyes hits me harder than anything else. 'Lauren,' he says, his voice fragile, like saying my name too firmly might shatter something. 'Are you okay?'

I blink, trying to find my voice. 'I'm fine,' I mumble, even though I'm not. My body feels heavy, like it belongs to someone else, and my chest is tight, the kind of tight that doesn't let go, no matter how much you try to breathe. All I want is to go home, crawl under my covers, and pretend none of this ever happened.

The nurse talks to Dad in that tone—sharp, clinical, like she's delivering bad news that I already know. Stress. Anxiety. Maybe dehydration. Nothing about ghosts, or dead sisters, or memories that cut deeper than skin.

Dad comes back, crouching beside me, his voice softer now. 'We're going to Dr Gregory's.'

I don't argue. I can't. My legs feel like jelly, and I don't have the strength to fight him. I just nod, too tired to do anything else.

Dad sighs, like he expects me to argue, and he reaches out, offering his hand. I take it, my grip weak as I push myself off the cot. His hand stays on my back as we walk towards the door, light but steady, like he's afraid I might fall apart if he lets go.

Savannah follows us, a few steps behind, her silence heavier than before. When we reach the hallway, she stops, arms crossed, eyes still locked on me, a worry on her face that I don't know how to ease. She doesn't say anything. She just watches, standing still as we walk away, leaving her behind in a place I don't know how to explain.

The car ride is quiet—there's too much left unsaid, and I don't know where to start. Dad keeps glancing at me from the corner of his eye, his fingers tapping against the steering wheel like he's trying to find the right words. Finally, he clears his throat. 'Lauren,' he begins, his voice tentative. 'That wasn't just an anxiety attack, was it?'

I turn my face towards the window, the cold glass biting into my skin as I press my forehead to it. The outside world rushes by, too fast, too blurry, as if the universe is trying to tell me something—something I'm not ready to hear.

'I saw her,' I whisper. 'I saw Elise.'

The words hang between us like mist, thick and unwelcome. I don't look at Dad. I can't. I don't want to see the pity, the disbelief, or worse—the look that says he doesn't know what to do with me any more.

At Dr Gregory's office, Dad squeezes my shoulder before I get out of the car. It's small, but it stays with me, like he's trying to send a message without saying a word. *I'm here. I'm worried. Please be okay.*

The chair inside is just as stiff as the cot, but it doesn't matter. The room smells like cinnamon and old books, and it settles into my lungs like something I didn't know I needed. Dr Gregory sits across from me, his notebook balanced on his knee, like he's waiting for me to explain myself.

'What happened today, Lauren?' he asks, his voice calm, too calm.

I try to make it sound normal, to explain it in a way that doesn't make me sound insane. The hallway. The notes on Elise's locker. The way she was there, like she never left. The words tumble out of me, jagged, messy. I brace for him to stop me, to tell me I'm imagining it. But he doesn't. He just listens, nodding, his expression unchanged.

When I finish, he leans forward, his voice steady. 'What you're describing . . . it has a name. It's called psychosis.'

The word lands like a heavy stone, cold and clinical. *Psychosis*. Like a wall between me and the world. I can feel it pressing down on me.

He sees the look on my face and adds quickly, 'It's not as scary as it sounds. It just means your brain is tricking you into seeing or hearing things that aren't there. It happens, especially after a major loss.'

I stare at my hands, watching the way they tremble. 'So . . . I'm hallucinating?'

'In a way,' he says, his voice soft, kind. 'But it's not something you're doing on purpose. It's how your mind is trying to make sense of what happened. You lost Elise, and your brain is still catching up.'

I nod, but it doesn't help. It doesn't explain the feeling that Elise was right there, breathing, alive, like I could touch her again if I reached out.

'But it was her,' I say, almost a plea. 'She was really there.'

Dr Gregory doesn't flinch. He just nods again, like he's seen this before. 'Grief is complicated,' he says. 'Sometimes, it feels like the people we love are still with us, even when they're not. Your mind is holding on to her because it's not ready to let go.'

It makes sense, in a way. But it doesn't make it hurt any less.

'So . . . I'm not crazy?' I ask, my voice small, fragile.

'No,' he says firmly. 'You're grieving. That's not the same thing.'

I release a breath I didn't know I was holding. For a moment, I feel lighter, but it's fleeting. The ache is still there, like a weight I can't get rid of.

'This doesn't mean you're broken, Lauren,' Dr Gregory says, his voice quiet but sure. 'It doesn't mean you'll feel like this forever. It just means your brain is handling the hurt the best way it knows how.'

The words should comfort me, but they don't. They're logical, they make sense, but they don't take away the heaviness in my chest, the hollow space where Elise used to be.

I nod anyway. It's easier than saying, '*This doesn't help*.' Easier than admitting that I don't know when—if—I'll ever feel okay again.

26

10 November 2021

The yelling drifts up from downstairs, but it's not as loud as it used to be. I don't even flinch any more. It's just background noise now, like the hum of the fridge or the creak of the floorboards when someone walks by. I've stopped trying to figure out what they're fighting about. I've stopped trying to care.

But then, I hear her voice. My mom. It cuts through everything.

'She's nothing like me!'

I freeze, my hand gripping the edge of my desk. Her words wound me, even though I don't know why. I should've shut the door, but I never remember until it's too late. And now it's too late.

The weight hits me then—the cold, suffocating feeling that makes it hard to breathe. It's familiar. The kind of weight that pulls you down, makes you feel like you're sinking.

I don't want to turn around, but I do.

And there she is.

Elise.

She's standing in the corner of my room, half-hidden in the shadows by the dresser. I blink, hoping she'll vanish, but she doesn't. She never does. Her eyes are on me, steady, unblinking.

'Why are you here?' The words escape before I can stop them. My voice is shaky, like I've been running, like I've been holding everything in for too long. 'You shouldn't be here. You're . . . you're supposed to be gone.'

But she doesn't say anything. She never does. She just stands there, the way she always did. Like a ghost, or a painting of a girl who died too young.

And then, suddenly, there's a swell of anger, sharp and hot, rising from deep in my chest. I don't know where it comes from, but it's there, swelling until I can feel my heart pounding in my throat.

'Say something!' I snap at her, the words coming out louder than I intend. My voice shakes, and I feel like an idiot, yelling at a shadow. 'Why won't you talk to me?'

But she's still silent, her eyes still fixed on mine.

'Is this what you wanted?' I ask, my words growing louder, edged with frustration. 'Is this your punishment? For me not knowing? For not seeing how bad it was?'

The walls of my room seem to close in, the air suddenly thicker, like there's not enough of it to breathe.

'You didn't say anything either,' I bite out. 'You didn't ask for help. You just—you left.'

I know I shouldn't say it. But it comes anyway, sharp and bitter, like a poison I can't spit out fast enough.

'And now look at me.' I gesture around the room, helpless, angry. 'I'm stuck. You left, and I'm stuck here, being compared to you, being ignored because of you, being less because of you.'

Still, she doesn't move. Still, she doesn't blink.

'You were perfect, Elise. Perfect grades, perfect smile, perfect everything. You got all of it—everyone's attention, everyone's love. And me? I'm just . . .' My throat tightens. 'I'm just here.'

I swallow hard, and the words hang in the air, thick and suffocating. Like I've just been punched in the chest.

I wipe my face before the tears can fall, but I already know it's useless. The room feels too still, too quiet. Elise feels too real.

'I never asked for this,' I whisper. My voice cracks, breaking under the weight of it all. 'I never asked to be the one left behind.'

She doesn't move. Doesn't say a word.

I know she's not really here, not in any way that matters, but it doesn't stop me from feeling like she is. It doesn't stop me from feeling like she's watching me, like she's seeing me.

And that's the worst part.

I feel seen. And I hate her for it.

'Just go away,' I mutter, my voice trembling. 'Just go.'

I turn my back on her, pressing my hands against the edge of my desk, my knuckles white with the pressure. My chest is tight, my breaths too shallow, too fast.

Downstairs, my mom and dad are still yelling. The same argument, over and over again. Like they don't even realize I'm here. Like I'm invisible.

I glance over my shoulder. Elise is still standing there, still silent, still perfect. She doesn't move, doesn't flinch.

And me? I'm still stuck.

Still nothing.

I sink into the chair at my desk, my hands covering my eyes, pressing hard to stop the tears from coming. But they do anyway, hot and stupid and angry, and I can't make them stop.

Downstairs, the yelling continues. The same fight, the same old words, the same old noise. Elise stays in the corner, as quiet as ever, a part of the room, a part of me I can't shake.

I wish I could hate her less. I wish I could forget her. I wish I could stop wishing for things I'll never get.

But nothing changes.

She's still here. And so am I.

And I don't know which one of us is haunting the other.

27

1 December 2023

It never gets cold in Manila, not like it did in New Hampshire. Here, it's just heat—heat that presses on everything, makes the air thick and still. It rains for half the year, but the rest of the time, it's just a constant weight, hanging in the air. Even December doesn't feel like December. There's no chill, no frozen breath in the morning air, no snow.

I don't get it. I don't get why my parents thought moving here would fix anything.

I don't remember much about New Hampshire, just bits and pieces—the way the air smelled, the sight of the bare trees in the winter, the sound of the wind rattling the windows. But I remember the cold. I remember the quiet of snow, how everything was still, like the world was holding its breath.

Mom and Dad moved us when I was too young to remember much else. They left that quiet, white place behind and brought us to Manila. Mom had been building her career here long before Elise and I were even born, and to her, coming back made sense. It was time, she said, to stop drifting. To live again.

But I'm not sure it ever worked out that way.

'Are you okay?' Aaren's voice breaks through my thoughts, pulling me back to the present. I hadn't realized we'd stopped walking.

I blink, forcing a smile. 'Yeah. Just . . . thinking.'

We're heading to Quezon City now, past rows of shops and vendors, the usual noise of jeepneys honking and people talking, haggling. It's familiar, in a way. But not the kind of familiar that feels like home. More like a place I don't belong to but can't escape.

'I think it's up ahead,' I tell him, adjusting my jacket even though I'm sweating. The humidity sticks to my skin, but I can feel my nerves turning my insides cold. The knot in my stomach keeps tightening, and I'm not sure if it's because I'm almost there or because I'm about to face something I don't know how to handle.

'Your mom's studio, right?' Aaren asks, glancing at me.

'Yeah.' I nod. 'She rented it from Bill back when things were just . . . starting. Before everything changed.'

We continue walking in silence, the noise of the city surrounding us. But my mind is somewhere else. The streets blur, and I can't shake the feeling that I'm about to uncover something I'm not ready to face.

Then, as we round a corner, I see it.

The building is small, tucked between two apartment complexes, its paint faded, the windows cracked and worn. It's nothing special. Just another forgotten spot in the city. But I stop when I see it, my heart stuttering in my chest.

'This is it,' I say softly.

Aaren looks at the building, then back at me, his brow furrowed. 'Are you sure?'

I nod. 'I think so.'

We walk towards it, slower now, like the air itself is heavy. I can feel my heart beating harder with every step. When I reach the door, I flag down an old man sitting on a bench, nursing a cup of coffee. His face is lined with age, his eyes squinting in the afternoon sun.

'Excuse me, sir,' I ask, trying to sound casual. 'Do you know if there used to be an art studio in this building?'

He looks at the building, then back at me. After a moment, he nods. 'Yeah, I remember something like that. Been closed for months, though. Bill ran it—he's trying to sell it now.'

The words hit me like a punch in the gut, and I feel the air drain out of my lungs. This place, my mom's studio, it's about to be just another memory. Something else that's slipping away.

I force myself to breathe. 'Do you know how we can get in touch with him? Or maybe someone else who could help?'

The man scratches his chin, thinking. 'Bill's ex-wife, Sally. She's part-owner. Lives close by. I think I've got her number. Hold on.'

He rummages through his pockets, finally pulling out a crumpled napkin. He writes something down and hands it to me.

I thank him and step away. Aaren looks at the number, already dialling before I even have a chance to react.

The phone rings a few times before a woman's voice picks up. 'Hello?'

'Sally?' Aaren's voice is calm, steady. 'Hi, we're interested in the studio here. We were hoping to take a look at it.'

There's a long pause. Then a sigh. 'You'll have to talk to my ex-husband. He handles all that.'

'We're already here,' Aaren says, his tone not wavering. 'We're leaving tonight. It would really mean a lot if we could see it now. Just twenty minutes.'

I watch him, amazed by how easily he keeps his voice light, persuasive, like he's done this a hundred times before.

After a beat, she speaks again, this time sounding resigned. 'Fine. I'll be there in fifteen minutes.'

Aaren hangs up and looks at me with a grin. 'Guess we'll have to wait.'

We linger outside the building, my heart pounding in my chest. The heat in Quezon City feels different—heavier, almost like it's pressing in on us. The jeeps rumble by, and the ground shakes just a little with each one, the movement vibrating through my feet. When Aaren finally gets the text with the location, we start scanning the crowd. Eyes darting between locals, we wait for the woman to appear.

It doesn't take long. She's standing near the entrance, leaning against the wall, like she's already decided what kind of people we are. She's tall, with sharp features that set her apart from the others. Her hair is cut short and styled with precision. It's not careless—it's calculated. She glances our way, eyes narrowing just enough to size us up, like she's already piecing together the story we're trying to tell.

'Aren't you two a little young to be buying a studio?' she says, raising an eyebrow, her tone amused, like she's enjoying this.

Aaren doesn't miss a beat. His smile stays in place, but I see the tension in his eyes, that little flicker of something tight. 'We're not the ones buying it,' he says, smooth but with an edge. 'We're just helping out. A friend of a friend needed someone to rent it while they're away. Temporary thing.'

She glances at the studio door behind us, then back at Aaren, her eyebrow still arched. 'A friend of a friend?' she repeats, voice dry.

I feel a twist in my stomach. We should've thought this through.

Aaren's voice remains steady. 'Yeah. They're travelling long-term. Needed someone to keep it running.' He lets out a little laugh, like he's trying to sell the lie even harder.

Sally's eyes flick to me, and I force a nod, hoping I don't look like I'm about to collapse. 'Yeah. We're just helping out.'

'Interesting,' she says slowly, her eyes narrowing, scanning me like she's trying to see right through me.

Her gaze feels like it's digging into me, probing, and I can feel the pulse in my throat, that little tremor in my chest.

'How does a business like that even stay open?' she asks, her voice laced with scepticism.

I feel my heart race. Aaren doesn't skip a beat. 'It's . . . sort of underground,' he says, like it makes sense. 'Word of mouth. Very exclusive.'

'Exactly,' I add, jumping in, desperate to keep the story moving. 'Artists like their privacy. Keeps things low-key.'

She tilts her head, still eyeing us with that sharp, almost predatory look. 'Interesting,' she repeats, but there's something in her tone that makes my skin crawl. 'I'll tell my brother about it. He's a photographer. Maybe he can help you promote it, get the word out.'

I force a smile, my teeth clenched. 'Actually, it's a private space. Strictly invite-only. We're keeping it small for now.'

For a moment, I think she might press us for more, but she just nods, a slow movement that feels like she's dismissing us. 'Of course,' she says, her voice dripping with fake sweetness. 'Best of luck. Young entrepreneurs are always so inspiring.'

We stand there for a moment longer, forcing smiles until she's far enough away, her footsteps fading out of earshot.

'Invite-only?' Aaren mutters, his jaw tight. 'Really?'

'Couldn't exactly tell her the truth, could I?' I snap back, trying to hold it together. 'And "sort of underground"? Genius, Aaren. Really.'

He exhales sharply, frustration flashing in his eyes. 'She's definitely suspicious now.'

I glance at the studio door, waiting for her to unlock it. The weight in my stomach doesn't go away, like we're walking into something we're not ready for.

Inside, the space is exactly what I expected—huge and empty, cold light flooding through tall windows, making everything feel exposed. Like we don't belong here. She walks us through, pointing out random things like they matter, her steps echoing against the concrete floor, and her voice flat. Like this place is nothing to her.

'The last person who rented this place,' she says, her tone matter-of-fact, 'was an artist. She left behind a bunch of her things when . . . well, when she passed. Suicide, I think. Poor thing.'

I stop in my tracks, my heart faltering. The floor drops away from me, and the air seems to thicken, pressing in on my chest.

Suicide. Artist. My mom.

The words swirl around my head, looping, repeating. I want to speak, to ask more, but my throat locks up. The room feels too small.

She goes on, her voice distant, like it's coming from far away. 'She was talented. Left a lot of paintings behind. God bless her soul.'

I don't even know how to respond. I want to scream, ask her what she knows, but nothing comes out.

Aaren notices the shift in me, and he steps closer, his voice pulling me out of the fog. 'Do you know where the paintings are? Are they still here?'

The woman hesitates for a moment, eyes flicking between us. Then she pulls a key from her pocket and hands it to Aaren. 'In the storage room,' she says, her words almost detached. 'It's locked, though.'

Aaren flashes that familiar, easy smile of his. 'Would it be all right if we take a look? Just want to get a feel for the place, see what's here.'

She shrugs, unconcerned. 'Sure, why not.'

We follow her down a narrow hallway to a small storage room, the door creaking open to reveal dusty canvases piled up like forgotten things. The air inside smells old—dust, paint, and something else, something stale, like it hasn't been touched in years.

I hang back, letting Aaren do his thing. His questions are smooth, a constant stream of words to keep her distracted. He's good at this. I watch him, his face unreadable, his voice calm and steady like he's done this a thousand times before.

I glance towards the room, towards the covered canvases. My chest tightens, a wave of unease crashing over me. I can't help myself. I slip further into the room, not thinking, just moving.

The door is cracked open behind me, and their voices—distant, like muffled whispers—fade. I know I should stop. I know I shouldn't be here. But I can't make myself leave.

My fingers hover over the edge of one of the sheets, trembling. Then, before I can think better of it, I pull it back.

The painting is of me.

At least, I think it is. The face is mine, but it feels wrong. The eyes are too wide, the smile too forced, like it's hiding something. The background blurs, slipping in and out of focus, like it's not even there.

This isn't just a portrait. It feels like something else. Like it's capturing a part of me I'm not ready to see. The brushstrokes are frantic, like my mom was trying to tell a story she couldn't finish.

I swallow hard, my throat dry. I move to the next canvas. And the next.

With each one, my chest tightens. The paintings grow darker, the faces melting into shadows, their eyes searching, reaching. I feel like I'm staring into parts of her I was never supposed to know.

And now it's staring back at me.

I almost give up when something catches my eye. Tucked behind a stack of canvases, barely visible, is a small easel. The legs stick out awkwardly, and there's a drawer beneath it, small and hidden in the corner. It calls to me, that drawer. Like it's important, like it's holding something I need to see.

I can't look away.

I glance over my shoulder, half-expecting someone to walk in. But the silence presses in, thick and heavy. My breath feels shallow, my chest tight as I reach for the drawer.

My fingers shake as I pull it open. Inside is a folded piece of paper—fragile, like it's been waiting to be found for years.

I freeze, the weight of it settling in my chest.

I don't know why I'm terrified. I should leave. I should run. But my hand won't move.

I pull out the paper, my hands unsteady. When I see the handwriting, everything inside me goes still.

It's hers.

Elise's handwriting—loops and curves that I'd recognize anywhere.

My heart stutters. I can't breathe. I should leave. I should walk away. But I can't.

I unfold the paper, my fingers trembling. The sound of paper crinkling fills the silence, and I feel like I'm holding onto something that could unravel everything I thought I knew.

In a sea of colours, where petals sway,
You led me through fields on a sunlit day.
With whispers of secrets, we laughed and we played,
Yet in this vast beauty, a feeling delayed.
What place am I, where nature's art plays,
A memory cherished, in sun-kissed days?

I read the note again, my heart pounding against my ribs as if it's trying to break free. Each word twists inside me like something I've almost remembered but can't quite hold onto—like reaching for a memory just beyond your grasp, or hearing your name in a crowded room and not knowing where the voice is coming from. My breath comes too fast, and my hands are shaking, but I can't stop reading. I can't look away.

Footsteps. Too close. Aaren's voice slides into the silence, smooth and casual, like he hasn't noticed the mess inside me. My stomach drops, and suddenly, the air feels thinner, like it's impossible to breathe. I feel the blood drain from my face. Panic rises, sharp and insistent, like a warning.

I scramble, shoving the note into my pocket. The paper crunches as I press it into the fabric, trying to hide it, to erase the truth I've just stumbled into. My heart pounds so loudly, I can't hear anything else. I need to move. I need to get out of here.

My hands fumble. I throw the sheets back over the canvases, the motion clumsy and awkward. It snags, and I tug at it, trying to smooth it down, hoping it looks normal, hoping no one sees. No one knows.

I don't even know why I'm freaking out. Aaren probably won't care. Or maybe he will. I don't know. The room feels too small now, too full of something I can't name—like it's watching me, waiting for me to slip up.

'Lauren?'

His voice is closer, closer than it should be, and I freeze. I'm still crouched beside the paintings, my mind spinning, desperate for something to focus on, something to make me look busy, to make it seem like nothing's wrong.

I grab the measuring tape from the table, my fingers stiff and shaky. Dropping to my knees, I start measuring the floorboards like it's the most important task in the world.

My movements are jerky, forced, like I'm trying to outrun everything I've just learned. But my thoughts are miles away, tangled in the mess inside my head.

The door creaks open behind me. I feel Aaren before I see him—his presence, that easy confidence that's too familiar, too close. Then, there's silence. He doesn't say anything, but I feel the weight of his gaze on me. He's watching, and I know he can see through the lie.

My neck burns. I can feel the heat crawling up from my chest, and I can't shake the feeling that he's piecing it all together, that he knows more than he's letting on.

'Yeah?' I ask, my voice cracking before I can stop it. It sounds too high, too tight. I clear my throat, trying to sound normal, but it's useless. 'Just measuring,' I add, forcing a smile, but I can't bring myself to look up. If I do, I know he'll see everything.

The sound of heels clicking against the floor interrupts the moment, sharp and quick, like a knife. 'Are we done here? Have you seen enough?'

Sally. Her voice is icy, but there's something else in it—a sharpness, a knowing.

Aaren steps in, glancing at me just as I meet his eyes. His shrug is so casual, so effortless. 'Yeah, I think we're all set.' But his voice doesn't match his words, the lightness masking something heavier underneath.

I nod, my stomach still tied in knots. 'Everything looks fine,' I mumble, my voice barely more than a whisper.

Sally looks between us, her smile tight, too controlled. 'Good to know,' she says, but her tone has shifted. It's colder now, like she's not buying what we're selling.

'So, are we renting it?' Her eyes flicker between us, sharp and calculating, like she's waiting for us to slip up.

I take a deep breath, steadying myself, and force my voice to sound calm. 'We'll update our client on what we've seen today.' The lie comes out too easily, like second nature, a practised mask.

'Yeah, they'll probably need more details, but we'll tell them to reach out to you directly for the specifics,' Aaren adds, nudging me with his elbow. I manage a smile, but it's strained.

Sally's smile tightens again, but she doesn't press further. She just nods, her eyes narrowing slightly as she studies us. 'All right,' she says, her voice clipped. 'I hope your client doesn't wait too long. This place is a great deal.'

'Of course,' Aaren replies smoothly, the politeness so practised it almost feels empty. 'Wouldn't want to turn down a good studio in such a beautiful place.'

Sally turns to leave, her heels tapping sharply on the floor, each step loud and steady, like a countdown. My heart races faster with each echo. I wait for her to turn around, to ask more questions, to see if she knows.

But she doesn't. She walks out, and the door clicks shut behind her.

I let out a breath, shaky and relieved, but the weight of everything I've uncovered still presses down on me, suffocating, relentless.

Aaren holds the door open for me, his gaze lingering as I step through. My legs feel heavy, like I'm carrying something far too big to hold.

The cool air outside doesn't do anything to settle the storm inside me.

Aaren glances at me, his eyebrow raised. 'You good?'

I nod too quickly, too forcefully. 'Yeah, I'm good.' The words feel hollow, like they don't mean anything at all.

Aaren doesn't press it, but I can tell he knows I'm lying.

28

6 December 2023

I'm walking past the booth selling tickets for the Christmas Festival when a girl I don't know steps right into my path. She has a clipboard gripped tightly in her hands, and her smile is wide—unnaturally wide, like it had been painted on and left to dry. The kind of smile that tried too hard to convince you that everything is perfectly, irrefutably fine. She has that 'I've sold thirty tickets today and nothing is going to stop me now' kind of energy.

'Hi! Are you interested in buying a ticket for the Christmas Festival?' she asks, voice bubbly enough to feel like it could pop any second. 'There's going to be food booths, arcade games, live bands! It's going to be *so much fun!*'

She's overflowing with cheer. The kind that makes me want to take a step back just to breathe a little more easily.

I give her a tight smile, fighting the urge to roll my eyes. It's always the same thing—overpriced food, people pretending to be festive when really, it's just a chance for them to make out with their crush under the glow of too many fairy lights. All while a band plays in the background, of course.

She doesn't let up, though. She rattles on, listing all the booths, the bands, the 'memorable' experiences I was apparently missing out on. I almost feel sorry for her. Almost. She's just trying to do her job. But I wasn't about to lie and pretend that standing in the middle of chaos is exactly how I want to spend my Saturday night.

'I'm good, thanks,' I say, stepping back. 'Not really my thing.'

Her smile wavers for just a second, but she quickly catches it, bringing it back till it adorns her face once again. She's still holding onto that hope, that belief that someone, anyone, would buy in. I could see it in her eyes.

I turn to leave but, of course, that's when it happens.

Bam.

I've walked right into someone.

'Whoa,' a voice says, startled but amused.

I look up, my face already burning. Aaren.

He stands there like it's the most casual thing in the world, balancing himself like he doesn't care that I've just knocked him out of orbit. His lips twitch, holding back a laugh, but his eyes . . . his eyes are warm and knowing. Like he's been waiting for this to happen.

'Hey,' he says casually, like we bump into each other all the time.

'Hey,' I mutter, brushing my sleeve off in an attempt to look nonchalant. 'You seem like you're in a hurry.'

'Band practise,' he says, like that explains everything.

'Right,' I reply, not sure what to do with the word. 'Christmas carols?'

He grins, the kind of grin that tells me he's up to something, and mischief dances in his eyes. 'Something like that. But we're working on more than just carols. Got a setlist ready for the festival next week. You should come.'

I almost snort. 'Why would I do that?'

'Because I'm sure you'll be there anyway,' he says, shrugging like it was already a done deal.

I frown. 'I'm not going to the festival.'

He raises an eyebrow, not buying it for a second. 'Not into the festival? Or just not into anything remotely fun?'

I cross my arms, feeling the weight of his gaze on me, sharp and a little too confident. 'It's just not my thing.'

He steps back, like he already knows exactly how this conversation is going to go, and it gets under my skin in a way I can't explain. I'm about to snap back, but he doesn't even give a chance for my retort to form before saying, 'That's it? That's your excuse?' His voice is teasing—not at all what I expected.

'It's not an excuse,' I say, shifting my weight and trying to keep my tone steady. 'It's a reason. A very valid one.'

He doesn't look convinced. 'Right. So, you're just going to let senior year happen without doing any of the things people are supposed to do?'

'Supposed to?' I echo, drawing out the word like it was a joke. 'Who decides what we're supposed to do?'

Aaren's smirk deepens, eyes glinting with amusement. 'I don't know, Lauren. Maybe people who don't overthink everything? It's a festival, not a life decision.'

I can feel my teeth clench. I want to tell him to back off, but it's not his tone that's pushing me—it's something else. Genuine curiosity. Like he can't fathom why anyone won't say yes to something so simple.

'Well, I'm not interested,' I say, my voice sharp now, trying to end the conversation.

He doesn't even flinch. Instead, he pulls something from his pocket and holds it out to me.

'Here,' he says, handing me a ticket.

I stare at it for a second, half-expecting it to leap out of my hand and run off somewhere.

'I already told you, I'm not going.'

'And I just told you it's senior year,' he says, pressing it into my hand more firmly—a responsibility I haven't asked for. His fingers brush mine, a quick touch, but it lingers just long enough to make everything inside me freeze. My heart skips a beat, but I don't let it show. Not even a little bit.

I glance down at the ticket. The Christmas Festival logo gleams at me, mocking me, practically daring me to say no again.

'What am I supposed to do with this?' I ask, barely managing to keep the bite out of my voice.

'Use it by going to the festival,' he says, matter-of-fact, like there was nothing more to it. 'You don't even have to enjoy it. Just show up and show some support. The proceeds go to a good cause. I'll be there, too.'

I blink. 'That's your sales pitch? You'll be there?'

'Yup,' he says, grinning wider now. 'What more could you want?'

'An actual reason?'

'You'll figure it out.' With that, he starts walking away, hands tucked casually into his pockets, like he'd already won.

I stand there, staring at the ticket in my hand. The red and green lettering seems to mock me, but for some reason, I don't toss it away. Instead, I just hold onto it. Maybe I am a little curious. Or maybe, deep down, I already know that Aaren has a way of making things happen without even trying.

29

14 December 2023

Zania drops me off at the entrance, and as I step out of the car, I notice that the soccer field doesn't look anything like the place I remember. The Christmas Festival had transformed it completely, the green grass almost unrecognizable beneath a blanket of colours and lights.

Bright, mismatched tents are scattered all over the field, their fabric flapping in the wind, like they've been put up in a hurry. The whole place buzzes with energy—music spilling out from the speakers, the sounds loud and familiar but somehow different, like everyone around me had already memorized the words to a song I hadn't yet learned.

The smell of popcorn and funnel cakes mix with the laughter of students, and it all blurs together into something that feels too big and too much for me to take in. It's electric, this frantic, messy energy, so far from the quiet of my room that it feels like I have stepped into someone else's world. A world where I don't belong.

Zania catches my attention as she leans across the passenger seat. 'Call me if you need anything,' she says, her grin wide and easy, like it was a promise she could keep.

I nod, but the words never come. She doesn't wait for anything else, just flashes me one more grin before driving off, disappearing into the crowd.

I stand there for a long moment, staring at the sea of people rushing past. I'm alone. Not just in that moment, but it feels like I have been alone for a long time. I try to push the heaviness in my chest away, but it won't budge.

The noise, the lights, the people—it all felt like it belonged to someone else. I had no idea what I was doing here, but it didn't matter. I couldn't keep running from everything that was waiting to catch up with me.

Hands stuffed in my jacket pockets, I wander across the field, trying to make sense of it all. My eyes move slowly over the booths and the game stalls, where people are laughing and shouting, daring each other to try their luck.

I pass the food stands, the smell of greasy sweetness curling into the air, and my stomach tightens. I try to ignore it, to keep moving forward, but it isn't easy. Everyone else seems so at home here. And me? I feel like I'm out of place, like I've just stumbled into a story that isn't mine to tell.

And then, I see her.

Savannah.

She's standing with a group of friends, laughing like the thing between her and me had never shattered. It wasn't forced or too bright, just effortless, like she hadn't spent years carrying the weight I'd left behind. Like she hadn't once looked at me with something sharp in her eyes and said, '*You've changed, Lauren. You've stopped caring.*'

I wanted to believe she hadn't meant it. That she'd said it in the heat of the moment, thrown it out just to make me feel something. But no matter how much I try to shake it off, it sticks. It clings to me in the quiet moments, in the spaces between my thoughts, refusing to let go.

She catches my gaze.

For a second, her smile falters, just barely, but I notice. And in that split second, I think I see something—something like regret, something like a silent *I miss you* or maybe just *I see you, too.*

Then she looks away. Turns back to her friends, laughter spilling between them. And I just stand there, my feet planted on the ground, my chest tight with everything I wanted to say but didn't know how.

And then she's gone.

Just as I'm about to turn and leave, I bump into him.

Aaren.

'Whoa!' I jump back, my heart thudding in my chest. 'You scared me.'

He laughs, the sound familiar and warm, like this is something I should have expected. 'You looked a million miles away. Sorry about that.'

We stand there for a second, the noise of the festival swirling around us, but for a brief moment, it feels like it's just the two of us.

'So, this doesn't really seem like your thing, huh?' Aaren asks, slipping his hands into his jacket pockets, his voice light, a hint of curiosity in his eyes.

I shrug, not really sure what to say. 'It's not. I thought I'd walk around for a bit. Maybe catch your band later.'

He raises an eyebrow, the corners of his mouth lifting. 'You're staying for the set?'

I hesitate, then nod. 'Yeah, I'll stay.'

His smile softens, his eyes looking at me like my answer means more than I think it does. 'I'm glad you're here.'

The words settle between us, and I don't know how to respond so I just nod.

He glances at the stage, then back at me, his expression shifting a bit. 'We go on in about fifteen minutes. Got some time to kill. Want to do something? You can't just stand here looking like you're lost.'

Before I can protest, he grabs my hand and pulls me towards the arcade section. 'Come on. Let's make this fun.'

I barely have time to protest before we're in front of an old racing game. Aaren slides into one seat and gestures for me to take the other. 'Prepare to lose,' he says with a wink, already twisting the wheel like he was born for this game.

The first round, I lose miserably. The second, I start getting the hang of it. By the third, I'm laughing so hard I can barely keep up. It isn't just the game. It's Aaren—the way he gets so caught up in it, like winning actually matters.

We play a few more rounds, the game and the laughter blurring together until everything else fades. Then, Aaren's phone buzzes. He checks it quickly, his face falling for a moment before he slips the phone back into his pocket.

'Okay,' he says, taking a deep breath. 'We're up in four minutes. You're staying, right?'

I hesitate. I had planned on staying but watching from the sidelines, staying out of the way. But the way he was looking at me, waiting for an answer, made me feel like I couldn't let him down.

'Yeah,' I say, my voice quiet. 'I'll stay. I'll find a spot near the stage.'

His smile returns, smaller this time, but more sincere. 'Thanks. I'll play better knowing you're there.'

I feel a warm flush rise in my cheeks, my heart doing a strange little dance. 'Don't let me distract you.'

'Too late.'

He shoots me a wink, his grin wide and easy, before heading off towards the stage with confident steps that betrayed just a hint of nerves.

The closer I get to the stage, the more the crowd thickens, pressing in with a buzz that crackles through the air. You can feel it—something's about to happen, something big, something that had everyone on edge. I find a place off to the side, not too close, but close enough to catch it all.

The lights snap on, casting everything in shades of purple and gold, sharp and vivid against the soft hum of voices. Aaren's band moves around the stage, their bodies familiar with the motions, each of them moving like they'd been doing this forever.

Cody, the rhythm guitarist, runs his fingers across the strings, checking his tuning, his face set with concentration. Jax, the drummer, spins a stick between his fingers before tapping a rapid roll on the snare, his foot keeping time without thought, like it was second nature. Bradon, the bassist, adjusts his strap, plucking out a few notes, nodding as if everything felt just right.

And then there's the girl at the keyboard. She looks new, her fingers hovering lightly over the keys, playing a soft, lilting melody that barely makes it past the crowd's buzz, but it's there. Just enough to add something else to the air.

Aaren stands front and centre, his mic stand in his hands, twisting it just a little until it was perfect. His guitar hangs from his shoulder, worn and comfortable like it belongs with him, like they'd been through too much together. He was calm. Too calm. Like this was exactly where he was meant to be.

The crowd's noise drops away for a second, thick with anticipation, every breath held, every eye fixed.

And then it hits—the first notes of the song shatter the quiet, raw and loud and sure. The sound hits my chest like it had a heartbeat of its own. Aaren's fingers dance across the strings, his voice cutting through the noise, clear and confident like he was speaking to each of us, one by one.

His bandmates fall into sync, their instruments locking together effortlessly. Cody's guitar ripples out, blending into Aaren's, building the song into something bigger than just noise. Jax's beat holds it all together, driving it forward, the rhythm already sweating into his skin. Brandon's bass grounds everything, steadying the chaos. And the girl at the keyboard—she adds something haunting with these soft, atmospheric notes that drift above the song, pulling everything together.

The crowd is already reacting, people rising to their feet, moving with the beat, the cheers rising up like the song had been the thing they'd been waiting for all night. I stay where I am, telling myself I'm fine, that I don't need to get any closer. But I can't stop looking.

Aaren moves across the stage, the guitar an extension of him, his fingers nimble and confident. His hair falls into his eyes and he brushes it away between chords, his body shifting with the rhythm like he was part of the song. When he sings, the lyrics feel like they aren't merely words—he makes you feel them. The sound isn't just his, it's ours, too.

Our eyes meet for a split second, and the world shrinks. In that instant, nothing else matters. His gaze doesn't linger, but it leaves something behind, something unspoken, a question, maybe, or a promise, or just an understanding between us that was too quiet to say.

The song swells, the lights flashing in time with the beat, and for a moment, I'm lost in it. In the sound, in the lights, in Aaren—lost in everything but the rest of the world.

And then he looks out at the crowd, scanning faces, searching for something. For a second I think—and maybe I'm imagining it—but I think his eyes lock on me again.

He smiles. Not the bright, easy grin from earlier, but something smaller, more private. Something meant just for me.

My heart skips a beat.

He doesn't look away. His fingers keep moving, his voice steady. And then the next line comes, and it feels like he's singing directly to me:

'I've been searching for something that feels real. But when I'm with you, it's all I need to feel.'

The words hit me like they'd been waiting there, sitting just under the surface. They settle into my chest, like they belonged there, but at the same time, they make everything inside me tremble with doubt.

I try to push it away. The voices in my head.

'He's not what you think.'

'You can't trust this.'

I squeeze my fists, my nails digging into my palms. The whispers always come when life starts feeling a little too good. They show up, ready to ruin everything, waiting for the perfect moment to tear it all down.

But then Aaren's gaze finds mine again. The voices in my head don't go away, but they quiet down—they don't hold the same weight any more. Because the way he looks at me, like I'm the only person in that crowd, makes everything feel worth it. Even if it scares me.

The song ends, and the crowd erupts into cheers. Aaren steps back from the mic, taking a breath, and shoots me another quick smile. It isn't big or showy, just enough to let me know he saw me.

30

14 December 2023

One minute, I'm caught in the rush of the crowd, swept up in the energy of students cheering and dancing as Aaren shreds on his guitar like he's been doing it all his life. The next, we're standing side by side in line for hot dogs, talking about everything and nothing, and it feels so easy—like we've always been here, in this quiet moment.

I never planned on coming tonight. The Christmas Festival? It wasn't even on my radar. Too much noise inside my head—my sister, those notes, the silent tension that seems to hang between us. But as we stand there, everything feels a little bit lighter. The music floats through the air, and I catch Aaren looking at me from the stage, a smile playing on his lips, like maybe he's actually glad I'm here. And for the first time in what feels like ages, I think, maybe this—this small, simple night—was worth it.

We grab our food—those flimsy paper trays they hand out at the snack stand, the kind that buckles if you hold them wrong. The warm scent of fried food mixes with the crisp night air as we head for the bleachers. We find a spot halfway up, balancing our food on our laps as we sit. Aaren turns to me, that familiar grin already curling at the corners of his mouth. 'So, what'd you think?' he asks, taking a bite of his hot dog like he's done this a thousand times before.

It catches me off guard, and the words spill out before I can stop them. 'I didn't know you sang.'

He freezes, mid-chew, his eyebrows lifting in surprise. 'Wait—what? You didn't know I sing?'

'Nope,' I say, trying to keep it cool, though I can feel his gaze on me, waiting for some explanation. 'I only knew you played the guitar. You never mentioned anything about singing.'

His face softens into disbelief, and I can't help but laugh a little. 'We've been doing this at the Christmas Festival since seventh grade,' he says, shaking his head. 'How did you not know?'

'I guess I don't pay attention to those things,' I reply casually.

Aaren stares at me for a second, his expression a mix of disbelief and amusement, before he chuckles, a sound that somehow feels more like a gift than a joke. 'Well, now you know.'

I smile back, and something inside me feels a little bit lighter, like his laugh just lifted a small weight off my chest. 'Yeah. And I'm glad I came.'

His eyes meet mine, searching—maybe for something more than just politeness. Then, he leans in slightly, his voice soft but curious. 'So, what did you think of the performance?'

I pause, not wanting to sound like I'm just saying the words because it's what people do. 'It was good. Really good,'

I say, lowering my voice, like it's a secret. 'You looked like you were having fun up there.'

His grin widens, and there's this spark in his eyes, a shift that makes my stomach do a strange flip. 'Good. That's what we were going for.' He smirks, teasing, 'I wasn't sure if you were paying attention.'

'I was,' I say, trying to sound casual, though there's a little flutter in my chest I can't quite explain. 'I just didn't expect you to be so . . . good.'

Aaren laughs, a deep, warm sound that hits me in a way that feels more personal than it should. 'Guess I'm full of surprises.' He shrugs.

We sit there in a comfortable silence for a while, eating and talking about the silly stuff—bands we love, weird food combos we might try if we didn't care what people thought. The kind of conversation that feels meaningless but also more meaningful than anything else.

Eventually, Aaren leans back on the bleachers, stretching his arms behind his head. He glances around the field, then turns to me with a thoughtful look. 'So, are you coming back tomorrow? We're playing again.'

I hesitate, not sure how to answer. I hadn't even thought about it. One night of this festival felt like enough. Big crowds, loud music, too much of everything. And I have enough on my plate without trying to make excuses to spend more time with Aaren than I probably should.

'I don't know,' I say, trying to sound indifferent. 'What's so great about tomorrow?'

He leans in, his voice dropping like he's letting me in on something special. 'It's the last day. We're playing a whole new set. And they're lighting the Christmas tree in front of the school. It's—'

'Magical?' I cut in, raising an eyebrow.

Aaren doesn't miss a beat. 'Exactly.'

I snort, shaking my head, a little laugh escaping me. 'It's just a tree, Aaren.'

'It's not about the tree,' he says, his grin widening. 'It's about the lights. The music. The vibe.'

I roll my eyes, trying to hide the smile tugging at the corners of my mouth. 'I don't know. I've never really been into all that Christmas "magic" stuff.'

'Fair enough,' he shrugs, totally unbothered. 'But I'll be there. You should come. It'll be fun.'

I look at him, trying to figure out what's behind his expression. He doesn't seem pushy, but there's something in the way he's looking at me, like he genuinely wants me to be there.

'I'll think about it,' I say, the words not quite promising but enough to satisfy him.

Aaren nods, not pressing me further. We sit there for a while longer, talking about everything and nothing, until he leans back again, stretching and staring up at the sky. The silence between us isn't awkward—it's the kind of silence that feels natural, like we both just need this moment of calm.

'You know,' he says, breaking the quiet, his voice thoughtful, 'I'm really glad you came tonight. Even if you don't come tomorrow.'

The way he says it hits me, somewhere deeper than I thought it could. It's a small thing, but it makes something shift inside me, makes the air feel heavier for a moment.

'Me too,' I say quietly, and to my surprise I find that I actually mean it.

Aaren smiles, a soft smile that feels like it belongs to this moment, to us, sitting here in the dark, with nothing but the sound of the festival in the background. 'This is nice, huh? Just . . . enjoying the moment, without thinking about everything else—about the notes, or what we're supposed to be doing.'

He finishes his hot dog and sets the empty paper tray off to the side, wiping his hands on his jeans like it's just another night.

His words land like a weight on me, heavier than I thought they would. I freeze, holding my hot dog halfway to my mouth. 'Yeah,' I reply, my voice small, feeling the weight of it settle in. The guilt creeps in just as quickly. 'Sorry, by the way, for dragging you into all of . . . this,' I add as I set the hot dog down on the paper tray and place it beside me on the bleachers.

Aaren's frown softens. 'That's not what I meant. It's just . . . nice. We should do this more often. Like, take a road trip or something. Just . . . enjoy senior year while we can. Before everything changes.'

The idea of leaving, of moving on, suddenly feels like a reality I'm not ready for. I nod slowly, trying to hold onto this moment for as long as I can. 'Yeah,' I reply, keeping my tone light. 'Maybe.'

He studies me for a second, his gaze sharp. 'You okay?' he asks, his voice soft now. 'You seem off. Did I say something wrong?'

I feel the weight of it all pressing on me. College applications, the pressure, the future. I haven't even started, and suddenly it's all I can think about.

'I . . . I haven't really thought about it,' I whisper, barely able to meet his eyes. 'I haven't applied to any colleges yet.'

Aaren leans in slightly, his voice steady, as if trying to reassure me without pushing too hard. 'It's okay. You don't have to have it all figured out. I mean, I'm thinking about taking a semester off, starting in January instead of August. No big deal.'

I feel the tightness in my chest loosen a little. 'You're right,' I say, exhaling. 'I just . . . I don't know what I want yet.'

Aaren nods, his expression understanding. 'It's okay. Don't rush it. And hey, if you want, maybe we both could just delay. Take some time to figure things out.'

I smile faintly, grateful for the offer, but there's still a knot in my stomach. 'I don't know . . . I guess I just want to be somewhere far away from here. Somewhere I can forget.'

Aaren's expression softens, something unspoken passing through his eyes. He looks away for a moment, as if searching for the right words. When his gaze meets mine again, the air between us feels heavy, fragile with words unspoken.

'I get it,' he murmurs, his voice quieter now, as if the words are more for himself than for me. 'But if I'm being honest, I hope you don't forget the good stuff. The memories we've made.'

We fall into silence, the kind that doesn't need to be filled with words. I don't know how to respond, maybe because I don't have to. I just watch him, my thoughts spinning, racing to catch up with everything he's said. The silence stretches until it feels like too much.

And then, without warning, everything shifts.

Aaren reaches for my hand. His fingers brush mine—just a whisper of a touch—but it shakes something loose inside me. My breath catches in my throat, my heart thumps so hard I feel it in my chest. It's just a touch, nothing more. But it's more than that. It's everything.

I look up at him, and he's watching me, waiting for something. Maybe for me to say something. Maybe for me to do something. But I can't. I can only hear the rush of my heartbeat drowning out everything else.

Aaren leans in just a little, his eyes flicking to my lips, then back to my eyes. I know what's coming next. My pulse races, pounding in my ears. This is it. The moment. Or maybe it's not. Maybe I'm imagining it. I can't tell any more.

But then, from across the field, a voice calls out. Aaren pulls back immediately, his expression shifting to something apologetic, like he's been caught doing something wrong.

'Sorry,' he says, as if it—whatever that was—is something that needs explaining. As if it was something that could be interrupted.

I watch as he glances at his bandmate, who's still waving his arms frantically, trying to get Aaren's attention. Aaren shoots him a look, annoyance flickering for a moment, but he keeps it casual.

'Five minutes, man!' his bandmate yells.

'Okay, dude,' Aaren mutters, turning back to me with a small smile, like everything is fine, like nothing just happened.

The Ferris wheel creaks in the distance, and the air smells like fried dough and roasted nuts. The lights blur behind us, a mix of colours spinning in a dizzying whirl, like everything around me is moving but I'm stuck in place.

I shove my hands into my pockets, trying to warm them, but it doesn't really work. The cold air bites into my skin. 'Actually, I think I'm gonna head home,' I say, my voice sounding smaller than I mean it to. 'I still need to figure out whatever Elise is trying to say with those notes and maybe try learning riddle-solving for once.'

Aaren doesn't answer right away. And that feels off. He's always the one to crack a joke or make some sarcastic comment, but this time, he just exhales sharply, his breath hanging in the warm air.

He drums his fingers against his cup, his eyes distant. It's like he's somewhere else, somewhere far away.

I start to stand, but something makes me pause. I can't just leave like this. Not with the silence stretching between us. I nudge his arm gently. 'You okay?'

He blinks, like he's just realized I'm there. 'Lauren, I just—' He exhales sharply, raking a hand through his hair. 'I don't know if this is gonna lead anywhere. What if there's nothing left to find?

I freeze. 'What?'

Aaren shifts, gripping the cup tighter in his hands. 'I mean, what if it's all pointless?'

I frown, not sure if I heard him right. 'Pointless?'

He runs a hand through his hair, clearly frustrated. 'I don't know if Elise meant for you to go on some kind of scavenger hunt. What if you're just chasing something that isn't there?'

For a moment, all I hear is the hum of the festival—the distant shrieks from the rides, the smell of oily food, the mechanical beeping of a game resetting.

Then, without thinking, I laugh. Not because it's funny, but because I can't believe this is coming from him.

'Okay, where's this coming from?' I ask.

Aaren shoves his hands into his jacket pockets. 'I don't know, Lauren. It's been on my mind, okay?'

'And you didn't think to mention it before?'

His jaw tightens, and he looks down at the ground. 'I didn't know how.'

I wait, hoping he'll explain. Hoping he'll say something to make sense of all this. But he doesn't. Instead, he shrugs, his eyes still focused on the ground. 'Look, maybe you're making this harder than it needs to be. Maybe there's no big secret. Maybe Elise just left stuff behind . . . because people leave things behind.'

His words hit me harder than I expect, a cold slap to the face.

'So . . . you think I'm wasting my time,' I say, my voice flat, though it feels like a punch to the gut.

'Honestly? Yeah. I do.'

The world feels like it's shifting beneath me. A few minutes ago, I thought he understood. I thought he got why I had to do this. But now? Now, it feels like I'm standing here alone, out in the cold.

I take a step back, my arms crossing in front of me, trying to hold everything together. 'Why are you saying this now?'

'I don't know,' he mutters, exhaling in frustration. 'Forget it.'

'No,' I say, shaking my head. 'Let's not "forget it". If you think I'm wasting my time, just say what you actually mean.'

He hesitates again, like he's torn between being honest and staying silent.

Finally, he sighs, rubbing his face, defeated. 'No. Just forget it.'

I wait. A part of me hopes he'll change his mind, that he'll say something to fix this. But instead, he breathes out slowly, and then says, in the most neutral tone he can manage, 'Let's see how long this takes us.'

And just like that, the conversation is over.

31

16 December 2023

I didn't think I'd end up here. But somehow, here I am—sitting in Aaren's old Jeep, my legs sticking to the cracked leather seat, the air thick with leftover heat from the lowlands. A breeze drifts through the open window, crisp and cool, a slow reminder that we're leaving the city behind, heading up to Baguio.

The temperature is changing, the sticky warmth giving way to something lighter, something that settles on my skin instead of clinging to it. I breathe in deep, hoping it might clear my head, but the weight in my chest stays right where it is.

The road stretches ahead, empty and endless. The tires hum against the pavement, steady, like a song with no words. Aaren hums too, under his breath, his fingers tapping a slow rhythm on the steering wheel. His eyes stay on the road, but his mind is somewhere else. Somewhere I don't know how to follow him to. Maybe I don't want to. Maybe I'm afraid of what I'll find if I do.

The city is long behind us now, and with every mile, the silence grows. Not just around us, but inside me, too. That's what unsettles me the most—not the quiet itself, but what it leaves room for. The thoughts I've been trying to keep at arm's length.

Savannah's voice lingers in my head, steady and sure—telling me I carry my grief like it's the only thing holding me together. And maybe she's right. Maybe that's why I keep searching. Because looking for the notes is easier than accepting they might not be there. Because as long as I'm searching, I don't have to ask myself what comes next.

And Aaren was right too—that night at the Christmas Festival.

I turn towards the window, pressing my fingers against the cool glass. The trees blur past in streaks of green, the sun dipping lower, throwing long shadows across the road. It should be beautiful. Something I'd normally reach for my camera to capture. But all I feel is tired. Like I've been running in circles, convincing myself I don't already know how this ends.

I glance at Aaren. His grip on the wheel is steady, but there's a tightness in his fingers, a quiet kind of tension that makes my stomach pull. Like he's waiting for something. Or bracing for whatever comes next.

And maybe that's the problem—he keeps running and waiting, all because of me.

But I think I'm done running.

I take a slow breath, feeling the weight of the words before I say them. 'Aaren.'

His eyes flick towards me, just for a second, before settling back on the road. 'Yeah?'

I curl my fingers against the seat, pressing down like I can steady myself that way. 'Let's not go.'

His hands still on the wheel. 'What?'

'The flower farm.' The words come out quieter than I mean them to, like they've been waiting in the back of my throat for too long. 'Let's not go.'

Aaren blinks, like he's waiting for me to take it back. 'Lauren, we've been driving for hours. You want to turn around now?'

I shake my head. 'It's not just that. I mean . . . maybe it's time to stop searching for the notes.'

His jaw tightens. Silence sits between us, stretching over the hum of the engine, over the empty road ahead. He exhales, slow and careful, like he's testing the weight of it. 'This isn't about the drive, is it?'

I hesitate, just for a second, then shake my head. 'It's about Savannah. And what you said that night at the festival.'

His hands tighten on the wheel, but he doesn't say anything.

'I keep telling myself that if I just find one more note, maybe I'll get the closure I need,' I say, watching the way my fingers curl into my palms. 'But I think . . . I think all it's done is keep me from moving on.'

Aaren doesn't answer right away. He just watches the road, the tension in his shoulders shifting into something quieter, something I can't quite name. Then, without a word, he eases his foot off the gas and pulls the Jeep onto the side of the road. Gravel crunches beneath the tires as we come to a slow stop.

The engine hums in the silence. He doesn't turn it off, but he doesn't move to start driving again either.

I stare at my hands, at the way my fingers twist together like they're trying to hold onto something that isn't there. The weight of his gaze settles on me, warm and steady. 'Lauren,' he says, my name soft in his mouth. Not a question, not a demand. Just a quiet acknowledgment, like he's letting me take my time.

I swallow. 'I think I knew it all along,' I admit, my voice barely above a whisper. 'I just didn't want to admit it.'

Aaren shifts, and out of the corner of my eye, I see him turn to face me fully. 'All right,' he says simply, and for some reason, that makes my throat tighten.

I let out a breath, shaky and uneven. 'I don't know why I thought finding another note would change anything. I wanted it to. I wanted it to tell me what to do, or how to feel, or—' I break off, shaking my head. 'But the truth is, I don't think I've been looking for answers. I think I've just been looking for her.'

Aaren doesn't say it's stupid or pointless. He doesn't remind me of all the times he told me this wasn't going to fix anything. He just nods, like he understands. Like he's been here before.

After a long moment, he reaches for the keys and turns off the engine. The quiet settles in around us, softer now, easier to breathe in.

'What now?' he asks, his voice steady, not pushing—just waiting.

I turn to him, the weight in my chest shifting, not gone but different. 'Now?' I say, like I'm testing the word, seeing how it feels. I let out a breath. 'Now . . . we stop.'

Aaren's fingers loosen on the wheel. His lips part like he's about to say something, but instead, he just looks at me—really looks—like maybe he's been waiting for this, too.

His voice is quiet when he finally speaks. 'Yeah?'

I nod. 'Yeah.'

For a second, we just sit there, the air between us settling into something softer. Aaren leans back, one arm draped over the wheel, the other resting on his knee. There's no urgency in the way he watches me, just something steady. Something sure.

'Okay,' he says. 'Then let's stop.'

32

16 October 2020

The bass is so loud that I can feel it in my ribs before we even get to Mason's front door. Savannah bounces next to me, her grin wide enough to swallow the whole night, like she's trying to convince both of us that this is something worth looking forward to.

'It's gonna be fun,' she says, like she believes it just as much as she hopes I will.

Maybe it will be. Maybe not. But it's certainly better than the mess I left behind at home, with my parents' voices breaking through the walls like cracks in glass. That's what Savannah said, anyway.

The house is packed when we step inside. Bodies pressed together like the walls are holding them in. People drinking, shouting over the music, making out in corners like the world outside doesn't exist. It smells like beer and sweat, and something sweet underneath it all—like candy and regret. Mason's parents must be out of town, because there's no way they'd approve of the chaos spilling into their living room.

'Kitchen,' Savannah yells, grabbing my arm. 'We need drinks.'

I don't argue. It's too loud to argue, and honestly, that would make me sound like the wet blanket I already feel like.

The kitchen is worse—red Solo cups litter the counters, and a group of guys are shouting like they're in the middle of the World Series, but it's just beer pong. Savannah hands me two Jell-O shots, one red, one neon green.

'To fun, chaos, and questionable decisions!' She grins, throwing back her shot like it's a glass of water.

I stare at mine like it might bite me. The gelatine jiggles, mocking me. 'Do people actually enjoy this?'

'Just try it.'

I tip my head back, swallowing the shot in one go. It burns, cold and slimy, tasting like cough syrup mixed with the desperation of a night gone wrong. I gag. 'This is fun?'

Savannah laughs, nudging me with her shoulder. 'You'll get used to it.'

She grabs my hand and pulls me towards the living room, where the air is thick with heat and the smell of spilled drinks. People move in time with the music, like the bass is controlling their every step. Savannah spins me around, her laughter cutting through the noise, her eyes bright with adrenaline. 'See? Fun!'

I don't know if that's true, but after a few more shots, everything starts to feel softer around the edges. Not great—just quieter, like my mind has stepped aside and left the noise to fill in the space.

We get roped into a game of beer pong. I'm terrible at it. Every shot I take misses by a mile, but the guys on my team don't care. They cheer like I've just won a gold medal. The enthusiasm is contagious. I laugh when Savannah sinks a ball and screams like she's about to be knighted.

Later, Savannah pulls me into the middle of the living room again, where people are dancing like they've forgotten anyone could possibly be watching. The floor shakes beneath our feet as the whole house bounces with the beat. Savannah twirls me around like we're kids again, and for a second, I forget the weight of everything else.

But then everything stops. Or maybe it just feels like it does.

A loud gasp cuts through the music—a collective intake of breath, the kind that comes right before something blows up. I follow the eyes of the crowd to the couch, and there's Mason, frozen like a statue. His shirt is covered in vomit, and he looks like he might throw up again any second. At his feet, a girl lies half-collapsed on the carpet, her hair covering her face as she struggles to stand.

Laughter erupts. A phone flashes. A voice yells, 'Oh my god, gross!' Then, she moves. Just enough for me to see her face. Elise.

Her eyes are wide, too wide, unfocused, like she's trying to piece the world together but can't quite see the edges. She sways when she stands, like she's walking on a tightrope no one else can see.

I don't think, I just move. I push through the crowd, but they part and swallow her up, and by the time I get there, she's gone. The laughter dies down, and Mason mumbles something under his breath before storming off to the bathroom. And just like that, the party resets. The music comes back up, and the noise spills over, just like before. But I'm still standing there, frozen.

'I need to—' I start, but Savannah's already dragging me towards the back patio, laughing as she almost stumbles in her heels.

'Fresh air!' she announces, throwing her arms up in the air. 'Not that we actually need it, but you know—vibes.'

'I think I need to find Elise,' I mumble, the words stuck like broken glass in my throat.

Savannah barely glances at me. 'She's probably fine,' she says, dismissing me with a flick of her wrist before turning towards some guy in a letterman jacket. He hands her a red cup, and she takes it like it's second nature. She grabs another and shoves it into my hands.

'Here. Less thinking, more drinking.' She clinks her cup against mine, nearly spilling both.

I take a sip, but the taste is sharp and sour, like something I shouldn't trust. Savannah doesn't notice. She's already back to swaying with the music, laughing at whatever the guy just said, completely lost in the moment.

I swallow hard. The taste clings to my tongue, like a mistake I can't undo.

The cold air on the patio feels like a slap, sharp against my skin. It's a relief, but my mind is still tangled inside, following Elise as she disappears into the crowd. Is she okay? Did she make it home? Or is she out there somewhere, feeling worse than she already looked?

I barely notice the guy from the football team until he's right in front of me, all smiles that don't reach his eyes. He starts talking, but it's all empty words, the kind that feel rehearsed. I nod, offering half-hearted responses, but he either doesn't notice or doesn't care. He leans in too close, like he thinks I'm interested.

I let it drag on for a minute before shifting away. 'I need to find my sister,' I say, turning to leave.

His hand catches my arm before I can take another step.

'Hey, don't be like that,' he says, eyebrow raised, like I owe him something. 'You're playing hard to get, huh?'

I blink, thrown off by his assumption. 'Playing hard to get? No. I'm just not interested. But hey, keep chasing a lost cause if you love setting yourself up for failure.'

He rolls his eyes and mutters something under his breath. I don't hear all of it, but I hear 'what a bitch'. And just like that, my hand is already moving. I slap him across the face. The sound rings out, sharp and sudden.

The patio goes dead quiet. People stop talking. All eyes are on me. Even Savannah's.

'Asshole!' I yell before I even think about it.

I don't stick around to see what anyone else says. I turn on my heel and march back into the house, my heart hammering in my chest, my face burning with a mix of anger and embarrassment.

Inside, I ask around, hoping someone saw where Elise went. No one really knows. The party's still in full swing, everyone too drunk or too caught up to care about one girl who's disappeared. Someone tells me they think they saw her leave a while ago.

I let out a breath. Relief and worry twist in my chest. At least she's gone. I pull out my phone and call Elise. It rings until it doesn't. I text her anyway.

Please be okay. Text me when you get home.

I just hope she's okay, or sober enough to make it home. I wish I could've been there for her, that I hadn't let Savannah drag me away, that I hadn't let my discomfort keep me from making sure Elise was all right.

33

18 December 2023

Aaren slides into the seat across from me, setting his tray down like he's trying too hard to be casual. He just looks at me for a moment, his gaze lingering, before finally letting his hands rest beside his untouched burger and neatly piled fries. Which is weird, because Aaren never lets good fries go cold.

I narrow my eyes. 'Okay, what's up? You're being suspiciously well-behaved.'

His expression stays neutral, but there's a twitch at the corner of his mouth, like he's holding back a smirk. 'Can't a guy just sit down and eat his lunch without being interrogated?'

'Not when it's you.' I steal a fry before he can stop me. 'So, spill.'

Aaren exhales, like he's been holding something in. Then, without a word, he reaches into his bag, pulls out a folded piece of paper, and slides it across the table. His fingers linger on the edge for a second before he leans back, watching me.

I hesitate before picking it up. Two tickets. Some kind of art event.

I tilt my head. 'You're inviting me to an art exhibit?'

Aaren drums his fingers against the table. 'Not just any exhibit. It's a showcase of local artists—new voices, timeless pieces, all that.' He pauses, just long enough for me to notice. 'And your mom's work is going to be there.'

The cafeteria noise fades into static.

I stare at the tickets, trying to swallow down the sudden pressure in my chest.

Not just an exhibit. Not just another night out.

I glance up, and Aaren's watching me differently now—not teasing, not pushing, just . . . waiting.

'I thought,' he says, voice careful, 'maybe we could start by actually enjoying art. Instead of, you know, staring at paintings and hoping there's a secret note taped to the back.'

I let out a breath of a laugh, but it comes out quieter than I expect. 'You mean like normal people?'

He shrugs. 'Something like that.'

My thumb traces the edge of the ticket, my brain buzzing with too many thoughts. This is—

I don't know what this is.

But I do know Aaren didn't have to do this.

I also know he doesn't do things halfway.

Instead of letting myself spiral, I glance back up, tilting my head with a smirk. 'Are you asking me out on a date?'

And just like that, Aaren—usually unshakable, usually too cool for his own good—flushes.

It's not dramatic, but it's there, creeping up his neck, tinting his ears. And because I am a mature and gracious person, I do not immediately point and laugh.

(Okay, I want to. But I don't.)

He clears his throat, shaking his head like he can brush it off. 'Not unless you want it to be.'

I tap the ticket against my chin, drawing it out just to mess with him. 'So, it *could* be a date?'

Aaren rolls his eyes, but the pink lingers. 'It *could* be.'

I grin, dropping the ticket onto my tray. 'All right. I'll allow it.'

He snorts, finally taking a bite of his burger like our conversation didn't just fry his brain.

Then, just as I reach for another fry, he says, 'I figured it could be a good start.'

I pause mid-grab. 'A good start to what?'

Aaren tilts his head slightly, like the answer should be obvious. 'To moving forward.' His voice is steady, but there's something careful about the way he says it, like he's testing the ground before stepping forward. 'You said you wanted to stop looking for notes.'

I tighten my grip on the fry, but I keep my expression light. 'I did,' I admit. 'And yet, somehow, I still check under every desk, behind every frame, in the margins of old books—'

Aaren gives me a look.

I sigh, tossing the fry onto his tray before I snap it in half just to have something to do with my hands. 'I'm trying.'

'I know,' he says. 'That's why I thought this might help. You love art, Lauren. Maybe it's time to just . . . be in it. Instead of chasing ghosts through it.'

I look at him, and for once, I don't have a comeback.

Because he's right.

And because he cares.

Aaren, the guy who used to chase after hidden notes with me in the strangest places, who once tried to convince me that the school vending machines were part of some elaborate conspiracy, who swore he wasn't good at serious conversations—he cares.

And somehow, that makes it harder to breathe.

'. . . Okay,' I say finally, softer than I mean to. 'Let's do it.'

Aaren nods once, satisfied. Then, just as the moment teeters on something too raw, too real, he smirks and slides his tray closer to his side of the table. 'Good. Now stop stealing my fries.'

I steal another one out of spite.

34

19 December 2023

The rain holds off as we step out of the exhibit. The air is thick, restless, like it knows what's coming.

Aaren grins as he unlocks the door to his ancient Jeep, the kind of grin that makes you believe things will turn out okay, even when you know better. 'Told you it wouldn't die on us.'

It dies fifteen minutes later.

Now we're standing at a bus stop, completely drenched, rainwater trailing down my spine in slow, unwelcome trickles. My dress sticks to my skin, my shoes let out a pathetic squelch every time I shift my weight. Aaren shakes out his wet hair like a dog, his grin widening as if this is the funniest thing that's ever happened.

'This is all your fault,' I say, arms crossed tight, trying not to shiver.

'My fault?' He gestures at the sky. 'Oh, sure, I totally control the weather now.'

I glare at him, but the effect is ruined by my own shudder. 'You could've controlled your busted Jeep at least.'

He shrugs, unbothered. 'Hey, I never said it was reliable. Just that it wouldn't die on us yet.'

I want to be mad. I should be mad. But Aaren has this way of making disaster feel like a plot twist instead of a tragedy.

The bus pulls up, packed to the brim, but we shove our way in anyway. Bodies press too close, the air thick with the scent of rain and damp clothes and whatever the guy next to me had for dinner. My shoulder bumps against Aaren's as we grab onto the hanging straps, his skin warm even through the dampness. He leans in, his voice low.

'Good date, though, right?'

I don't answer right away. I think about the way he placed a hand on my back when we wove through the exhibit, how he steered me towards the paintings he knew I'd love, how he whispered things that made me laugh when the art felt too heavy.

It was a good date.

I don't say that, though. Instead, I roll my eyes and elbow him lightly. 'Ask me again when I'm dry.'

We reach his stop after what feels like a lifetime, and the rain hasn't let up. If anything, it's worse. The kind of downpour that makes everything blur—the streetlights, the sidewalks, the spaces between. His house is only a few blocks away, but by the time we reach the front door, we're completely wrecked all over again.

Aaren unlocks the door and gestures me inside. 'Welcome to Casa de Soggy.'

I step in, dripping onto the hardwood. The house is quiet, save for the low hum of the fridge and the occasional groan of the pipes. It smells like detergent and something faintly familiar, like old books and whatever cologne Aaren wears. It's warm, though. Lived in.

He toes off his wet sneakers, then nods toward the hallway. 'Bathroom's that way. I'll grab you something dry while I call my dad about the car.'

I hesitate. 'Are you sure?'

He smirks. 'Unless you wanna stay in that soaking dress all night?'

Fair point.

I follow him down the hall, and he rummages through a drawer before tossing me a hoodie and a pair of basketball shorts. 'Here. Not exactly designer, but at least they're dry.'

I take them carefully, my fingers brushing his. Neither of us pulls away first.

'Thanks,' I say, my voice quieter than I mean it to be.

Aaren clears his throat. 'Yeah. No problem.'

I change in the bathroom, peeling off my dress and pulling on the hoodie. It's too big, swallowing me whole, but it smells like detergent and something else that's just . . . him. I tug the sleeves over my hands and take a second to breathe before heading back out.

Aaren's on the couch, scrolling through his phone. When he looks up, his expression changes—just for a second, subtle but noticeable.

'You look . . . cozy,' he says, a teasing smile tugging at his lips.

I roll my eyes and drop onto the couch beside him, tucking my legs beneath me. 'Very funny.'

He chuckles, his voice softer this time. 'My dad's on his way. We'll tow the Jeep the old-school way once he gets here.'

I raise an eyebrow. 'By driving it?'

'More like dragging it,' he corrects, stretching his arms over the back of the couch. 'We can't afford a tow truck right now, and my dad's a fix-it-yourself kind of guy.'

I glance down at my hands. I don't know why, but that tugs at something in me. Maybe it's the way he says it like it's normal. Like doing things the hard way has always been the only way.

'Sorry about your Jeep,' I murmur.

Aaren shrugs. 'Eh. It's just a car.'

But I can tell it's more than that.

I don't say anything, though. Instead, I rest my head against the couch, listening to the rain hammer against the windows. Aaren does the same. We sit there, quiet, just breathing in the moment.

Then, after a while, he says, 'This was still a good date.'

I let myself smile, just a little. 'Yeah,' I admit. 'It was.'

His phone buzzes against the table, rattling the wood. He glances at the screen, and for a second, his expression flickers—too fast to read before he presses the side button, ignoring the call. But before he can even set it down, it rings again. More insistent this time.

His dad.

'Give me a sec,' Aaren mutters, pushing himself up. His voice is even, but his fingers tighten around the phone, his jaw set like he already knows the conversation isn't one he wants to have.

Before he reaches the door, I clear my throat. 'Hey, uh—you wouldn't happen to have an iPhone charger, would you?'

Aaren hesitates, his fingers curling like he's about to reach for something—me, maybe—but instead, he just nods towards the hallway. 'There should be one in the nightstand drawer. My room's down there.' His voice is softer now, like he already knows I won't like what I find.

Then he's gone, the door clicking shut behind him.

The silence stretches, pressing in at the edges. I stand there for a second, my phone clutched in my hand, its screen flashing that desperate red warning—1 per cent—before I exhale and move.

The hallway is dim, the kind of quiet that makes your own footsteps sound too loud. When I push open his bedroom door, it's like stepping into someplace that belongs entirely to him. Not just a room, but a whole world.

There's a mess, but not the kind that says careless—it's lived-in, familiar. His bed is unmade, sheets kicked to one side like he left in a hurry. A pair of sneakers by the door, one tipped over. A desk scattered with notebooks, some open, some stacked, like he was in the middle of figuring something out and just walked away. The walls aren't bare. There's a framed photo of him and his dad by the window, a concert ticket taped up beside it, a faded sticky note stuck to the edge of a shelf. I can't see what it says from here.

I sit on the edge of the bed, pressing my palms into the mattress, grounding myself before reaching for the nightstand. My fingers curl around the drawer handle.

I pull open the drawer, expecting the usual—a mess of tangled cables, loose change, maybe an old receipt or two. But my fingers still when I see something else instead.

A single sheet of folded paper.

It shouldn't mean anything. Just a piece of paper. But my chest tightens because I know that fold, that thickness, the way the edges are slightly worn, like it's been opened and closed too many times.

Like it's been read. Like it's been kept.

I don't think. I just move, pulling the drawer open wider, reaching for it. My hands are careful, but my heartbeat isn't. It pounds in my ears as I lift the paper, unfolding it—

And then I freeze.

Because she's here.

The woman.

The same one from Dr Gregory's office. The one who pointed at the painting on my wall like she recognized it.

She stands by the window, exactly where she always does, quiet and still except for her hair, shifting even though the air in the room is dead. There's no breeze. No reason for it to move.

She hums, a soft, barely-there melody. It crawls under my skin, settling in my ribs.

And then, for the first time, she speaks.

'You shouldn't be here.' Her voice is even, like she's telling me something obvious. 'You should leave before it gets worse.'

I grip my phone, fingers tightening around it. 'What . . . what do you mean?' The words barely make it out. My throat feels tight. 'What's going to get worse?'

She doesn't answer right away. Just looks at me. Calm. Unreadable.

'Just leave.' This time, the words feel heavier, pressing into my chest.

A buzz cuts through the air, my phone vibrating in my hand. Aunt Clarissa's name lights up the screen. I barely register it. The woman is still there, still watching, still taking up space like she belongs here.

'What are you even saying?' My voice cracks. 'Just tell me what you mean.'

Another buzz. My fingers slip. The paper tumbles from my hand, and my phone follows, landing with a dull thud before sliding under the bed.

'Shit.' I drop to my knees, fingers scrambling across the floor, searching. My palm skims over smooth glass—my phone—but my eyes catch on something else.

The paper.

No longer folded.

It lies open, the edges slightly curled, the creases still visible where it had been carefully pressed together. And then I see it—

The handwriting.

Familiar in a way that makes my chest go tight, my pulse a little too loud in my ears.

I don't breathe. I don't move.

I stare at it as I gather the courage to pick it up and read it.

dear jAmes,

there ARE No perfect words to explain how your presence changed me. you brought light into my life in ways i stilL can't quite express. but even with all the peace you gave me, it didn't feel like enough—not enough to quiet the rEst of it.

so i started lookinG for something bigger . . . something beyond what any of us can see. and if you're reading this, it meAns i've finally found it.

i'm sorry for leaving the way i did, for the hurt i know it caused you, and for the weight i left behind. i hope, in time, you can forgive me for that. but i also want to thank you for keeping your promise, foR holding onto it like i asked.

you know, whoever gets the chance to know you is going to be lucky—luckier than i coulD've ever been. keep this note safe, like you always kept me safe, at least for a little while.

thank you for sAving me, even if it was just temporary. i'll always be thinking of you, and what could've been.

The name at the top of the note catches me off guard: James. It's bold, the letters standing out in sharp contrast to the paper's muted background. My eyes trace the name again, and my stomach lurches. No. This can't be right.

A cold sweat prickles along my spine. My pulse stutters, uneven and sharp, like my body can sense something my mind isn't ready to accept. The edges of the note blur. I blink hard, but the letters remain, unmoving, undeniable.

I turn the note over in my hands and grab a pencil, my right hand moving faster than my thoughts. I rearrange the letters at the bottom of the note, my breath coming too fast, too shallow. The world tilts, the weight of realization pressing in on my chest.

Slowly, painfully, the name starts to form, one letter at a time.

AAREN LEGARDA.

The air in the room thickens. The sound of my own breathing is too loud, drowning everything else out. I grip the edge of the desk, my knuckles white, but it doesn't stop the nausea rolling through me.

My breath catches in my throat. I glance around the room, frantic. My eyes land on a school ID resting on the desk—Aaren's. I grab it, hands trembling, and read his full name: ***AAREN JAMES LEGARDA***. My chest tightens, the air in the room suddenly thick, and everything in me tilts.

How did I miss this?

How did I not see it sooner?

Aaren—*the* Aaren—was here all along, helping me search for my sister's notes, and now, I'm holding one of them. A note meant for him.

The hurt hits first, sharp and deep, sharper than the confusion that's twisting in my gut. I've been wrong before, sure. My mind loves to play tricks on me, twisting things into knots. But this—this feels different. This feels real. I feel like I'm looking at a version of the truth I never wanted to see.

The door creaks behind me. My heart jumps, my grip tightening around the note as I spin around. Aaren steps into the room, holding a bottle of water.

His voice breaks the silence, soft, cautious. 'Hey, my mom wanted to know if you're staying for—'

The words stop as he sees the note, sees my face. And in that instant, everything about him changes. His smile falters, replaced by something unreadable. He's still, watching me with eyes I'm not sure I recognize any more.

I don't speak at first, just stare at him, as if I can somehow find the answers in his eyes. But there's nothing there. Not really.

'Why do you have this?' My voice cracks, barely rising above a whisper.

Aaren's gaze flickers from the note back to me, and then, for a second, he looks like he might speak—but nothing comes out. He opens his mouth again, but this time, his jaw tightens, his shoulders stiffen, and all I can hear is the heavy silence between us.

'Were you hiding this from me?' I barely manage to choke out, the words coming so fast, I can barely breathe. 'Does this mean . . . I—' The thought hits me suddenly, a realization that makes my chest tighten. 'Were the notes for you all along?'

The truth is staring me in the face and I feel like I'm suffocating in it.

Aaren steps closer, hands raised like he wants to calm me, but I don't want calming. I want answers. I want to understand why everything feels like it's falling apart.

'Is that why you wanted to help me?' I ask, the words sharp as they scrape against my throat. 'Because you knew my sister wrote these notes for you? You just stood there, letting me run around thinking I was solving something—*my* story to solve—and you let me look like an idiot. You let me get so caught up in it, and it wasn't even *my* story. It was yours.'

The words spill out, cutting between us, each one more desperate than the last. I can feel my heart in my throat, a dull ache spreading through me.

Aaren's face tightens, and I can see the regret there, but it doesn't reach me. Not now. Not yet.

'Lauren, it's not like that—' he starts, but I can't hear him any more.

I shake my head, nearly stumbling as my legs wobble beneath me. I take a few shaky steps back to steady myself, the door just ahead. I can't stay in this room for another second—not with him, not with the weight of all these unsaid things.

'Don't. Just . . . don't,' I whisper, but the words are already fading behind me.

I step carefully around him and move into the dim hallway, my footsteps quiet and uneven. When I finally reach the front door and step outside, the humidity clings to my skin—no relief for my tangled thoughts. Then the tears come—fast, unstoppable. Once they start, there's no stopping them.

I press myself against the side of the house, gasping for air, clutching the note to my chest like it's the only thing that's real right now. The world is spinning, and I'm caught in it. But this time, I let it happen. Let the truth settle, heavy and unyielding, in my chest.

The notes weren't for me. They were never for me.

They were always meant for Aaren.

35

19 December 2023

I shouldn't have looked.

I should have left the note where it was—hidden away in the drawer, out of sight, out of mind. But something kept pulling me, like a quiet whisper that wouldn't let go. I kept going. Kept digging. Because maybe—just maybe—this one would be different. This one would finally make sense of everything, would finally piece things together.

It didn't.

It slammed into me like a blow I wasn't prepared for, knocking the breath right out of me.

dear jAmes,

My mind keeps stumbling over the words, each one feeling like it belongs to someone else's life. *James.* Not just any James. *Aaren James Legarda.*

The name hits me like a quiet shockwave, rippling through everything I thought I knew. I can't shake it off. I can't stop asking myself—had they been something? Had Elise and Aaren shared something I'd never seen?

The thought follows me, relentless and stubborn. Elise and Aaren. Aaren and Elise. Their names won't stop, circling in my mind like a song I don't want to hear.

I remember how casually she'd mentioned him, like it didn't matter. Always just a passing thought. No big deal. But now, all those little moments came rushing back—like a flood I hadn't expected. The way her smile shifted when his name came up, the small, soft laugh that followed her words about him.

Now it all feels different. Like I'd been blind to something that was right in front of me. Something I should have seen, but didn't.

you brought light into my life in ways I still can't quite express . . .

My stomach twists, an uncomfortable knot that won't loosen.

I can't stop thinking about today—standing in front of that painting at the gallery in Pasig. Elise had always spoken about it so casually, almost as if it were just another painting. But when I stood there, staring at the swirling colours, the delicate strokes, something clicked. It wasn't just a painting. It was *her* message, something she wanted me to see, to understand.

I thought these notes—these strange pieces of her scattered through my life—would give me clarity. I thought that if I could just find them all, if I could piece them together, I'd finally understand her. Maybe then, I wouldn't feel so lost.

But this note?

This wasn't an answer. This was something else. Something that cracked everything open.

Elise and Aaren. Aaren and Elise. The words pound in my head, relentless, impossible to ignore.

Had they ever been together? Were they more than what I'd seen? More than what I knew? I'd always heard her mention his name, but it was so casual. So . . . distant. But now, every look, every mention of his name felt different. Like there was something buried beneath the surface, something I wasn't supposed to see, something I had missed.

I stare at the note again, feeling the weight of it like a brick in my chest.

Tears prick my eyes, hot and fast. I wipe them away quickly, hoping to stop them before they have a chance to fall. But it doesn't work. I can't stop it. I can't stop the wave of grief, confusion, and rage flooding through me.

I feel hollow. Like someone's reached inside and pulled out the part of me that used to be whole, leaving me with nothing but a sick ache in my gut.

I can't stay here, not with that note in my hand, not with my thoughts a jumbled mess of things I wasn't ready to face.

I need air. I need to move.

The streets stretch out, empty and quiet, the glow of the streetlights pooling in uneven patches. I focus on the cracks in the pavement, counting them, grounding myself in something solid. *Keep moving. Keep moving. Don't stop.*

Then, everything shifts.

The air thickens, heavy and wrong, pressing against my chest like something unseen was wrapping around me. The streetlights flicker—just for a second, like the world itself was hesitating.

And then, I hear it.

'Lauren . . .'

My breath hitches. My pulse hammers against my ribs, the sound so loud it drowns everything else out.

I stop, every muscle in my body locking up. My mind screams at me that it isn't real. It can't be real.

But then I turn.

And there she is.

'Elise . . .' My voice barely rises above a whisper. It's a name, but it feels like a question. Like an admission I don't want to make.

She's standing at the end of the street, barely visible in the dim light, half in shadow and half bathed in the pale glow of the streetlamps. My breath hitches, and my chest feels tight as I stare at her.

She looks the same. But she also doesn't. She looks . . . *frozen*. Like time had stopped for her, like she hadn't been touched by the things that had broken me.

I should've said something. I should've screamed, run, anything. But I couldn't. I just stood there, staring at her, my body paralysed.

'Lauren.' Her voice is quieter now. It's real. It isn't in my head.

My knees grow weak. My pulse thunders in my ears, loud enough to drown out everything else. I open my mouth to speak, but no sound comes out. My lips part, but nothing escapes.

This can't be real. This can't be happening.

But there she is.

Elise.

I swallow hard. 'What do you want?' My voice is hoarse, a rasp that barely makea it past my lips. 'Why are you here?'

She doesn't say anything. Doesn't move. She just stands there, her gaze fixed on me with an intensity I can't understand. It's as if she was waiting for me to figure something out—waiting for me to make sense of it all.

I take a step towards her, the ground beneath me unsteady. 'Is this what you wanted? For me to feel stupid? To hate myself forever?' I can feel the words rising in my chest, bubbling over before I can stop them. 'Is this why you left all those stupid notes?'

My voice cracks on the last word, and I don't care. My chest feels tight, my heart is slamming against my ribs, and my mind is a hurricane of grief and anger.

She doesn't move. She doesn't flinch. She just watches me, silent and still.

And then it hits me.

Like a door slamming open, memories flood back—memories I'd buried deep and hadn't allowed myself to feel in years.

I remember the night my parents died.

I hadn't let myself remember it. Not in years. It was a wall I'd built to protect myself, but now, standing here, the cracks were too wide. I could see it all again—every detail rushing back like a film reel on fast forward.

The hallway felt like it was too long, stretching further than it should. The silence was thick, unnatural, pressing down on me, like the world was holding its breath. And I remember thinking that something wasn't right.

The air didn't feel right. It was heavy, like I was trying to breathe underwater. Like something was about to happen, but I didn't know what. It was the feeling you get just before everything changes—before everything you think you know shatters.

I can see it so clearly now. My feet echoing as I walked down the hall. The quiet creaking of the floorboards under me. And then—*there it was.* The figure. Standing still in the corner of their room, its shape barely there, but I could feel it. Something cold, something wrong.

I couldn't see its face, but I could *feel* it. The kind of wrong that settles deep in your chest, the kind that sticks to your skin, like when you walk into a room and just know something's broken, but you can't explain why.

'Lauren . . .' The voice was soft, but the words landed hard. 'I'm going to kill them.'

I froze. My body locked, my muscles refusing to obey, as if I wasn't even in control any more. I couldn't move. I couldn't scream.

'You're not real,' I whispered, but even as I said it, doubt curled at the edges of my mind.

I could barely breathe, the air in the room's too thick. My chest tightened like something was pressing in from all sides. I blinked, and my eyes landed on the utility knife sitting on the edge of my mom's drafting table. It was just a little thing—nothing like what I thought a knife should be. Not one of those kitchen knives that could slice through anything, but one of the tiny ones Mom used for her art projects. I had held it a thousand times, and never once had I thought it could be dangerous.

But now? Now it felt like it could tear through the world.

My hands were shaking as I wrapped my fingers around the handle, even though my brain told me to run, to *do something.*

'Leave,' I said. My voice came out in a whisper, broken and thin. 'I'll—I'll call the cops. I mean it.'

The figure didn't flinch. Didn't even blink. It moved, slow and deliberate, towards my mom, who was still lying there, eyes closed, completely unaware.

And then I saw it. Its hand reaching for her throat.

Her breathing was shallow, but she didn't wake. She didn't know what was happening.

I didn't think. I just moved. I lunged forward, my body acting on instinct, and I swung the knife, the motion jerky and desperate. The sound of metal cutting through air was the loudest thing I'd ever heard. It landed with a thud, but the figure didn't fall.

It didn't stop.

My heart was in my throat, pounding so hard it felt like it was choking me.

I didn't know how many times I swung, or how long I fought, but I couldn't stop. My body wouldn't let me stop. I kept going, stabbing, hitting, trying to make *it* go away.

And then, just like that, the figure disappeared.

I staggered back, breathless, like I had just run a marathon. My legs wobbled, and the knife dropped from my fingers, landing on the floor with a clink that echoed in the silence.

And I was still standing there, shaking, trying to catch my breath.

But the room—it didn't feel empty. Not any more.

I turned, and there it was again. The figure was by my dad now, its hand around his neck, and his eyes—his eyes were wide open, but they were empty. Not seeing me. Not seeing anything.

I couldn't think. I couldn't breathe. I didn't know what I was doing.

I grabbed the knife again, hands trembling, and I swung—again and again, no thought, no reason. My arms burned, and everything blurred around me. The ringing in my ears was all I could hear, and the world felt like it was closing in.

And then it was gone.

Just like that, vanished.

I stood there, gasping, heart pounding in my ears. The knife was still in my hand, but it felt like it didn't belong to me.

Then my eyes found them.

Mom. Dad.

The blood was everywhere—on the bed, the walls, on me. It was on my hands, dripping from my fingers like it had always been there.

I couldn't breathe. My vision swam, and I thought I might collapse right there. But I didn't. I just stared at them. My knees felt like they might buckle under me, but I stayed.

I let go of the knife. It dropped to the floor, but the sound it made was so loud it felt like the world was shaking.

And then it hit me.

I killed them.

The thought sliced through me like a blade, and I didn't know what to do with it. Tears flooded my eyes before I could stop them, hot and fast, spilling down my cheeks. I couldn't make them stop, no matter how hard I tried. My chest ached, and I gasped for air, but it wouldn't come.

I wanted to scream. To throw something. To *rewind.* To take it all back.

But I couldn't.

The blood—it wouldn't go away. It was on me. On the walls. In the air. It clung to me, to everything. I could see it, feel it, taste it.

It wouldn't go away.

I don't know how long I stayed there, knees pressed into the cold floor, hands still shaking. The tears came faster, and the room felt too small, too tight.

And in the quiet, broken pieces of my mind, I knew.

It was too late now.

Too late to fix it. Too late to make it right. Too late for anything.

36

28 November 2021

The bathroom light flickers above, its hum buzzing in the air like a faint memory I can't quite place. It should bother me. I should care. But I don't. I can't.

I don't know what I'm doing. My hands hover in front of me, stiff and foreign, like they belong to someone else. I flex my fingers, watching them move slowly, clumsily, as if each motion takes more effort than it should. I'm just . . . here.

The sink is cold when I lean against it. The porcelain feels sharp against my palms, like it's reminding me of something I should be feeling. I stare at my reflection, but it's a stranger's face looking back at me. The blood, still red and vivid, trails down my face in slow, heavy streaks, slipping into the sink like it's just another part of the day's events. It should matter. It should make me feel something. But it doesn't. It just . . . is.

I don't know what's worse—the blood or the way I'm not reacting to it. I see it, but it doesn't seem real. Not in the way it should. There's a smear across my forehead, tangled in my hair. My throat feels tight, like something sharp is lodged there, something that refuses to move. My chest rises and falls, but it doesn't feel like I'm breathing. It's just a mechanical motion.

I'm on autopilot, waiting for something to change, knowing it never will.

I turn on the faucet, and the water rushes out in a sudden flood. It makes me jump, the sound too loud, too jarring. I shove my hands under the stream, watching the blood thin, swirl, trying to wash it away. But it doesn't leave. It just clings to my skin, sinking into the cracks of my fingers, slipping under my nails. I scrub harder, my nails biting into my palms, but the reflection in the mirror doesn't change. She's still there, bloodstained and wrong, staring back at me like she knows something I don't.

The sound of the rushing water fills the space. It echoes in my ears, rattling around in my skull until I can't hear anything else. I turn the faucet off, but the ringing remains. A ghost of noise, like the world's still trying to pull me into something I don't want to be a part of.

My hoodie feels heavier than it should. Then I realize why.

It's still in my pocket. The thing I didn't want to remember.

I move slowly, like I'm underwater, like I don't have the strength to pull myself out. My fingers brush the cool handle, and a shiver runs down my spine. I don't remember putting it there. I don't remember how it ended up in my pocket. But it's here now. And I have to do something about it.

I pull it out, the metal slick and cold against my skin, too real. Too final. It's like a weight pressing down on me, reminding me that I'm not in control, that I'm just a passenger in my own life.

I shove it back, my hands shaking, my body moving on its own, like I'm not really here. I reach for my phone, the screen glaring against the harsh bathroom light. I scroll past names I don't recognize, names that don't matter. But then, I find the one that does.

My thumb hovers over the screen. A hesitation. And then I press.

'911, what's your emergency?'

The voice is distant, like it's coming from somewhere far away, like I'm underwater. I open my mouth, but the words won't come. I try to speak, but my throat is a dry, hollow place, and nothing escapes.

And then—'My parents are dead.'

It's not me. It doesn't feel like my voice, it feels like I'm watching someone else say it. But it's out there now. Too big. Too final. And it won't go away.

'Ma'am, can you tell me where you are?'

I blink. The mirror is still there. The blood is still there. And my parents' room is just down the hall, their bodies still there, like they're frozen in a moment I can't escape.

'Magnolia Crest Street. Verenna Heights Village.'

The questions keep coming, but they don't matter. They don't mean anything. I stare at the phone, the screen blurring like I'm losing my grip on reality. And then, before I can stop myself, I drop it. It clatters on the floor, but it doesn't make a sound. Or maybe it does, but I don't hear it.

I stand there for a long moment, feeling the air in the bathroom pressing down on me. It's thick, suffocating, like I can't breathe right. My stomach churns, but I can't seem to move. Eventually, I push myself forward, my legs shaky as I step out of the bathroom.

The bed is the same as it was when I left it, untouched. My mother's body lies there, silent, still. The blood has spread, soaked into the sheets like ink, and her hand is limp, lifeless.

I can't let them think it was me. I can't let them know.

The knife in my pocket feels heavier now, like it's absorbed everything—the terror, the guilt, the last thread of anything that could resemble me. My fingers tremble as I pull it free with my sleeve, the metal cold even through fabric. I can't stop thinking about what it remembers. What I've already given it. It's too much. But it's mine now. I can't get rid of it.

I kneel beside the bed, my body moving without me, as if I'm watching someone else. I set the knife gently beside her open hand, close enough that it could have fallen there, but not quite touching. A story I need to tell. A lie that has to be believed.

I sit back, watching, waiting. For what, I don't know. But it feels like I'm waiting for something to fix all of this, even though I know nothing can.

I wipe my hands on my hoodie, but the shaking won't stop. Nothing stops.

And I don't even know if I'm still here.

The sirens cut through the night, high-pitched and relentless, like they're tearing through the walls, through my mind. Red and blue lights flash against the windows, turning the room into something unreal, like a crime scene from a show on TV, like none of this is really happening.

I stand still in the middle of it all, frozen, like my feet are glued to the floor. I don't remember deciding to stay here, but I can't seem to move.

The officers flood in, their boots pounding against the tile, their voices sharp, their words too loud. One of them stops, his eyes flicking between me and the bed. He speaks into his radio, the words broken by static. But I can't hear them. My ears are ringing too loud.

'What happened here?'

The question is so simple, so clean. But it hits me like a punch to the gut. I open my mouth to answer, but the words don't come. My throat is tight, dry, like it's no longer my own. I rub my face, but when my fingers come away, they're streaked with red.

'I don't know,' I say, my voice so quiet I barely recognize it. 'I just . . . I remember them arguing. Before I went to bed.'

I don't know if it's a lie or if it's the truth. I can't tell any more.

The officer's gaze lingers too long. His eyes flick to the blood on my hands, then back to my face. He doesn't ask if I'm okay. He doesn't offer comfort.

He just watches.

Like he's already deciding if I belong in handcuffs.

And then—Clarissa.

She crashes into the room like she's breaking through something invisible, her face pale, her breath coming in shallow gasps. But when she sees me, she's at my side in an instant, pulling me close, her arms wrapping around me so tightly I feel like she's trying to hold me together.

'It's okay,' she says, her voice shaking, though I'm not sure if it's for me or for her. 'You're okay.'

She's lying.

I know it because I don't feel okay. I don't feel anything at all.

'I removed the knife from her throat,' I whisper, barely above a breath. I don't know why I say it. Maybe because it makes it real. Maybe because saying it out loud makes me feel less crazy.

Clarissa pulls back, just enough to look at me, her hands still on my shoulders. I see something shift in her eyes—something sharp and unreadable. Without a word, she turns towards the officers, planting herself between me and them like a shield.

'The kid's in shock,' she says, her voice steady and cold. 'Can we do this later?'

They hesitate, but don't argue. They step back.

Clarissa doesn't let go of me as she leads me out, guiding me away from the flashing lights, the sharp voices, the wreckage of my life. We move slowly, one step at a time, like she's afraid I'll slip away if she lets go.

The only thing that anchors me is the weight of her arm around me. It's the only thing that feels real right now. And she doesn't let go. Not once.

Not since we left that place for good.

37

20 December 2023

The first thing I notice is the sheets—too stiff, too rough, like they've held onto every person who's been here before me. They trap warmth, but not the comforting kind. It's the kind that lingers too long, like the heat of fever, of restless nights spent in places you don't belong.

Then comes the smell. Antiseptic, too sharp, clinging to the air, like someone's tried to scrub away every trace of sickness, every mistake, every ghost.

Hospital.

I blink, my head thick and heavy, like my thoughts are trying to push through mud. The room is too bright, too white, too clean in a way that doesn't feel real. I try to move, but my body is slow to catch up, my limbs heavy and unfamiliar, like they belong to someone else.

And then I see her.

Clarissa.

She's curled into the chair in the corner, her elbows on her knees, hands pressed against her temples. A rosary dangles from her fingers, the beads shifting slightly as she exhales.

Her hair is a mess, a loose knot that's barely holding together, strands falling into her face like she's forgotten they're there.

She looks exhausted.

When she finally lifts her head and sees me staring, her whole body tenses, like she's afraid I might disappear. Her eyes are rimmed with red, raw at the edges, the kind of tired that doesn't go away with sleep.

I open my mouth to speak, but my throat is raw, scraped dry.

'Clarissa?' My voice barely makes it past my lips. It cracks, hoarse, like I've swallowed a handful of gravel.

She straightens, blinking at me like she's not sure I'm real. 'You collapsed,' she says, her voice steady, but there's something underneath it, something sharp that's unravelling. 'Someone found you and brought you here.'

I press my hands into the mattress, trying to sit up, but my body protests, slow and sluggish. My fingers curl into the sheets, and that's when I see it—the dirt beneath my nails. Faint, but there.

I don't remember how it got there.

Clarissa leans forward, her voice softer now, but edged with something else. 'What were you doing out there, Lauren?' Her fingers tighten in her lap, knuckles white. 'Why were you alone?'

The question presses against something inside me, something I don't want to touch.

'They wouldn't stop,' I whisper, the words barely audible, my throat burning. 'The voices . . . they wouldn't stop.'

Clarissa's face tightens. She doesn't speak right away, but I see it in her eyes—the weight of it, pressing into her shoulders, pulling her down.

She exhales sharply, rubbing at her face before looking at me again, this time with something harder, something fraying at the edges. 'Do you have any idea what went through my head?' Her voice trembles, just barely. 'An unknown number calls me—tells me you're in the hospital. And for what? Some project Zania says you've been obsessing over? You're never home any more, and now—'

The words slip out before I can stop them. 'And now I know.'

Clarissa stills. Her eyes lock onto mine, searching. 'Know what?'

I look down at the sheets, at the small loose thread between my fingers, pulling it, twisting it, anything to keep my hands from shaking.

'What really happened,' I murmur. 'That night. The truth.'

The air in the room shifts. It thickens. The space between us feels smaller, pressing in.

Clarissa leans in, her voice quieter, careful. 'What truth?'

I shake my head. I can't say it. Not yet.

'Lauren,' she says again, softer this time, like she's trying to hold me together with nothing but words. She shifts her chair closer, reaching for me. 'Talk to me.'

I bite the inside of my cheek, tasting copper, holding onto it like it might keep me steady. But Clarissa's watching me like she already knows. Like the words are already there, just waiting for me to let them out.

'I've been finding notes.' My voice barely makes it past the lump in my throat. 'The ones Elise hid. In Mom's paintings, mostly.'

Clarissa's expression shifts, but she doesn't move, doesn't react—not at first. But her hands still, fingers curling into themselves like she's holding onto something, like she's trying not to let go.

'What are you talking about?'

'The first one was in my room,' I say, my voice picking up now, like the words have been waiting too long to be spoken. 'It led me to the library . . . then somewhere else, and somewhere else. I thought if I followed them . . . if I uncovered everything, I could understand why Elise did what she did. Maybe even let it go.'

I pause, exhaling shakily. 'But I only found more questions. So many questions. Especially about Mom.'

Clarissa looks away, her jaw tight, her fingers tapping against her knee.

The silence presses down.

And when she finally speaks, her voice is careful, measured—like she's choosing her words one by one, afraid of what might slip out if she isn't careful.

'Your mom . . . she was schizophrenic.'

The words slip from Clarissa's lips like they've been waiting too long, pressing against her ribs, begging to be let out.

Everything tilts. The room, the bed beneath me, the air in my lungs—it all shifts, like I've lost my footing, like I'm falling and there's nothing to catch me.

'She was . . . what?' The words barely make it out. They don't sound like mine.

Clarissa doesn't flinch. 'Schizophrenic,' she says again, gentler this time.

The words press into me, filling up all the spaces I don't know what to do with.

Clarissa exhales, tapping her fingers against the chair, like she's thinking through every word before she says it. Like she's trying to figure out how much of this I can take.

'She didn't want you to know, at least not anyone,' she says, her voice steady but careful. 'But when you were born, Lauren . . . things got worse for her. She kept trying to hold on, trying to be okay, but it was like something inside her cracked, and she couldn't put it back together.'

My chest tightens. 'But why didn't she say anything?'

Clarissa's eyes soften, like she's seeing something in me that I can't. 'Because she was afraid,' she says. 'Afraid of you becoming like her. When she looked at you she saw herself, and that scared her more than anything.'

I swallow hard, but it doesn't make the lump in my throat go away.

'She didn't know how to protect you from it,' Clarissa continues. 'So, she kept her distance. She thought that was the best thing she could do.'

My breath stumbles in my chest. I don't know what hurts more—the fact that she saw me and only saw herself, or the fact that she left because she thought that was love.

'But she was proud of you,' Clarissa adds, her voice softer now. 'She saw how strong you were, even when she couldn't be.'

I press my fingers into the sheets, grounding myself, trying to make sense of something that has never made sense. Maybe I always thought she didn't love me. Maybe I thought she couldn't.

But maybe . . . maybe she just didn't know how to love me without falling apart herself.

Clarissa reaches for my hand, squeezing gently, her grip steady. 'She never hated you, Lauren. She loved you more than you'll ever know. But she was too afraid to let that love show. She was afraid of what it might do to you.'

I blink, trying to hold back the tears that burn behind my eyes. Because I want to believe her. I want to believe that love, even when it looks like distance, even when it hurts, is still love.

Clarissa looks at me, her voice quiet but sure. 'But you're not her. You never were.' She pauses, like she needs me to hear this, really hear it. 'Your mom and I both knew that. Because you're stronger.'

Her words sink into me, deep and unshakable. They don't soothe. They don't absolve. They sit there, lodged somewhere behind my ribs, pressing outwards.

I don't believe Clarissa nor my mom because I don't feel stronger. I feel *awake*.

Because something else is rising alongside the ache—something I don't know what to call yet. Not grief. Not guilt. Something sharper. Something that doesn't let me look away.

All this time, I've understood myself as the aftermath. The one left behind. The one things happened to. Elise. Mom. Dad. Loss after loss, crashing into me like weather I had no control over.

But now . . . now I can't ignore the shape of my own hands in the wreckage.

The dirt under my nails.

The way the night disappeared around me.

The way the truth doesn't arrive all at once, but in pieces that keep cutting deeper.

I didn't just survive this.

I *acted*.

The thought makes me stomach turn. Not because I'm evil. Not because I meant to hurt anyone. But because intention doesn't erase impact. Because love doesn't cancel damage. Because wanting to understand doesn't excuse what understanding cost.

I look down at the sheets again, at the loose thread twisted tight around my finger. I pull until it bites into my skin, grounding myself in the fact of my body, my presence, my responsibility.

Clarissa's hand is still wrapped around mine. She's here. I'm here. And whatever happened didn't disappear just because I know more now.

For the first time, I see myself clearly—not just as someone shaped by other people's choices, but someone capable of shaping the world in ways that don't always look like love.

That realization doesn't crush me. But it doesn't free me either.

It settles in, heavy and unresolved, asking something of me I'm not ready to give yet.

Not forgiveness. Just honesty.

I draw in a careful breath, testing what it feels like to stay with the weight instead of dropping it. To hold the truth without turning it into punishment or release.

This isn't the end of it.

It's the beginning of knowing what I'm capable of.

And I don't look away.

38

28 December 2023

Clarissa knows.

She must have known for a while now. Maybe longer than I wanted to admit. But she never said anything. She never had to. It was in the way she looked at me, how her eyes lingered just a little too long, like she was waiting for me to crack open and spill everything.

Maybe Dr Gregory told her after I finally opened up to him three days ago. Or maybe she just figured it out on her own. Either way, pretending wasn't an option any more.

I'd spent so long trying to keep her out, hiding the worst parts of myself like if she couldn't see them, they wouldn't be real. But now, there was nothing left to hide behind. The walls I'd built between us didn't matter any more. *She knew.*

And when she walks into my hospital room, I see it before she even speaks.

Her eyes are rimmed with red, her face carefully neutral, like she's trying to hold it together for both of us. She crosses the room without a word, pulls me in close.

I freeze.

It isn't the kind of hug you give in passing or the kind that's meant to fix something. This is different. This is the kind that fills the silence when words won't do. The kind that says, *I see you. I know you're hurting. I don't know how to fix it, but I'm here anyway.*

Her shoulders shake, just barely.

'It's not your fault,' she whispers. 'You know that, right?'

I don't answer. I can't. My throat locks up, my body still caught between wanting to sink into her or push her away.

The words don't settle. They hover, unreal.

Not your fault.

I look at her and all I can think is: *How?*

I killed your sister. I ended a life. *Two* lives.

My chest tightens, heat crawling up my throat. I don't understand how she can sit here and say it like it's true—how she can still look at me the same way, still let me stay, still choose me, knowing what I'm capable of.

The gratitude is there, heavy and sickening, tangled up with something darker. I don't know what kind of love forgives this. I don't know what kind of person deserves it. But she's giving it to me anyway.

She pulls back slightly, searching my face. Her gaze is soft. 'None of this is your fault.'

I don't realize I'm crying until I feel the tears hit my chin. And I'm not even sure why I'm crying—relief, guilt, exhaustion, all of it tangled together in a knot too tight to unravel.

'I didn't mean for any of it to happen,' I whisper. 'I thought I was—' I swallow hard. 'I thought I was losing it. I didn't know what was real any more. I never meant to . . . kill them.'

Clarissa shakes her head, her gaze steady. 'You don't have to explain.' Her voice is soft but firm. 'It doesn't matter any more.'

I want to believe her. I really do.

The silence stretches between us, pressing down on my chest. The hospital lights hum overhead. The monitor beeps steadily, a quiet reminder that my heart is still beating.

By the door, a strand of tinsel droops, hanging limp. Zania's half-hearted attempt to make the place feel festive. But it doesn't feel like Christmas. Not here. Not now.

Clarissa wipes her face with the sleeve of her sweater. She starts talking then, her voice calm, careful. The doctors want me to stay another week for observation. I nod. I was too tired to argue. Too tired to pretend everything was fine when I was barely holding it together.

I turn my head to the window, watching the heavy grey sky press down on the world. I let my head rest against the cold metal of the bedframe and try to breathe.

Clarissa stays, talking about anything and nothing, her voice a steady hum in the room, grounding me in the only thing that felt familiar right now.

And then, there was a knock at the door.

For a second, I think it might be Dr Gregory, back with more questions. But when the door opens, the person it reveals isn't him.

It's Aaren.

'Hey,' he says, his voice barely above a whisper.

I can't bring myself to answer. I just stare at the tinsel on the wall, tracing its shape with my eyes, pretending it's the most interesting thing in the world. Anything to avoid looking at him. To avoid the weight of him standing there.

Clarissa, with that quiet understanding only she has, gives me a smile—a little sad, but kind—and kisses my forehead. 'He's the one who brought you here,' she murmurs, like that explains everything. Then, without another word, she leaves, closing the door behind her with a soft click that echoes in the space between us.

The silence that blankets the room in her absence is thick.

Aaren stands there, not moving, not speaking. I can't take it. My voice breaks through the quiet. 'You shouldn't be here.'

I don't mean to sound as unaffected as I do.

I don't look at him but the words slip out, a confession that had been sitting in my chest, waiting for him to appear.

I'm not sure if he's here because of me or because I'm some shadow of Elise—someone who didn't matter beyond the fact that I reminded him of her.

'Lauren,' he says softly, his voice quiet but certain. 'Please, let me explain.'

His voice pulls at me, but I stay silent.

'I knew Elise,' he says, his words careful, measured. 'Not well, at first. We met at a party a couple of years ago. It wasn't anything special—just one of those nights where you go because there's nothing better to do.'

Aaren pauses, shifting his weight, like the memory was something heavy he was trying to carry.

'She wasn't having a good night,' he continues. 'People were awful to her. They whispered behind her back, laughed at her. Treated her like she didn't even matter. At one point, she got sick, and instead of helping, they just stood there, watching, like it was entertainment.'

His jaw tightens, his eyes darkening as the past crept into the present.

'I couldn't just stand there,' he murmurs, as if the words were hard to admit. 'So, I grabbed her some water, made sure she was okay. When I offered to take her home, she wouldn't go back. She didn't want to face your mom. She didn't want to go back to all that. So, we just . . . we drove around.'

His voice softens, like he's talking to himself now, lost in the past. 'We didn't talk about anything important at first. Just random things to fill the silence. But then it started to feel real. She told me about how people treated her, how some days it didn't bother her. But on others, it was too much. She said it felt like she didn't belong anywhere. Like the world was too loud, and she couldn't keep up any more.'

His words slow, and there's a vulnerability in his tone, like he's exposing something raw, something unhealed.

'She said she'd been thinking about death,' he whispers. 'Not in an "I want to die" way. More like . . . she wanted to understand it. What it felt like. What came after. She said it was always there. The thought. Just . . . waiting. Like a door she wasn't sure if she wanted to walk through.'

I feel my throat tighten.

'I didn't know what to say,' Aaren admits. 'I thought listening was enough. But I should have noticed the signs—I should have seen it. But I didn't.'

His fingers flex at his sides. His gaze drops to the floor, like the memory was too much to face directly.

'And then she disappeared for a while,' he continues. 'And when I found out what happened, it hit me hard. I kept thinking about that night. How I should've done more. Said more. Maybe if I had just—' He stops, shaking his head. 'If I had been there, maybe things would've been different.'

His voice wavers, and for a second, I see it—the weight he's carrying, the guilt that has never let him go.

'That's why I wanted to stop looking.' Aaren finally meets my eyes, and it knocks the breath out of me. 'After the note I found—the one meant for me—every new one felt like walking straight back into everything I couldn't fix.'

The silence that follows is thick with things neither of us know how to say.

'I didn't want to do it,' he admits, voice raw. 'I didn't want to miss the signs again. I didn't want to be too late.'

And in that moment, I know—he wasn't just carrying Elise's absence.

He was carrying his own.

The weight of what he couldn't do. The ache of all the ways he thinks he failed.

Aaren lets out a slow breath, steadier this time. 'And the notes . . .' His fingers twitch like he's reaching for something that isn't there. 'Even if they were meant for me, I don't want to find them.'

Something in my chest tightens. 'Why?'

'Because they won't change anything.' His voice is calm, but there's an edge to it, something sharp enough to cut if I look too closely. 'They'll just remind me of everything I didn't do. Every word I didn't say. And that's what regret does, Lauren. It doesn't just hurt. It sticks. It makes you replay everything over and over until you can't tell the difference between what really happened and the version of the past you wish you could rewrite.'

He's staring at me then, searching, like he's waiting for me to understand. Like maybe if I do, he won't have to say it out loud.

'We all want to believe we can save the people we love,' he says, softer now. 'That if we say the right thing, if we do the right thing, maybe they'll stay. Maybe we'll fix them. But sometimes . . .' He swallows hard, and for the first time, I hear the weight in his voice. 'Sometimes, we can't. Some people don't want to be saved.'

His voice cracks just slightly, and I see it—the guilt, the ache, the quiet grief that never settled, never stopped pressing against him, waiting to be felt.

Aaren exhales, quieter than before. 'It doesn't matter how many notes I find. They won't bring her back. And picking apart every word she left behind . . . it won't fix anything. It won't help her. It won't help me.'

I stare at him, my throat tight. I know what he means. I've spent so long looking for something—anything—to explain why Elise is gone. I've spent even longer telling myself that if I just find the right note, the right answer, it'll stop hurting. But it won't.

Aaren takes a slow breath, like he's bracing himself. 'I don't think Elise left those notes for us to chase forever,' he says. 'I think she just wanted us to remember her. Not to punish ourselves. Not to make sense of something that never will. She just wanted us to know that she mattered.'

The words hit something deep, something I haven't been ready to admit to myself.

'That's why I helped you,' he continues, holding my gaze. 'I wanted you to see that no matter how many notes you found, they wouldn't fill the hole. They wouldn't make it hurt less. And I hoped you'd stop before it hurt too much.'

His words crack something open inside me—some small, desperate hope I've been clinging to, thinking that maybe, just maybe, an answer would be enough.

'There is no answer, is there?' I whisper.

Aaren shakes his head.

I close my eyes for a second, letting it sink in.

Aaren exhales, watching me. 'I know you, Lauren,' he says, steady. 'You push people away because you think you have to figure everything out alone. Because you think pain is something you have to carry by yourself.'

He pauses, then adds, 'But the difference between you and Elise is—you want to move through it. You don't want to stay here forever.'

His words knock the air out of me. Because he's right.

'I'm sorry for keeping the note I found.' His fingers rub at the back of his neck, like he's trying to steady himself. 'That day at your house, when we went back. It was in the basement. And it was for me.'

Something in my chest tightens.

Aaren glances at me, unreadable. 'I kept it because . . .' He exhales, shaking his head. 'I thought if I held onto it, you wouldn't think I had anything to do with what happened to Elise.'

The words don't sting the way I expect them to. They just sit there, waiting for me to take them in.

And I do.

And it isn't anger that fills me. Not betrayal. Just something softer. Something closer to understanding.

He didn't keep the note to hurt me. He kept it because he thought it was the only way to protect me.

Because he thought that if I kept searching, I might find something I wasn't supposed to.

Something I wouldn't be able to come back from.

His voice drops lower, careful. 'And that night. At the Christmas Festival . . .' He hesitates, his hand curling into a loose fist before he lets it fall open again. 'I didn't mean to tell you that.'

A slow, uneasy feeling settles in my stomach.

He doesn't say it like he regrets it. He says it like he hopes I don't hold onto it. Like maybe I should stop looking before I find something I can't unsee.

Aaren meets my eyes, steady and certain. 'What I meant was—I know what it's like,' he says, his voice quieter now. 'Digging through the past, hoping that if you just find the right piece, everything will finally make sense.'

He shakes his head. 'But it doesn't work that way. It just keeps you stuck—running in circles, asking the same questions, chasing answers that never feel like enough.'

His words settle into me, into the cracks I've spent so long trying to ignore.

Aaren's eyes search mine, like he's trying to make sure I really hear him this time. Like he's afraid I'll keep slipping through his fingers if he doesn't say this right. His voice is quieter now, steadier.

'I didn't want you to feel stuck,' he says. 'I need you to know that you don't have to keep searching just because you haven't found the answers. Some things . . . they don't have answers.'

His eyes don't leave mine, waiting.

He exhales through his nose, shaking his head slightly. 'We can't keep punishing ourselves for all the ways we think we failed her. Carrying the guilt like it's proof we loved her, like it somehow makes up for what we didn't do.' His voice is softer now, but not uncertain. 'It doesn't change anything. It just keeps her here in all the wrong ways.'

The words hit like a sudden drop, like stepping off a ledge before realizing there's nothing beneath you.

I blink at him, my throat tight. Because the truth is—I have blamed myself. Over and over. For every moment I wasn't there. For every word I didn't say. For not knowing how to save someone who maybe never wanted saving.

Aaren looks at me like he knows. Like maybe he's been carrying the same weight, waiting for someone to tell him it's okay to put it down.

He exhales, slow and measured, his fingers curling and uncurling against the edge of my hospital bed. 'You can let her be a memory—not something you have to keep trying to fix.'

The words lodge under my skin, impossible to ignore.

I swallow, gripping the thin sheets beneath me, grounding myself. The air is cool, but it doesn't take away the weight in my chest.

'And maybe that's what she wanted,' he says, his voice unwavering. 'Not for us to forget her. Just . . . to keep going. To live. To be okay, even if she couldn't be.'

Aaren takes a breath, watching me carefully. 'That's what I want for you,' he says, his voice quiet but certain. 'To stop waiting for answers that don't exist. To start living again. For yourself this time. Not for her.'

39

30 December 2023

'Are we really doing this?' I whisper, glancing over my shoulder, half-expecting someone to come storming after us.

Aaren shoots me a grin—the kind I haven't seen in a long time, the one that makes it seem like anything is possible. 'Of course. Come on.'

He doesn't wait for me to catch up. He's already moving, feet light, like the night is carrying him forward. I try to hold back the laugh bubbling in my throat, but it slips out anyway, blending into the hum of the city below.

We round the corner, and there they are—the emergency stairs. Aaren doesn't hesitate. He takes them two at a time, like he's racing against something. I follow, my heart pounding from more than just the climb.

'You're not gonna tell me where we're going, are you?' I ask, breathless.

Aaren glances back, eyes shining under the dim stairwell light. 'You'll see.'

When we reach the rooftop door, he pushes it open in one swift motion. A gust of cool air greets us, sharp and clean, curling around my skin. I step forward, and for a second, it feels like stepping out of the world entirely.

The sky stretches above us, caught between the last threads of daylight and the quiet hum of night. The city sprawls below, glowing in soft yellows and scattered blues. From here, it looks almost peaceful—like nothing bad has ever happened. Like the world hasn't fallen apart a hundred times over.

Aaren walks straight to the edge of the roof, leaning against the railing, his gaze fixed on the skyline. I join him, resting my arms against the cool metal. The space between us is filled with the quiet kind of understanding that doesn't need words.

Then, he turns to me, holding out an earphone. His smile is easy, familiar. He taps something on his phone, presses play.

A soft guitar riff fills my ears, steady and slow. Then a voice joins in—his voice.

I turn to him, blinking. 'Is this . . . you?'

He scratches the back of his neck, looking almost embarrassed. 'Yeah. We recorded it after the festival. It's called "Lauren".'

My brain struggles to catch up. 'You wrote a song . . . about me?'

Aaren nods, his eyes steady on mine. 'Yeah. You kind of inspired it.'

The words land softly but sink deep, settling somewhere beneath my ribs, in the quiet spaces I don't always know how to reach. The music drifts between us, filling in the gaps, saying things neither of us has figured out how to put into words.

I listen, letting it hold me there.

Then he says it, like it's the simplest thing in the world. 'Not every day do you meet someone who makes everything feel a little brighter. And when you do, it's impossible not to like them.'

The song fades, leaving only the hum of the city below and the sound of my heartbeat pressing against my ears.

I exhale, shifting my weight, grounding myself in the feeling of my shoes against the rooftop, in the way the air feels cooler now, lighter somehow. Aaren just gave me something real, something I wasn't expecting, something I don't quite know how to hold.

And I know—I can't just stand here and pretend I don't have my own truths waiting to be spoken.

I inhale, steadying myself, then remove the earphone, handing it back to him. My fingers graze his for half a second, and it feels like something closing, something opening.

'You're not the only one who's been keeping secrets.'

My voice is quieter than I meant it to be, like I'm still not sure I want him to hear it. But he does.

And he waits.

I force myself to hold his gaze. 'I have them, too.' My fingers curl into the fabric of my jeans. 'And if I tell you this, you can't take it back. You can't unknow it.'

Aaren tilts his head slightly, unreadable. 'Okay.'

I exhale, forcing the words out before I lose the nerve. 'I don't feel right in my own head.'

The silence that follows is sharp enough to cut through me. My breath catches, waiting for something—pity, hesitation, fear.

Aaren's eyes don't move from mine, but he doesn't speak right away. My stomach twists. I brace myself for it.

But then, in the most nonchalant voice, he says, 'I'm aware.'

I blink. 'What?'

Aaren shrugs, like I just told him I like my coffee black. 'I know.'

I search his face, trying to make sense of it. 'What do you mean you know?'

That's when he finally looks away, out at the city, like he's pulling a memory from the back of his mind. 'I was there,' he says, voice softer now. 'That day at school. I saw when you had the anxiety attack. You passed out. Your dad showed up at the nurse's office to take you home.'

He pauses. 'Then I overheard Savannah telling the school nurse that she heard you talking to someone in a bathroom stall. She thought you weren't alone. But then there was a crash . . . and that's when she found you on the floor, unconscious.'

I nod slowly, piecing together the moments I don't fully remember.

Aaren takes a breath, his gaze dropping to the ground before meeting mine again. 'And that night, when you ran out of my house . . . I saw you. You were screaming at something that wasn't there, crying so hard, like you couldn't catch your breath. And then you just—' He swallows. 'You collapsed. I had to carry you here.'

His hand runs through his hair, like he's carrying something heavy. 'I looked it up after that. But I wasn't sure. Not until I overheard the nurses talking before I left. Your Aunt Clarissa finally showed up at the hospital and told them you were seeing a psychiatrist. She gave them his name. Then, when your doctor came in, he said you needed to be closely monitored. . .'

He hesitates.

'... for schizophrenia.'

I swallow, but it doesn't help. My throat feels tight, like my body is trying to keep the words down, keep them from ruining everything.

'I didn't want you to find out like that.' My voice is barely mine at all. 'I didn't want anyone to.'

Aaren doesn't say anything right away. He just sits there, quiet, waiting. Maybe he knows that if he speaks too soon, I'll lose my nerve. The silence stretches between us, heavy with everything I'm afraid to name.

Then, finally, he nods. Like he understands. Like this isn't the kind of thing that needs a big reaction, just space to exist.

'It doesn't change anything,' he says, steady, certain.

A dry laugh slips out before I can stop it. 'It changes everything.'

Aaren looks at me, and he isn't smiling, but there's something solid in his expression. Like he's already made up his mind and nothing I say will shake it. 'It doesn't. Not to me.'

I study his face, waiting for the shift. The carefulness. The distance. The moment he realizes what this actually means, what I actually am, and starts seeing me differently.

'You're not scared?' My voice is smaller than I want it to be. 'You don't think of me differently now?'

His brows pull together, like he doesn't understand why I'd even ask. 'No.'

I search his face for hesitation, for anything forced. 'Not even a little?'

His gaze softens, and he shakes his head. 'Lauren, I don't look at you and see someone I have to be careful around. You don't scare me.' He exhales, steady. Sure. 'I like you. All of you. And that doesn't scare me. It doesn't change anything for me.'

I open my mouth, but nothing comes out.

Aaren leans back slightly, watching me, giving me time. Like he's waiting for me to believe him.

Then, casually, like he's talking about the weather, he says, 'It's not like the voices in your head are telling you how to act around me, right?'

Something inside me twists—not in a bad way, not in the way I'm used to. He isn't flinching. He isn't careful. He isn't treating me like something breakable.

I let out a shaky breath. 'No.'

He nods, like that's all he needed to hear. 'Then we're good.'

I exhale, my gaze drifting past Aaren, past the edge of the rooftop, past everything that felt too close.

He presses his lips together, like he's sifting through his thoughts before settling on the right words. 'I think you're doing better than you think,' he says, his voice softer now. 'You should be proud of yourself.'

I turn to him, a small, quiet smile tugging at the corner of my lips. He's watching me carefully, the way he does when he's trying to figure out what's happening inside my head.

'So . . .' He tilts his head slightly, his voice steady but careful, like he's giving me room to think, to feel. 'Do you still want to keep searching for the notes?'

The question settles between us, heavier than I expect it to be. I've been asking myself the same thing for days but hearing it out loud made it feel different. More real. More final.

I let it sit inside me for a moment, turning it over like something fragile, something that might shatter if I wasn't careful.

The urgency that had lived inside my chest for so long—the desperation to chase every answer, to pull apart every clue—it wasn't there any more. Like a door I hadn't realized was open finally clicking shut behind me.

I open my mouth, ready to tell him I'm not sure. That I need more time. That I'm not ready.

But then I realize—*no*. I don't think I want this any more.

The urgency that had once pressed into my ribs wasn't still there, even if the ache still was. I let the silence settle around me, turning the thought over, testing its weight. If I let go now, if I stopped searching, would that mean she was really gone? Would that mean I was ready to live without her shadow pressing into me?

Maybe it wasn't about being ready. Maybe it was about choosing to move forward anyway.

I didn't need more time.

I didn't need to keep looking.

The truth had been there all along, waiting for me to catch up.

'No.' My voice comes out quieter than I want it to be, but there's no hesitation. No doubt. 'I don't care about them any more. And I mean that.'

Aaren doesn't speak right away. He just lets the quiet stretch between us, making sure I believe my own words.

A breeze sweeps past, cool against my skin, pushing my hair into my face. I don't move to brush it away. Aaren's hand reaches for the strands first, his fingers tucking them behind my ear, like it was the easiest thing in the world. His touch lingers for just a second longer than necessary.

I let out a slow breath, something shifting inside me, something lighter. 'I keep thinking the answers would change things,' I admit. 'That if I just found the right note, the right explanation, then suddenly it wouldn't hurt so much.'

Aaren doesn't say anything, just watches me, like he knows I'm not finished.

'But answers don't fix people,' I continue, the words coming out slow, careful, like I was hearing them for the first time as I said them. 'They don't pull you out of the dark. They don't make the past hurt any less. The only person who can fix me is me.' I swallow. 'And maybe . . . maybe that's the answer I've been looking for this whole time.'

Aaren's lips twitch into something small, something knowing. 'I'm glad you finally realized that.'

The rooftop stretches out before us, the city blinking in the distance, alive and moving, like it hasn't been waiting for me to catch up.

'I've been meaning to ask you something,' Aaren says after a while. His fingers trace invisible lines against the metal railing. 'Do you have an answer now? About why you wanted to find those notes in the first place?'

I smile, but it's not because the question is funny. It's because I realize I had known the answer all along—I just hadn't wanted to admit it.

'I needed someone to blame,' I say, and the words feel foreign, like they belong to someone else. 'I thought if I found the right note, if I got the answer I wanted, I could finally stop feeling guilty—for not doing more, for not saving her.' My voice dips lower. 'I wanted to pass the weight onto someone else.'

A stretch of quiet follows. Aaren doesn't rush to fill it. He just stands there, his fingers tapping against the railing, waiting for me to finish finding my own way through the words.

Then, finally, he exhales. 'You really think finding those notes would've changed anything?'

I swallow, my throat tightening. The answer sits heavy in my chest, one I had known for a while but hadn't wanted to say out loud.

'No.'

'Then why did you keep looking?'

I bite my lip, pressing my nails into my palms to steady myself. 'Because Savannah was right. I carried this grief like it was something I wasn't allowed to set down. Like if I let it go, if I stopped searching, then it would mean she was really gone. And I wasn't ready for that.' I take a breath. 'I wasn't ready to live my life knowing there was no missing piece, no final answer that would suddenly make everything okay.'

Aaren doesn't push, doesn't rush me. He just waits.

I let my eyes drift past him, past the edge of the rooftop, down to the city below. The headlights. The steady movement of people. The proof that the world hadn't stopped for Elise.

And there were other truths I couldn't afford to look at yet, sitting just beneath the surface, heavy and waiting. Maybe that was the hardest part—knowing that no matter how much I tried to hold on, nothing would bring her back. Nothing could undo what was already done and gone.

'And now?' Aaren asks gently.

'I think . . .' I exhale, the words settling into place. 'I need to let it all go.'

Aaren doesn't speak, just watches me, making sure I mean it.

I close my eyes for a second, then meet his gaze. 'Because looking won't change anything. And maybe I don't need a reason to let go. Maybe I just need to do it because she's gone.'

Saying it doesn't make it hurt less. But it makes it real.

The moment stretches between us, full of the weight of everything I had just said.

Aaren lets out a breath, his voice steady but softer than before. 'I'm proud of you.'

I blink at him, surprised. 'For what?'

'For getting here.' His eyes soften, like he was seeing something I wasn't. 'For realizing you don't have to keep looking just to hold on to her.'

I let his words settle.

'She meant a lot to you,' he says, his gaze steady. 'She always will. But you're still here, Lauren. And that counts for something.'

I nod. 'Yeah.'

There's a shift between us, small but undeniable. The wind pushes against my skin, but I barely notice it. Aaren is still watching me, and I'm not sure who moves first—maybe it was him, maybe it was me—but suddenly, the space between us doesn't feel so wide anymore.

His fingers brush against mine, just a fleeting touch, but it sends something electric through me, something I hadn't expected. He tucks my hair behind my ear again, his touch lingering just a second longer than necessary, like he was memorizing this moment.

I should pull away. Should ask if this is a mistake, if it will change everything between us. But I don't want to.

I want this.

And so, I stay still.

Aaren exhales. His fingers stay close, barely touching mine—a quiet reminder that I am *still* here. That I *am* real.

Maybe life isn't about solving every mystery or tying up every loose end. Maybe it's about learning to carry the questions without letting them weigh you down.

There is still so much I don't know. About Elise. About myself. About whatever this was between Aaren and me.

But for the first time, the unknown didn't feel like something to fear.

Maybe, just maybe, not knowing wasn't a weight to carry.

Maybe it was a door waiting to be walked through.

ACKNOWLEDGMENTS

To feel is human—but to be consumed by those feelings is often what leaves us isolated. Even so, the heaviest, most unnameable emotions are not signs of weakness; they are proof that we are alive.

Mental health should never draw lines between generations. Just because some were taught to carry their pain in silence does not mean those who choose to speak deserve to be dismissed. Healing is not linear, nor does it bow to age or experience. It is a quiet, necessary journey—one that belongs to each of us. We owe it to ourselves, and to one another, to keep listening, to keep speaking, and to keep the conversation alive, so no one has to walk through their shadows alone.

Writing has never been just about telling stories—it has always been about telling the truth, especially the truths we hide even from ourselves. This book was born from heaviness, from the need to give shape to thoughts and feelings I didn't always have the language for.

And this book—this dream—would not have found its way into the world without the people who stood beside it. Their presence, guidance, insight, and belief shaped these pages as much as I did. Without them, this story would have remained a fragile hope in my hands, instead of something I now get to release into the world, wishing for it to reach greater heights and endless possibilities.

To Nora, thank you for seeing something in this story and choosing to take a chance on it. Your belief gave this book the wings it needed to fly beyond the walls of my own fear.

To Thatchaa and Swadha, thank you for pouring your time, energy, and heart into this manuscript as deeply as I did. Thank you for reading between the lines, for understanding what I meant even when I said it imperfectly, and for helping me refine this into something stronger, clearer, and truer. Thank you for polishing the messy, emotional parts with such patience and care, and for treating my words with gentleness.

To Penguin Random House SEA—one of my dream publishers—thank you for opening the door to a dream I've carried for years. This story found its home because of you. Working with you has been more than I ever imagined. Thank you for your trust, support, and belief in both this book and the person who wrote it. You helped turn a quiet hope into a shining reality.

To Jayal, thank you for reading one of the earliest drafts and for offering your wisdom, kindness, and unwavering encouragement. I wouldn't have made it here without you. And to Angelo, thank you for celebrating every small victory as if it were your own. Your joy made this journey brighter.

To Clap, my first-ever proofreader and the first person I shared this idea with—I'll never forget that walk to the library in Qatar Foundation, me rambling about the story, and you stopping mid-step, eyes wide, saying, "Holy fucking shit?!" That was exactly the reaction I'd hoped for, and I'll carry it with me forever.

To my family, thank you for trying, for learning, and for shifting from disbelief to compassion. For listening even when it was difficult. For reminding me, in your own quiet ways, that even when I felt lost, I was never unloved.

To my partner's mom, thank you for welcoming me into your home with open arms and even more open love. Your house became my sanctuary, a place where I could breathe and write freely. Thank you for giving me that creative haven, for letting me heal, and for becoming the second mother I never expected to find. It was in your warmth that I found the courage to finish this book—years in the making, finally ready.

To my partner, thank you for riding every emotional wave with me: the highs, the lows, the storms, and the silence. For giving me space when I needed it and presence when I didn't know how to ask. For whispering 'read well' and 'write well' like blessings tucked into my pockets. Thank you for staying. Always.

To my best friend's family—her mom, dad, and sister—thank you for raising someone who loved so fearlessly and so fully. You gave the world a beautiful soul, and because of her, I never gave up on this story. Your daughter was the steady voice in my corner, the reminder of why I had to keep going.

And to my best friend, Renzelle, you were the first person to read the very first draft of this book. You watched it grow, storyline by storyline, character by character. I miss you more than words can carry. Thank you for seeing the writer in me long before I ever dared to see her myself. For nudging me towards that school newspaper application—the earliest doorway into the world I now get to stand in. For meeting me in the spaces only we understood. You believed in me on the days I couldn't lift my own pen—or myself. You stayed, even when life didn't.

B, ito na. Published author na ako.

Just like I always told you I wanted to be.

Just like how you wished it badly for me.

Thank you for dreaming my dreams with me for as long as you were here to hold them with me.

I love you. Forever and always.

If you or anyone you know is struggling or in crisis, know that you are not alone. You can reach out to crisis support services.

The NCMH Crisis Hotline is available 24/7 for those in the Philippines. All you have to do is dial 1553.

The Lifeline International Organization is a resource that can be availed by anyone. You can access their crisis hotlines on https://lifeline-international.com/